THE DEAD GIRLS DETECTIVE AGENCY

The Dead Girls Detective Agency

HARPER TEEN

An Imprint of HarperCollinsPublishers

Y A

HarperTeen is an imprint of HarperCollins Publishers.

Dead Girls Detective Agency

Library of Congress Cataloging-in-Publication Data
Cox, Suzy.
    The Dead Girls Detective Agency / Suzy Cox. — 1st ed.
        p.   cm.
    Summary: "When Charlotte is pushed in front of the F train, she
wakes up as the newest member of the Dead Girls Detective Agency and
learns that she must solve her own murder before she can pass to the
Other Side"—Provided by publisher.
    ISBN 978-0-06-202064-2
    [1. Mystery and detective stories. 2. Dead—Fiction.
3. Murder—Fiction. 4. New York (N.Y.)—Fiction.] I. Title.
PZ7.C83933De   2012   2012006567
[Fic]—dc23   CIP
                                                            AC

Typography by Torborg Davern
12 13 14 15 16 CG/RRDH 10 9 8 7 6 5 4 3 2 1
❖
First Edition

FOR PAT, MY FAVORITE STORYTELLER

A Big Red Door (and then some)—sized thank you to:

The amazing Sarah and Kari at HarperTeen, for your patience and guidance; Lindsey, for your support, creativity, and awesome taste in handbags—this page would not exist without you; the ladies of Slayerfest, for being my own personal Scoobies; Emma, Suse, and Hattie, for reading and not laughing; Anna and Martin, for being cooler than me; Lyndsay, for everything; my parents, for always reading me "just one more page"; and Christian, for showing me New York—and being the right combination of David and Ed.

THE DEAD GIRLS DETECTIVE AGENCY

Chapter 1

POP QUIZ: WHAT WOULD YOU DO IF YOU *only had one day left to live? Just one clear day. A few short hours to fill with a list of your "lasts." Tough call, isn't it? Would you steal your mom's credit card and brutalize Barneys, because—let's face it—you might as well go out looking your best. (And you can't be grounded in the grave.) Go tell that senior you've always had a crush on just how much you heart him and end it all on a kiss? Get blind drunk, act obnoxious, vandalize something—just because you could? Or would you find your family, apologize for any time you've let them down, and spend the day telling them you don't want to let them go?*

Me? Well, if you'd asked me on that *morning, my answer would have been simple: I would have wanted to spend my last precious hours with my boyfriend, David. Yeah, whatever, I know how that sounds—all Bella and Edward bleh—but give me a break, I was really into him. His floppy blond hair. His skater boy pants. Those* sea-blue eyes that made me think of . . . Oh God, I'll stop. I'm even making myself feel sick. Anyway, if you'd asked me then, I would have wanted to grab David's hand, walk through New York's autumn-air streets to the Plaza, duck into Central Park, and climb our rock. We'd lie back, talk about books we'd read and places we wanted to see, and watch the perfect blue sky above us. Then, when the sun started to slide, we'd laugh and do shots until the edges of the world began to blur—so that when I left it, I wouldn't be sure what had happened, much less be aware of everything I'd just lost.

How I wouldn't want to spend my last day? By sleeping through my alarm because I'd been up watching reruns of Gilmore Girls (I know: tragic). Being late for first period and a chem test that had completely slipped my mind. Or, afterward, slamming into Kristen, head cheerleader/head bitch extraordinaire, causing her to drop all her books and me to (probably) be the recipient of her evils for the rest of the semester. To leave school, step right into a muddy puddle crossing Fifth and 49th, writing off my mom's new suede DVF boots. Which I'd borrowed without asking. I certainly didn't want to get down to the F-train platform, hot, sticky, stressed, and—for once—desperate to get home, only to find the train delayed. And when it finally did steam in, I didn't want to die after feeling the sharpest push to the small of my back, then falling—as someone behind me screamed—onto the tracks.

But when I woke up that morning, I didn't know I only had six hours of my life left. Why would I? When it comes to the end—biting the bullet, kicking the bucket—it's not like someone walks up and *warns you. You don't see blond girls dressed all in white, flapping their big old angel wings. Or a particularly menacing black crow. Your iPhone doesn't suddenly install a Reaper app.*

Because life's not like that. Life—as your mom says—isn't always fair. And when it comes to your afterlife, well, there's a whole new book of rules to learn. Not the normal ones like, "Only go for the hot meal in the cafeteria on a Monday" or "Don't make eye contact with the lacrosse team unless you're in twelfth grade." Oh nooo. Rules far more serious than that. Ones that actually matter. Ones that can change your death forever . . .

Chapter 2

WIND SUCKS BACK HAIR. THE F TRAIN CHUGS. *Foot feels wet. Headlights in the dark. There's that push. Heat. Someone screams. Then . . .*

"Charlotte! Charlotte! Open your eyes. It'll be fine, I promise."

For pretty much the first time since sixth grade, I did as I was told. I opened my eyes. And saw a girl in a blue-and-white-striped top standing over me, smiling in a nervous way. I blinked.

"Charlotte . . ." The girl pushed a strand of her thick squirrel-red hair behind her ear, making the black frames of her glasses wiggle. She looked about my age, sixteen, maybe seventeen.

"Okay, so this is going to be incredibly weird, but please try not to freak out. It'll only make things worse." She was talking above me, looking at me hard. Like she really, really needed me to concentrate, but wasn't sure I could. She paused. "Do you remember being on the train platform?"

The platform. Oh yeah. How did I get from the F train to here? Did I miss my stop? And where *is* here anyway? I sat up—too fast, I guess, because the room whirled. It looked like I was in some sort of art deco hotel lobby. The floor tiles were black and white and there were these plush red-velvet drapes around the doors. Yes, it must be a hotel, because there was a reception desk and above it a sign with—duh—Hotel Attesa, written in curly, swirly letters.

"Charlotte. I need you to listen."

I looked at the girl and tried to think back, but it was as if I were looking at my memories through a window smeared with Vaseline. I was on my way home after class. I was getting on the train. So how did I end up in a hotel? Oh God, I bet I blacked out on the platform. It *was* hot down there, and I'd fainted that one time during detention last summer. Now, that was mortifying. What if I was one of those people who pass out on the platform, then have to be taken off someplace to sit down—someplace like this old hotel—until they feel better. I hoped I wasn't that lame. I'd die of embarrassment if . . .

"There's no easy way to say this, but something bad has happened to you, Charlotte."

Oh no, I *was* pass-out girl. I knew I should have eaten breakfast and had more than a salad for lunch. Mom was always telling me that. It's just that I couldn't face food that early in the morning. It feels weird to eat straight after you've brushed your teeth and . . .

"Charlotte, you're . . . dead."

"I'm d— *What*?"

Suddenly, I was focused. Focused enough to know this girl was deranged. Who the hell thought it was a good idea to leave an ill person like me with a psycho like her?

Or, wait a minute, I knew what was happening! This was all some weird fainting-dream thing. I was *still* passed out on the platform. In a minute I was going to come around, then they'd call my mom and everything would be fine. Maybe I'd even get out of school tomorrow.

"You're dead. And from what we can tell"—she looked down at an ancient-looking letter in her hand—"someone pushed you onto the tracks just as the F train came in. And, well, I'm sorry, but you didn't make it." She smiled in a nice "oh well" way. Like she'd just told me I didn't make the swim team or that the last dress in my size was out of stock in every branch of Urban Outfitters.

Wow, I must have really hit my head, and hard, because this was some trippy Dorothy-goes-to-Oz hallucination I was having. My English teacher, Ms. Jackson, would totally pass me if she knew I was subconsciously *this* creative.

I looked down at my body. Nope, it was the same as always. I hadn't imagined myself with train-track marks or anything. Instead I was sitting, all nice and comfortable, on this big, black, squishy leather couch in this hotel lobby.

"This is a very confusing time. I know that. Which is why I'm here to help you all I can. I'm Nancy, by the way. Nancy Radley. I'm dead too."

The girl held out her hand. And because I had no better plan of action right then, I smiled and took it. She was super-polite for a figment of my imagination.

"Now, I think the best way to get you acclimated to the situation is to just throw you in at the deep end. Tell you everything you need to know in one go, then you can absorb it at your own rate."

Acclimated? Absorb? Dead Girl Nancy must have been working her way through the SAT word list before she "died."

"Sure." I smiled serenely and stood up to follow. I just hoped I'd remember all this when I woke up. David would get a total kick out of my imaginary friend.

"Come on then, let's get you up to your room. I'll fill you in on the way."

Ha! Here we go. This was totally not right.

"Room?" I asked. In what underworld would a ghost actually need a room? This was so dumb. I just wanted to wake up, call David, and dry out Mom's shoes before she realized they were missing.

Nancy looked at me with a little smile. "Well, to be honest you don't *need* a room," she said. "After all, ghosts don't sleep. But we figured, seeing as we've got this hotel, and there are rooms here, why not give them to people when they arrive? You had a room while you were alive, right? So we give you one when you're newly dead. We think it makes the transition from that life to this one feel a little less weird. Well, we hope it does."

"*We?* So you're not alone?" Jeez, my imagination must be

doing overtime. I'd not just dream-invented one ghost but a whole bunch of them.

"Yes, of course. You'll meet the others later." She opened a door and led me into an elevator. Which also seemed a little stupid. If I were a ghost, surely I'd be able to walk through walls? I tried pinching my arm.

"Right now you are in the Hotel Attesa, just off Washington Square in New York City," Nancy explained. "It's right next to a regular old human hotel. Of course, the Living can't see the Hotel Attesa, only we can. Otherwise you'd get all these ghost hunters popping in with their electromagnetic detectors or PKE meters or whatever other crap they saw in *Ghost Busters* trying to prove we exist. Which is the last thing we want—especially when we've got such important work to do."

I pinched again. And again. Nope, still not awake.

Ping! The elevator stopped and Nancy led me down a red-carpeted corridor. I couldn't help but think that, if I were conscious and this hotel didn't just exist in my dream, it was exactly the kind of place I'd love to stay in. If my parents didn't think hotels were "a complete waste of our money," that is. It was super-classy, old yet pristine.

Nancy opened the door and the room inside was even more gorgeous than the lobby—white walls, antique lights, prints of old Hollywood movie stars in sleek black frames, a sink-into-me bed and floor-to-ceiling windows on one wall. I walked over to the windows, which looked out on Fifth Avenue and the Empire

State Building. Wow. Nice imaginary view.

"Don't get *too* excited by the location," a high-pitched voice said. I turned around to see a blond girl standing über-close to me. Another ghost? Awesome. This one was like something from an Abercrombie ad, all glowing skin, Mac-counter makeup, and perfect hair. She wouldn't look out of place in one of those frames on the wall.

"Want to know the suckiest thing about the afterlife?" she asked. "It's all look, look, look, but don't touch. Like, there's all this on our doorstep . . ." She motioned to the streets below. "And us? We can't even enjoy it." She leaned on the window so closely she would have left a breath mark. If she was still breathing, that is. "I'm Lorna by the way."

This was getting ridiculous. "What are you talking about?" I asked.

"Oh, Nancy didn't tell you that little Rule yet? It's a bummer. Totally and utterly hideous. I mean, there are some great things about being dead: no eating equals no dieting. No more split ends or breakouts. Of course, style-wise, death sucks. The rule is that we ghosts have to spend all our time in whatever outfit we died in. Which as you can see, for me, is a baby blue Marc Jacobs Spring/Summer '06 dress. Not a bad choice. I mean, I'd totally be seen dead in it. It's just that I'll never get to wear anything else. Ever."

I looked down at my outfit and saw my gross school uniform: a blue-and-yellow plaid skirt, white shirt, my navy blazer . . . and

Mom's DVF heels. Wouldn't my favorite Seven jeans and Converse have been more eternity appropriate?

I smiled politely, all the while pinching my arm like a crazy person. Like the worst thing about being dead would be the limited clothing decisions. What about missing your family or your friends or, I don't know, being alive? Then, on the eighteenth pinch, something in my brain clicked. A memory broke through. When I was on the platform, right before I opened my eyes here in the hotel, I felt something. What was it? A push. In my lower back. So hard I lost my balance. Then there was that scream. And the heat. And then I was here.

What if this *wasn't* a dream? What if I had been pushed? Right onto the tracks and under the F train. What if . . . what if, like Nancy said, I was dead?

Shut up, Charlotte, I told myself, stepping backward and landing awkwardly on the bed. I mean, come on. There was no tunnel with bright lights at the end, no big pearly gate, no old bearded guy welcoming me in. I held up my hand to the light—I couldn't suddenly see through it. I hadn't turned into Casper or anything.

"So what else do I need to know?" I asked, trying to play along and make sense of whatever was happening. Maybe this was some elaborate practical joke. "I mean, this whole hotel thing is nice and all, but I always thought heaven would be more sitting on a cloud with unlimited Ben and Jerry's and less downtown fancy hotel."

"Sorry, sorry," Nancy said, turning her attention back to me.

"I was getting to that. So here's the deal." She sat on the bed beside me and gave me another of her reassuring smiles. Worrying, I realized that she had the air of someone who had done this before. A lot.

"When teenagers die in mysterious circumstances—like you being pushed under that train—they don't pass straight over to the Other Side, as people do when it's their natural time to go. Instead, in New York, they come here, to Hotel Attesa—"

"It's kinda like a waiting room," Lorna interrupted. "But adults, they go to this other hotel uptown. It's, like, way nicer because it's more modern and it's nearer the park and whoever decorated it did this thing with pink paint and . . ."

"Lorna! Be quiet?" Nancy glared at her friend. Note to self, do not cut Nancy off mid-sentence. "While you're here, you're stuck. You can't go over to the Other Side until you've worked out who killed you and why. Basically, you need to set things straight before you can move on. And we—me, Lorna, and Tess—"

"Yes, you so need to meet Tess," said Lorna.

"*And* Tess." Nancy ignored her this time. "We're here too, trying to help out those who come in because, you know, then they might get to the Other Side faster."

"Nancy calls us the Dead Girls Detective Agency," Lorna said, smoothing down her skirt. "And she's actually proud of it."

I tried to focus. Maybe, just maybe, if this actually was some big, stupid, fainty dream, if I solved my murder, I'd wake up. Like, it was a coma and not a dream. Ohmigod, if I was in a coma my mom was going to freak. And she was going to know I stole her boots.

"So this Other Side," I said, trying to stay calm. "If we figure out who killed me, how do I get there?"

"Through the Big Red Door," said a new voice behind me. I spun around to see a brunette standing in the doorway. She was not channeling Nancy's reassuring smile or the kindness in Lorna's eyes. Instead she looked bored. As if she'd been here a million times before and couldn't care less. I wondered how long she'd been standing there, just listening.

"That's Tess," Lorna said, checking out her cuticles. "She's been here the longest of all of us girls. Tess is the best, but she can be kind of . . ."

Nancy shot Lorna another look and gave me an eye roll. "Subtle, Lorna."

"I can be kind of what?" Tess asked. "Honest? Harsh? A mega-bitch?"

When Lorna shrugged vacantly, Tess turned to me. "Well, seeing as I appear to have a rep, I may as well live up to it. All those little fantasies you're currently having? The ones where you're trying to convince yourself that this isn't real and any second now, Mommy dearest will come into your bedroom and wake you up? Forget them. They're all lies."

She carried on talking before I could tell her I'd already worked out I was in a coma.

"These two"—she paused to gesture toward Lorna and

Nancy—"they're all, 'Let's make it easy for newbies, let them come to terms with it in their own time.' Well, that tactic didn't help me. In fact, nothing helped me. So here's the truth: You're dead. End of story. The only thing you can do is deal with it and hope you're lucky enough to move on."

Tess gave me a look that practically screamed *capisce?* and walked out of the room, leaving Lorna and Nancy gaping after her. Outside a cab horn honked.

"Got to say it," Lorna said eventually. "That girl has a way with words. You're totally dead, Charlotte."

And that's when I tried to throw up. Except I couldn't throw up anymore. I couldn't do much of anything anymore. I, Charlotte Louise Feldman, of Twenty-One West Seventy-First Street, was, apparently, no more.

My head was swimming. I wasn't sure if it was the having-just-died part or the it's-impossible-to-take-in-all-this-information part of the situation that was freaking me out the most; but on reflection, I guess it was probably the part where I was dead. That morning all I had to worry about was where to meet David for lunch, whether I'd get tickets for the portrait exhibit at the Met, and what Dad was going to say when he heard I'd flunked chemistry. Again. Now? Now I had to deal with the fact that (a) I was dead, (b) OMG, I was dead, and (c) someone really didn't like me. As in, didn't like me so much that they decided to murder me.

What about my poor parents, did they even know yet? And David? Did this mean we'd broken up?

Tears welled at the corners of my eyes. I tried my hardest not to think about the "Living," as Nancy had called them. Come on, Charlotte, I told myself, biting down on my lip and waiting for it to hurt. But it didn't. Hold it together. There must be a way to fix this.

"I better show you the Door," Nancy said, all businesslike again, desperately trying to distract me. "I know it's a lot to take in, but we have to get moving. Every second we waste could mean we miss out on a vital clue to what happened to you and we can't have that, or we'll never find your Key."

"My what?" I asked, pressing my finger to my lip. No blood.

"Your Key," Lorna said. "Don't worry, it's taken me four years to understand all this stuff. It's more complicated than applying a streak-free fake tan!"

I followed Lorna and Nancy out of the room. My new room. For that moment, at least. One thing was for sure: dead or not, I wasn't ready to leave my life behind just yet.

Chapter 3

I'D LOVE TO SAY THAT THE BIG RED DOOR— the mighty gateway to the Other Side that Tess had so *kindly* told me about without so much as a sit-down-this-is-major—was the most impressive thing I'd ever seen. But honestly? I'd seen more impressive entrances to clubs on the Lower East Side.

"This," said Nancy, with all the drama someone under five foot five could muster, "is it: the Big Red Door."

I politely pretended to take a moment to admire it (Mom didn't raise me *that* badly), but in truth? Nancy hadn't given me a minute to deal with the whole train/death/afterlife issue. Sure, I heard her when she said that, if we were going to find my murderer, we didn't have time to waste, but I was too thrown to take it in. What felt like seconds ago I was standing on the subway platform. Now I was expected to be all breezy about my death and impressed by a door that might take me to some Other Side.

"Um, wow?" I finally managed.

You didn't have to be a Mensa member to see how the entrance to the Other Side got its name. It was big (say, one story tall), red (wood, in case those kind of details interest you), and a door. Though it was hard to check off the last point, seeing as it was firmly shut. And apparently staying that way until I solved my murder and found my Key. Whatever that meant.

Big Red sat—almost hidden—in an unassuming alcove just off Hotel Attesa's main lobby. So this was what my way out of this nightmare looked like. So far, so unhelpful.

"Run me through how it works again." I turned to Nancy and tried to look super-interested. Maybe the sooner I got the hang of things, the sooner I'd feel less . . . messed up, confused, and low-level terrified.

"Well, *where* shall I start?" Whether she sensed my bewildered horror or not, Nancy was clearly loving this part of her job. "Rule One: The Door can only be opened by a ghost's personal Key. So, when we solve your murder . . ." She smiled as if that was a sure thing—like getting your period on the day of an important swim meet or your cell battery dying just as the guy you like finally calls. "You'll get your Key, put it in the door and—whoosh!—off you go to the Other Side."

Whoosh. Just the sort of noise I imagined the entrance to the next world making.

Finally Nancy sensed my lack of okay.

"We have no idea how long it's been here," she said, desperately trying to get me involved. "It could have been around for hundreds or thousands of years in some form or other. After all, kids must have been murdered in New York ever since time began." Nancy took a second. I got the impression that, for once, there was something she hadn't thought through. Shocker.

"Well, definitely since the Dutch rocked up anyway. Or the Native Americans. Or the . . . Or maybe even years and years before that," Nancy finished unconvincingly.

Super. Now she was giving me a *history* lesson. This was getting more and more surreal.

"Though getting pushed under a T. rex was probably more painful than the F train," Lorna said. She was examining the ends of her hair like a pathologist from *CSI*. I bet she massively regretted not booking a pre-death spa day. Imagine spending eternity with split ends or an imperfect manicure. How did she end up here? Someone spike her Mac lip gloss with cyanide?

"Let's start with the basics," Nancy said. "Rule Two: In the Attesa, things work in pretty much the same way as they did when you were alive—give or take a few little changes." From the back pocket of her pristine, pressed jeans, she produced an equally pristine, pressed booklet with *The Rules* typed on its front cover. It was about as thick as the length of a thumbnail.

Nancy handed the book to me, way too eagerly for someone about to talk about my death. "Everything is covered in here"— she smiled encouragingly—"but obviously it's my job to talk you through things too."

Lorna groaned.

"As the Attesa exists in—what we assume to be—a kind of limbo, you interact with everything in here as you did when you were Living." I looked at Nancy blankly.

Nancy sighed. I wasn't catching on as fast as she'd hoped. "In other words, in here, you act like you did when you were alive. So you can open this curtain, use the elevator, move these pieces of paper." She ruffled some stuff on the table in front of the Door for effect. "Of course, as you're a ghost now and formed of a ball of kinetic energy rather than cells, you *can* walk through the walls if you really want to." She put her hand clear through the white plaster to my left. "But that's just showing off. Oh, and before you ask, no, you can't fly. That would be stupid."

Riiight, trying to find Keys to another dimension and walking through walls = fine. Flying = stupid. Of course.

"On to Rule Three: Like I said before, the Attesa is protected, which means the Living can't see it or us when we're in it. When we're outside, in the human world, the Living can't see or hear us *unless* we want them to."

Wait a second—the Living could see us if we wanted them to? *This* sounded interesting.

"But we'll get on to that later." Bummer. "Right now, what I really want you to see is HHQ."

"H-H- *what*?" I asked.

Nancy led us out of Big Red's alcove and pulled aside a velvet curtain to the left of the reception desk. Behind it was a set of winding stairs. I followed her down them, Lorna and her perfectly respectable split ends trailing behind, to a badly lit corridor below. From what I could see it was dark, dingy, like the areas of any hotel that guests weren't meant to see. Clearly the glamour of the Attesa didn't extend to the lower floors. Why were we here?

At the end of the corridor was a regular-size door. Above it was a cardboard sign with HHQ written in very neat, deliberate letters. Whoever made that sign had probably practiced writing the letters over and over to make sure they were perfect. That said, the sign's effect was slightly ruined by being placed over the door's original, professional hotel sign. The first and last letters (an *O* and an *E*) peeked out behind the cardboard. I decided the original sign had probably spelled out Office.

"Now this," said Nancy, opening the door, "this is the *heart* of our operation: HHQ."

She swung the half-wood, half-frosted-window door open a couple of feet and I squinted inside.

The room was about twelve by twelve feet in size. More than enough to "swing a jackrabbit," as my grandmother would have said, but certainly not as big as I'd expected from an HHQ. Whatever that was.

Nancy walked inside and beckoned for me to join her. Three oblong windows spanned the top third of the facing wall. Through them, I saw a pair of feet walk past. I realized that, having come downstairs, those windows must be at street level with the road outside. And, from down here, you could see people's shoes as they walked by.

It was so weird seeing them—Mr. Nike, Ms. Stiletto, oh and hello, Mr. You-*Really*-Need-to-Visit-the-Shoe-Shine-Guys-in-Grand-Central—and thinking that even if they bent down right now, they couldn't see me.

I looked at the passing feet and wondered, Had I walked past the Attesa before? I must have. After all, there was that amazing boutique at the end of the street that always had great sales. And that basement dive bar where they never asked for ID. Even when David's mom had just made him get a haircut and he looked, like, two years younger than the week before.

Had some newly dead girl stared up at my sneakers as I stomped past? Wondering what kind of person stood in them? Had she thought how much easier everything had been before? Before some idiot stole her future away and she ended up in this place, trying to solve her own murder.

I sighed and looked around the room properly. On the wall to the left of the windows was a map. A massive map of Manhattan. I leaned in more closely. Someone had drawn sharks in the Hudson (um, not cute) and put a pin in a spot labeled School on East 49th Street and Madison Avenue. Another on West 71st labeled Home. And another at the Rockefeller Center F train stop, labeled Murder Scene. And another . . .

Hey, wait a minute! That was *my* school and *my* home and most definitely *my* murder scene. This map was all about *me*.

I swallowed, even though I had nothing to gulp down. School, my apartment, the subway . . . those things I could deal with. But murder scene? Seeing it written out like that was so . . . disturbing.

Someone had carefully tagged this map with all the places I'd visited on my last day—was that *still* today?—the very same person who had neatly written HHQ over the door. And I'd bet my afterlife that I knew who that was.

"Um, Nancy, not to sound all drama queen when we've only just met, but this map? It's all about me. I know it is. And it is freaking me out. What gives?" I asked.

Nancy took a step to her left—to reveal a large blackboard behind her, opposite the map wall. Oh, great, so we were back in school. Then I read what was on it.

17:01 Police arrive at CF's house.

17:04 Police enter.

17:10 Mother of CF informed of her death.

17:16 CF's mother contacts her father to pass on the news.

17:22 Police rule out foul play.

17:30 Case closed. Cause of death: Accidental.

"Will someone *please* tell me what is going on?" I heard myself say.

"Okay, Charlotte, sit." Nancy patted a chair beside her.

Sit? Sit on the black couch, sit on the bed, sit on the weird spinny office chair in HHQ. "Sit" seemed to be Nancy's default setting when I looked like I was dangerously close to fainting.

I sat down with a thump.

"So when I got to Hotel Attesa—two years ago now, Tess and Lorna were here, but so was another girl called Lyndsay. She was the longest resident, so she taught me some stuff, just as she'd taught Tess and Lorna when they first arrived."

My head was whirling more than ever.

"Lyndsay said that, when she'd arrived, another ghost had given her the Rules book—and told her to pass it on to whoever came in next before she left."

So the Rules were passed down from dead girl to dead girl?

"But the rules clearly didn't help you solve your murder," I said. "You're still here."

"It might have," Nancy admitted quietly. "I'm sort of ninety-nine percent sure who killed me."

"So why haven't you gone through the Big Red Door?" The words tumbled out before I had a chance to worry that it might be too early to ask something like that.

Nancy looked down at her feet, tilting her head until a wave of her thick hair fell over her face. "I guess I . . . I don't want to move on yet," she said in a small voice. "The information Lyndsay gave me when I first showed up here . . . well, it was invaluable to me. In helping me, um, come to terms with things. I kinda figured: if I could stick around and help other kids the way she helped me, then maybe I wouldn't have died in vain.

"What I'm trying to say is that I have my reasons for sticking around." Nancy gave me a small smile. "You may find yours. Anyway! We've solved the murders of the last—what?" She looked at Lorna for reassurance. "Six kids who have come through these doors."

Six? *Six?* Um, that did not sound like a Series-winning stat to me.

"It seems that when we die, some power in the Attesa takes our stories from out there"—Nancy pointed to the window where the outside world was going on as normal—"to here," and waved the ancient-looking letter she was still holding at me. "One of these arrives just before each new ghost does. We don't know how or who sends it, but it's always the same. It tells us basic information: your name, how, and when you died."

So there was some spectral scribe out there sending letters about teenage deaths? Awesome.

"Er, so if another one of those letter-things arrives, another dead kid is on the way?" I managed.

"Well, yes, but—aside from our current residents—it's not often that we have two new ghosts here at the same time. I mean, it does happen. But if you look at the *New York Times* murder map, around seventy-four people are unlawfully killed each year in Manhattan and only six percent are under eighteen. Which means, in theory, we get less than one new case a month. Quite a manageable workload, wouldn't you say, Lorna?"

I tried not to audibly gulp.

"Now, as you can see from the board, both of your parents

know," Nancy continued, as if she were reading out a grocery list. "We did some basic recon when we got your letter before your arrival, and the police had already ruled your death an accident. That's quick, really. Especially considering how you went."

"There must have been a real mess on the tracks," Lorna said. "They shut down the F train line for a whole two hours for you. Two hours! *And* in rush hour."

My final achievement. Man, I hoped Mom was getting that put on my gravestone. "Here lies Charlotte Feldman. She pissed off commuters. A lot."

"Since the police have no clue you were murdered and in the absence of your murderer confessing in the next few days, finding out who pushed you is down to us," Nancy said.

Super. Down to a Nancy Drew wannabe, AWOL Tess, the Abercrombie model, and me. What murder squad wouldn't want a lineup like that? I better get some posters for my bedroom wall. I was going to be here for some time.

"That's why Nancy calls this room HHQ," Lorna explained with a look that said, *If you thought Dead Girls Detective Agency was lame, just wait till you get a load of this one.* "It's the official dead girls' *Haunting* Head Quarters."

Inspired. "And the map?" I asked.

"I just put it up on the wall because it helps me visualize a case."

"What about the sharks drawn in the Hudson?" I asked. Did I really want to hear the answer? Was the river haunted by some supernatural sea life they'd failed to warn me about?

"Rule Four," Lorna said. "Ghosts can't travel over water. Nancy just drew those in to show that we can't go in the river."

Of course. I turned to Nancy hoping she'd explain.

"Basically, ghosts are landlocked. Who knows why? Maybe so we'll stay in the city and concentrate on solving our cases. But if you are going to be stuck on an island, I can't imagine a better one than Manhattan, can you?"

Awesome—so now that I was dead and didn't appear to have a curfew, I still couldn't go and watch bands in Brooklyn. Double, triple, quadruple *fun*. Uh, unless I was about to find out that Rule 5 was that all teen ghosts did have a curfew after all.

"So is that it then?" I asked. "Are those all the Rules? No water walking, lots of crime solving, and don't forget to treat the hotel and everything in it like you would if you hadn't been pushed under a subway train?"

Nancy tucked her hair behind her ear. "Oh no, there are a *load* more." She pointed to the thin red book. "I just thought I'd ease you in with the simple stuff."

Great.

"And what if I don't abide by these Rules?" I was getting sick of all the dos and don'ts. "What happens to me then? According to you, I'm already dead. How much worse can it really get?"

Nancy looked shocked. Lorna actually looked up from her split ends. Crap. Had I gone too far?

"Now you sound like my kinda ghoul," a low voice deadpanned behind me.

I swung around to see a guy with a sarcastic look on his face, leaning on the door frame. His coloring was as dark as David's was fair. His black bangs were swept to one side, but fell across his face, threatening to obscure his green eyes. He was wearing a tight black T-shirt and black skinny jeans. Even his Adidas—which were either vintage or a proof he'd been dead a lot longer than everyone else—were black. Something in the way he looked at me made me want to put my hands over my face and hide like a kindergarten kid. Why had everyone failed to mention that there was a dead boy next door?

"Just ignore him," Nancy warned. "He's used that line many, many times before. And not one new arrival has laughed at it yet, have they, Edison?"

"Tess did," he shot back.

Tess? Was *he* friends with *her*? Not that I knew the girl, but I strongly suspected that made this Edison guy trouble.

"So you say, but seeing as you were both here before Lorna and me, we don't have any proof that's the case," Nancy said. One thing I could not imagine Tess doing was cracking a smile.

Edison raised an eyebrow at her and smirked at me. Oh boy.

"See you around." He walked out of the room. No "hey, nice to meet you," "who are you?" or even a "how did you die?" Men: Clearly some were as incommunicative in death as in life.

"So, um, these Rules," I said, trying to keep my voice steady.

"Sorry to sound stupid, but I'm not really getting them. Can we run through the important stuff again?" Without making me read the book because it looks really, really dull, I silently added.

"Oh, we can do better than that," Nancy said, brightening and leading the way out of HHQ. "I'll show you how they work—out in the real world. In practice."

Chapter 4

I'D BEEN IN WASHINGTON SQUARE PARK A million times before. After all, I'd lived in New York all my life. Me and my best friend, Ali, used to cut through to go shopping in Soho (the thought of that gave me an instant pang). Mom's favorite Italian was around the corner (double pang). But if you said "Washington Square," I always thought of one person: David.

I'm not one of those boyfriend name-droppers. I hate those girls—who doesn't? Ali and I used to say they had broccoli syndrome. Like, they could work their boyfriend's name into any conversation. So even if you were discussing something as blah as broccoli, they'd be like, "Oh, Pete, my boyfriend, he *loves* broccoli."

I'm so not a broccoli girl. But, being here, I couldn't help thinking about how we met.

David transferred from his super-fancy private school uptown to my regular one near Rockefeller Center last spring. When he walked into my homeroom, all shy looks and baggy pants, I decided he was probably the hottest guy I'd ever laid eyes on right then and there. He was tan, had messy blond hair, and a guitar case permanently slung over his shoulder—he looked like a cute surfer who'd run away from the beach to join a rock 'n' roll band. But I also figured the omnipresent Strat and remnants of last weekend's guyliner meant he was probably one of those try-hard prep kids too. You know, the ones who figure they're hip, but blow it by thinking it's okay to actually use words like *summered* and *supper*.

After school one day in his first week, I was walking down Fifth, when I saw him smiling across the street. If I'm being honest, I had to stop and take a second to check he was waving at me and not some other girl standing behind me.

"Hey, where are you going?" he asked, bouncing across the street like an overenthusiastic puppy dog. Was he for real?

"Just down to the Village."

"Great! Me too!" He smiled and I noticed that, when he did, his eyes crinkled. "Mind if I go with you?"

I was totally prepared for this to be the most awkward subway ride of my life. But the bizarro thing was, as soon as we started talking, we couldn't stop. It was like he'd read every book I had and downloaded all of my favorite songs. We talked about discovering Hole *years* before *Jennifer's Body* came out, how we knew we should have read *A Clockwork Orange*, but hadn't made it past the first page, and how—even though he'd only just started—David could totally tell our school sucked and was full of a bunch of vapid morons.

Before I knew it, we'd hit West 4th Street and walked over to Washington Square. We sat on the gray walls of the fountain, our backs to the water. It was a scorching May day, but there was this breeze that, every so often, would pick up out of nowhere, making the leaves on the trees rustle and wave. I remember that, not because I'm some weird weather obsessive, but because when it did start up, the spray bubbling up in the fountain would catch on the breeze and fall on our backs like mist. And, even though I am so not into my looks, I kept thinking all that moisture in the air was going to make my wavy black hair frizz. And that David, this cool muso boy I'd just met, was going to decide then and there that he didn't want to date a big ball of hair fuzz like me.

Which was pathetic, I know. But everyone's allowed to be vain once in a while. Especially where cute boys are concerned. Especially cute boys who have three Cure albums on their iPod—instead of just downloading "Pictures of You" because it was on that commercial—and actually know who Emily Dickinson is.

It was all going great. Way too great as it turned out. Because then *she* appeared.

"David! Hey!"

I looked up from Mr. Probably-as-Perfect-as-a-Guy-Can-Get to see a sickeningly cute, slender redhead wearing a maxi-dress I'd never look that good in, waving at us across the square.

David jumped away from me as if we were six and I'd just told him I had cooties.

"Oh, I . . . I've gotta go," he said, pushing his iPod into his bag and racing off across the baking concrete. "Bye!" he shouted at me, without even turning back. When he reached the redhead, he slung his arm around her shoulder. As he pushed his Wayfarers up his nose, she threw back her head and laughed. They looked like something off the front of a Bob Dylan album.

Maybe I shouldn't have been surprised that, looking at the fountain now—a year and a half later—I still felt nauseous at the memory, so badly I wanted to sit down.

Of course it all worked out. Eventually. But what did that matter now? What did it matter that, back in the Living world, I had a boyfriend who totally got me. And a family who loved me. And a best friend who, well . . . What did it matter? Not one bit.

Not now as I stood here, on the evening of the day I died, with only two dead girls for company.

What if I never spent another afternoon like that with David—or any guy—again? What if this was it for me? What if the only people I would ever talk to now were Nancy (Her Geekiness), Lorna (signs of intelligence yet to be discovered), Tess (not my biggest fan for who-cared-why), and Edison (tall, dark, and probably trouble)?

Uptown, the lights on the Empire State Building twinkled in the evening air. Tonight they were orange and green—in honor of Halloween, which was less than a week away. While I'd totally never admit this out loud, I liked them best when they went pink for Valentine's Day. I hadn't been up the Empire State since I was about eleven. Not since me and Ali went through our super-lame *Sleepless in Seattle* stage (triple pang). That felt eons ago.

"Now, porting is actually quite easy. Though most newbies don't manage it on their first try." The sound of Nancy's voice snapped me back to the here and now. Unfortunately. The now where I was meant to be learning how to be a good ghost instead of thinking about David or Ali or stupid old movies or signs or whatever.

"Por— *What?*"

"Porting. Well, transporting, to give it its full name. Jeez, Charlotte, have you never seen a scary movie? Read a supernatural book?"

Not recently. I was more of an art gallery girl. I shrugged.

Nancy went on. "In order to solve our murders we need to be able to travel around the city. To spy on the Living. Maybe haunt them a bit. But only if *absolutely* necessary. And it's not like we can hail a cab or get the subway."

The subway. No, I was definitely not super-keen to jump on the subway anytime soon. Glad to hear I now had a new mode of transportation.

"So here's the good news: Ghosts have their own way of traveling—porting. And it means we can get anywhere in the blink of a human eye."

"Anywhere?" I asked. This could be kinda neat.

"Anywhere!" Nancy said. "Well, anywhere in Manhattan. Rule Four. Remember Rule Four?"

I nodded. Yes, I remembered it. Ghosts don't do water, therefore no going anywhere remotely interesting like London or Venice or Paris . . . or Williamsburg. Which big-time sucked.

Guess saving for a summer backpacking around Europe had been a total waste of my time then.

"If we need to go somewhere in the city to investigate your murder, all we do is shut our eyes"—Nancy crinkled hers tightly for effect. Or maybe just because she thought I was *that* dumb—"concentrate really hard on the place we want to go, and when we open them again we should be there."

"Do we need to have been there before?" I asked.

"Nope," Nancy said. "Just as long as you know where it is and can concentrate on the location, that should be enough."

Sweet. That sounded easy enough. I screwed up my eyes. Where to?

"No! Wait! I don't think it's a good idea for you to port on your own on your first go," Nancy said. "You could end up anywhere. Do you remember that time we lost the new dead boy, Lorna?" She nodded. "He was seventeen, but he wasn't really all that smart. To put it mildly. Anyway, he got overexcited and ported to some part of Central Park up near the East Meadow where he and his friends used to go to smoke pot when he was alive. But because he'd never been there at night before—"

"Or not baked," Lorna interrupted.

"He got lost," Nancy said, being very careful to keep her eyes on me. I don't think Nancy wanted to give Lorna any encouragement. "For some reason, he hadn't been listening when I'd told him where the Attesa was"—I wondered why—"so he couldn't port back here. It was a whole day before we found him walking around the zoo and got him back. He was hiding out in the penguin enclosure. I estimate that held up his investigation by weeks. Weeks! We don't want that happening again."

Hell no.

Lorna stood beside me. "So we'll take you on your first port, get you used to the feeling, then after that you can go wherever you like." She winked at me. "In the line of investigation of course."

Hmmm, maybe this was going to get interesting. Nancy walked over to my other side. I felt surrounded. Just as I was about to ask them to give me some space, both girls lifted their hands, making an arm circle around me. What the . . . ? "So," Nancy said, "where do you want to port to on your first trip? Bearing in mind that we can't leave the island, of course."

Where? I honestly had no idea. Where *did* I want to go? Nowhere near the F train, that was for sure. Or my apartment. I couldn't handle seeing my parents upset. Or knowing that they couldn't see me when I was right by their side. Not yet anyway. Ali's place? That could also be, well, weird. And the other option? The obvious one that involved going to the one person I *really*, deep down, wanted to see? That was way too painful right now.

I shifted my eyes back to the Attesa. There was a quick

movement in one of the upstairs windows. A chill ran through me. *Come on, Charlotte,* I reasoned. *You've got nothing to be afraid of in there.* I focused on the window. I could just about make out a figure dressed in black. Edison. Why was he bothering to watch me? He must have seen this whole training session BS a trillion times before.

"Charlotte, pick a place," Nancy said.

But where? I looked over to the Attesa again. The figure in the window pointed upward. At something high in the skyline, way above the hotel.

I looked up, following Edison's lead. But before my eyes even found it, I knew which building he was pointing to. The one looming above the rest of the skyline, standing proud like the tallest kid in class.

"There," I said to Nancy, pointing to the Empire State.

"Then we'll take you," Nancy said. She and Lorna lifted their arms.

I looked back to the hotel, to make a sign that somehow thanked him for the suggestion, but the window was empty.

"Let me guess, the spookabee requested you take her up the Empire State?" a voice drawled.

I looked to my right and there was Tess. How had she snuck up on us?

"You know, statistically, that's the second-most-picked place for the recently murdered to choose when Nancy gives them this part of the induction," she said, walking around the three of us.

"Of course, number one is usually 'home,' but you never let anyone go there, do you, Nance?"

"Of course not," Nancy said. "There's a time for that and I don't think it's so soon after . . . arrival."

"No, not at all," Tess said. I wished she'd stop walking. She was making me feel kinda dizzy. "Don't you ever wish though, Nancy, that someone would pick somewhere more exciting? Like the Chrysler? Or Harlem? Or maybe a subway track?"

Wow, that was unnecessary.

"Tess . . . ," Nancy warned, in a voice that told me Tess was in control of this one, no matter what Nancy said. "Where do you suggest we go then?"

"I'd love to stay and think of somewhere good, but in case you haven't noticed I'm not the local limbo guide," she said. "That would be you. And I—unlike you losers—have *much* better things to do. See ya."

Tess turned. There was a *pop!* and she disappeared.

"How did she . . . ? Where did she . . . ?" I asked, hoping maybe she'd gone forever, even though that was totally not something I could say out loud. Yet.

"So that was your first introduction to porting," Nancy said, shaking her head. "Not quite the one I had in mind, but I guess at least you know what it looks like from the outside now. Anyway, let's get this lesson back on track."

Nancy and Lorna resumed their places around me, arms curved.

"If I were you, I'd shut my eyes," Lorna said.

Suddenly Washington Square started to spin. The white arches melted into the trees and the streetlamps and the sidewalk and the buildings and the bricks. When I was a little kid, Ali and I played this game where we whirled around and around and around until we felt sick and couldn't walk in a straight line. Urgh, this was that feeling squared. Being dizzy wasn't any better when you were dead. Leave it to me to be the only ghost to develop porting sickness.

I scrunched up my eyes, hoping that if I didn't watch the world twirl, I could fool my body into thinking I wasn't moving and the grab-me-a-bucket feeling would pass. Tighter, tighter. I concentrated on nothing but squeezing my eyes shut.

Then—just like that—with a *pop!* my own personal merry-go-round stopped.

"Charlotte, it's cool," Lorna whispered into my right ear. "We're here. Open up."

I did as she said. A surge of reassurance rushed through me. The whole of New York lay out beneath us. Its lights winking in the moonlight. There we were—on top of the world.

Chapter 5

LIKE I SAID, THE LAST TIME I VISITED THE EMPIRE State Building, I was eleven years old and kinda easily impressed. Even though I'd been up there before—once for some kid's birthday, another time on an elementary school trip—I'd still walked around the viewing platform gawking like a tourist. I wanted to be cooler about it, but I felt a buzz the second the elevator doors opened. Eighty-six stories up, you were on a level with the clouds. It felt like you ruled the city and anything was possible. Anything at all.

That day, Ali and I spent ages trying to pinpoint my apartment building and find where she lived, a few blocks west and nearer to the river. Mom pointed out our school, and the New York Times building where Dad worked on the sports desk. There was a Yankees game on, and Mom joked that, if you looked closely enough, you could see him jumping up and down at his desk with excitement. I was too young to make a face and tell her to stop being so dumb, and looking back now, I was kind of glad about that.

Now, at night, even after everything that had happened to me today—and it was a *lot*—it was just as impressive.

"Does everyone feel beyond dizzy the first time they port?" I asked Lorna, who was staring wistfully at a group of girls our age in super-fashion dresses, carrying so many shopping bags they could hardly lean on the rails.

"Yes, it's fine. Don't sweat it. You'll get used to it. Do you see her adorable Marc Jacobs bag?" She pointed at the girl gang again with a pout.

"Lorna . . ." I tried to get her attention, but she was still obsessing over the girls, nibbling on a hangnail that would never come off, and scrunching up her eyes.

"Lorna!" I practically shouted.

"Yeah?" She finally stopped staring and turned back to me. I tried not to think about the fact I was sentenced to eternity in clothes Mom had bought from the school supply shop. Hopefully her kick-ass boots saved me. A bit.

"Why did you and Nancy circle me with your arms like that? Just before we ported."

"To make sure we all traveled together," she explained. "When you get the hang of porting on your own, we can all just think of the same place—like the hotel or a particular street—close our eyes, and end up there. But until you've passed Nancy's port test, it's safer if we act as the TomTom and guide you. It worked though, right? The hotel to here in less than ten seconds. How cool?"

Lorna lowered her voice—though not *that* much—and leaned in. "Honestly, I am so glad you're here, Charlotte. It's the best when new people turn up. Even if it's just for a few days before they get their Key. Keeps me sane what with all the Rules and the clues and the Scooby-Dooing."

I was so glad my untimely death was good news for someone. I nodded and tried to smile. Maybe it was time to ask the question I'd been dying to ever since Nancy admitted that she could probably find her Key if she *really* wanted to.

"Haven't you tried to get to the Other Side? To find your own Key," I asked, hoping she wouldn't get upset. Lorna might be ditzy but she was way friendlier than Tess. Though so was a rabid rottweiler. Still, this was the first chance we'd had to talk. I didn't exactly have unlimited friend options.

"My Key? Not really." Lorna shuffled. "I mean, I know how I died, but I'm not totally Key focused, if you know what I mean. My family"—Lorna's face softened—"they live just up there." She pointed to the Upper East Side, somewhere past the Guggenheim Museum, which glowed dental commercial white in the moonlight. "And I kind of like the fact I can still go visit them. See what they're up to. Talk to my cat, Tiger. Find out how my little sister, Emma, is doing. See how much cuter she gets every day."

Lorna kept staring out, as if she could see her home. "The idea of giving that up—of moving on to somewhere where there are no guarantees that I'll be able to watch them as much as I can now? Well, that just makes me sad. So for now, I'm staying put. It's not like I'm in a rush or anything, is it? In theory, I have forever, so I figure I'd rather spend a little more of it in New York with the people I love. Even if they don't know I'm here."

I was not the touchy-feely link-arms-on-the-sidewalk type, but right then I wanted to give Lorna the biggest hug. But I wasn't really sure if ghosts could even hug each other. I might fall right through her. So instead I hung back, said nothing, and thought that, yep, there was definitely more to Lorna than first met the eye.

"Besides, like Tess is always saying, finding your Key might not be such a good idea—after all, we don't know what's through the Door, do we?" Lorna said. "We only know that no one has ever come back through it. And that might not be because they don't want to." She shuddered.

Tess. There she was again. It seemed like Nancy and Lorna were almost scared of her. Or at least weren't about to get on the wrong side of someone with such a stellar mean-girl act.

"I mean, what if when you go through, that's it? You're trapped?" Lorna said. Tess had shook her up about this, hadn't she? "What if what's behind the door is . . . hell?"

I must have been looking at her strangely because Lorna stopped, got a hold of herself, took a second, then smiled. "I'm sure it's not though. I'm sure you'll be fine," she said.

"This may be a totally rude question so please just tell me to get lost—I'm not up on the dead-etiquette thing yet—but, um, how *did* you die?"

Way to lighten the mood, Charlotte.

"No, it's fine. I don't mind telling you," Lorna said. "I made out with the prom queen's date during the slow dance section. Some bitch hit me over the head with her crown as soon as I left the floor."

I unsuccessfully suppressed a giggle. I was being sarcastic about the whole cyanide-in-the-lip-gloss theory, but turned out I wasn't that wide of the mark.

"Well, that's a much better conversation starter than 'some psycho pushed me under the F train,'" I said.

Despite ourselves, we both giggled. Hmmm . . . maybe I liked Lorna. Which was weird because I hadn't had a whole lot of girl friends when I was alive, apart from Ali, who I'd known forever. And especially not ones who looked like they'd stepped off the pages of *Teen Vogue*.

"Come on, let's go find Nancy," Lorna said. "I'm sure she's going loco somewhere because we're wasting 'valuable lesson time' gossiping. Though, in my humble opinion, gossip is never a waste."

We found Nancy on the north-facing side of the observation deck, looking out in the direction of the New York Times building. For a second, I felt a pang for my dad, and had to tell myself to stop with the pity party and just get on with the matter at hand. Haunting for beginners.

"So how did you find your debut port?" Nancy asked.

"About as much fun as my last trip to the dentist, but I'll get over it." I was trying not to think about the dizziness or if it would be as hard on the way off this thing as it had been on the way up. "I just need to train my brain to realize that, now I'm dead and can't breathe anymore, it's pointless making me feel like I am going to blow chunks. Because I can't, right?"

Nancy nodded. "Now that you don't have a body, it's all in the mind. Which brings us to Rule Five . . ." Of course. I patted my blazer pocket and felt its outline. Red book—passed down from teen ghost to teen ghost—at the ready. "Which is that ghosts can appear to humans if we need to—to solve a case."

What? Ghosts could appear to humans! So there *was* a way to make my parents and David see me again?

"We can?" Rein in the overenthusiasm, Charlotte, or they'll get suspicious.

"Oh yes!" Nancy said. "I mean, we don't make a habit of it. No one wants to be freaking out the Living for no good reason or doing anything that's going to end up on YouTube or *Most Haunted* or whatever reality TV show Bravo's commissioned this week." No, God forbid. "But sometimes we do need to let the Living know we're here in the course of an investigation. A little light haunting can be extremely effective when we're trying to get information out of people—information they don't necessarily want to tell us."

"Nancy Radley, are you suggesting that sometimes you scare the Living in order to make them confess?" I asked.

"Not exactly," she said, using a voice that should have had subtitles reading *yesss*. "It's for the sake of justice. And your Key."

"So essentially what you're saying is that if we think one or more of the Living know something about my death or they seem to be acting all suspicious and hiding something, we are entirely within our rights to scare them until they 'fess up?"

"Um, no. Well, yes?"

Uh-huh. Maybe there was more to Her Geekiness than met the eye too.

"Now, the key to making yourself visible to the Living is to focus on your fingertips, then push until the energy spreads out over your whole body," Nancy said. "You'll materialize to the Living as an apparition—and look just as you did before you died. Well, before you were killed horribly. So that means normal, but with a bit more of a glow."

Oh, good, I'll appear as a glowing ghost to my loved ones. That won't mess them up even more than my murder.

"So, in order to apparite, you need to push," she continued. "Push all your energy down to the ends of your fingers, everything inside of you—and there's a lot of kinetic energy there—and that power will make you visible whenever you need it to. Sure, it takes time and practice, but you can do it. And you will get the hang of it."

"Um, Nance," I said. "Is it wise doing this here? There's so many peo— I mean, so many of the *Living* hanging about. Won't they freak out if they start seeing free-floating hands while they're trying to make the telescopes work?"

"Actually this is a perfect place to practice," she said, all trust-me and breezy. "I always bring new recruits to public places. Everyone here is so busy gaping at the city, no one looks at what's happening next to them. Look, I'll prove it."

She walked over to a young couple who were snuggling up like newlyweds. Miss Snuggler was pointing in the direction of Brooklyn, while her guy spooned her from behind and whispered the kind of sweet nothings in her ear that made me want to barf. Wait until one of you dies before your time, I wanted to say to them, you won't be so smug and huggy then. Because one of you will be down there in the city probably crying your eyes out and looking at pictures from last semester's trip to the Smithsonian while the other one of you will be floating around somewhere inappropriate, like the top of the Empire State, learning how to make her pinky finger reappear just to scare humans.

Nancy stood next to Spoon-a-lot and a look of extreme concentration filled her face. She stared hard at her hand and slowly, like a glass filling with cherry soda, her fingers changed color. They began to look, well, more alive again. Until that moment I hadn't even noticed that she—we—could have auditioned to play one of the Cullen family, but now Nancy's hand was back to full rosiness, it was beyond obvious. So that was what happened when a part of you became visible to the Living again. Her hand glowed with a pinky hue.

Nancy looked back at me, then back to Hug-boy and smiled. If he stopped paying attention to his date and did a 180, he'd see that there was now a neat little hand floating right by his ear. A hand without a body. No body that he could see, anyway.

Nancy waved her visible hand about for a few seconds, before putting it behind his head and making a bunny ears sign. Neither he nor his girlfriend noticed a single thing. They were far too busy planning what sights they were going to see the next day. Or which street corner they were going to make out on next. Yuck.

As usual, Nancy was right. Busy places were actually perfect to practice my new skills without upsetting the Living. I hoped I didn't suck at apparition as badly as I did at chem.

"Your turn," she said, relaxing as she put her hand back down by her side. It paled until it matched the chalky color of the rest of her body. "Try it out. Make your hand appear."

I held out my fingers in front of my face and stared at them hard. In fourth grade, my piano teacher told me I was lucky to have such long, thin fingers. Apparently I could have been a natural. Like Alicia Keys or something. That was if I'd ever bothered to practice and Dad hadn't canceled the lessons after two months on account of me missing three to watch cartoons with Ali instead.

Right, apparition. How hard could this be? My fingers were ready. All I needed to do was find my energy. I could do that. I'd watched enough yoga shows on the Fitness Channel. (Admittedly while eating cookie dough ice cream on the couch, but still . . .) I patted my stomach. Maybe my power was hiding in there. I strained and clenched and stared at my hand. Boy, was this unattractive. I strained again. Nope, nothing. My hand still wasn't going to be seen by any breath-takers tonight.

"Relax, don't try so hard," Nancy said. Which, actually, was so not helpful. I smiled through my clenched teeth at Lorna, silently thanking her for hanging back and letting me take my time.

I lifted my hand again and stared at my fingers. This time, instead of thinking about my stomach, I thought about them and how much I wanted them to appear. To look the way they used to when I was alive. How they did when David held my hand. If I could just make this work, then he could see me. I could appear to him one last time and let him know that I might be dead, but I was okay. And that he would be okay someday too.

My toes felt warm. Then my calves. Then my knees. Then that balmy perfect-bath feeling traveled all the way up my body—like the sensation you get when you drink a mug of hot chocolate on a winter's day—until, eventually, all of me was nice and toasty.

I examined my fingers, wiggled them again. They felt buzzy like the top of a stereo speaker. And they were pink! Pink! Had I made them apparite? I turned back to Nancy and Lorna expecting to see them smiling all encouragingly because I'd done it. I'd made my hand appear!

But both of their mouths were on the floor. Not literally. But they *were* looking at me like I had three heads.

"Charlotte, whatever you do, don't move," Nancy said, edging toward me. "You've somehow managed to . . . You, well, you . . . It seems you have a *gift* for apparition."

What was she talking about? I'd done what she asked, right? My hand was pink, just like hers had been. "Nancy, what's *wrong* with you?" I asked. "Since I got to the Attesa, I've done everything you've asked of me," I waved my hand around and up in the air. "And it seems all you can do is . . ."

Um, hang on a minute. What was that? I waved my arm again. It was glowing. *All* of it. My fingers, my forearm, my elbow. Like a neon party sign. I looked down at my other arm, my legs. Same story.

Uh-oh. Somehow I hadn't just made my hand visible to the Living—I'd done my whole body. Which meant that people—human, not dead people—could see me and . . .

"Miss, can I see your ticket?" A security guard in a uniform was standing in front of me. I swiveled around, desperately hoping there was some alive girl behind me who he was talking to.

"Miss?" Darn, there was no one but two preppy guys in dorky pastel polo shirts and khakis. Which meant he had to be talking to me. Which meant—oh, *help*—he could totally see me. And he was looking at me very strangely indeed.

"Er, I think I lost it when I came up here," I said. My voice sounded strange. Like it was lower than normal and had a bit of an echo. Now he could see me, could he hear me too?

"Lost it?" He parroted back. So we'd established that, yep, apparition made my voice audible to the Living too. "And where do you think you did that exactly? You do need a valid ticket to be up here, I'm afraid. Plenty of signs told you that before you got in the elevator. Where do you think you lost it, miss? Your ticket?"

Oh, crap. Should I just make myself disappear? Or would that make him madder? Actually, I didn't even know how to do that. Nancy had stuck me at the wheel of a speeding car and forgotten to point out the brakes. Come to think of it, where *was* Nancy?

Then I saw her. Behind the security man, she and Lorna were waving madly. They kept pretending to hold something in the air, then miming that it had fallen out of their hands and . . . where were they pointing?

What was with them? This was not the time to start playing charades. I was knee-deep in smelly stuff here and I needed their help. Nancy pointed over the edge again.

"What? What are you trying to say, Nancy?" I asked, feeling myself getting annoyed.

Security man looked behind him to the spot where Nancy stood. Where I could see her. But he could just see air.

"Have you been drinking, young lady?" he asked, starting to get stern with me now. He obviously thought I was wasted—why else would I be asking the air behind him questions? "Because one thing we at the Empire State Building do not allow is any person under the influence of any alcohol . . ."

Lorna giggled. Nancy was too busy madly pointing to find it funny.

"Now, you'll have to show me your ticket or I'm going to have to ask you to leave."

"Sir, I told you: I lost it," I pleaded. He was so not buying this.

"It went . . ." I looked back to Nancy, who was waving at me—she did her little mime again, something in her hand, it flew out and over the edge. Oh. I got her now. I turned back to the security guard and gave him the same polite smile that I usually reserved for David's mom.

"I did have a ticket, but when I got up here there was a big gust of wind and it went over the rails." I pointed to the street below, like that was going to make him believe me any more than he already didn't.

"That may be," he said, his cheeks getting redder by the second. I shouldn't have added the polite smile. It never worked on David's mom either. "But if you don't have your ticket now, you'll have to leave. If you'll just follow me to the elevator . . ."

He turned his back to me and started to lead the way off the observation deck and back into the building. Ohmigod, what was I going to do? What if he tried to touch my arm? He'd go right through it—just like Nancy's arm had gone through the wall in the Attesa. Or worse, he was going to take me in the elevator, where there weren't as many lights, then he'd see I was glowing. *Glowing.* He'd get all freaked out. And call the police. Or maybe Ghostbusters. I bet they had a number for that here. I can't have been the first spook to show up. What if they caught me with some ghost ray and locked me up in a special, secret prison and I was stuck in there forever and ever and . . .

"Quick! Charlotte! This is your chance. Blow!" Nancy said.

"What?"

"Don't think about it, just as hard as you can blow—blow all the energy out through your mouth and you'll disappear."

Blow? Blow. I didn't think, I just did what Nancy said.

Cold crept down my body. Quicker than the warmth had come. It made me wince, like a milkshake headache did.

"Miss, if you'll just walk this way . . ."

The security guard turned around. And around again. I hadn't moved an inch, but—please—it seemed as if he could no longer see me.

"Miss? Miss?"

I looked down at my body. It was washed out and pale again. No glow. Result!

"Well, I . . ." He stomped off into the building. No doubt to find a colleague to come and hunt for me. Or—worse—so he could look at the security camera footage. Now *that* was going to make for interesting viewing. Now you see me, now you don't. Was that how it went? Did apparitions even appear on camera? Maybe he'd think he'd fantasized me. That I was just a figment of his imagination. He'd probably had a long day after all.

I turned back to Nancy and Lorna. "That was a close one, hey?"

"That's one way to put it," Nancy said, tucking a stray strand of hair behind her ear.

"How did you do *that*?" Lorna asked, her blue eyes wide. "It took me weeks to even make my little finger glow and you—you made your entire body go on your first try. You're even better at apparition than Nancy!"

Her Geekiness scowled.

"I have no idea. I just thought of how much I wanted it and *bam!* there I was. Weird."

"Wait a minute," Nancy said, looking uneasy. "He's coming back."

She gestured behind us. We turned to see the security guy striding over—with another guard. Even though I knew I was invisible again, what if I hadn't blown hard enough? What if they could still see my foot or my ear?

"She was here. Just *here*," the guard told his friend. "Then poof! She was gone. Like she disappeared into thin air. Where can she have gone to? There's only one way out."

"Guys, we should get out of here," Lorna whispered. She seemed to have forgotten that the security men couldn't hear her either. "We don't know when Miss Apparite here"—she pointed to me—"will get her glow on again." Lorna walked in between the two men, who were busy arguing about my whereabouts. "And these guys look, like, ancient. I don't think either of their hearts could take seeing a ghost again this evening."

"You're right, Lorna," Nancy said. Possibly for the first time ever. She turned to me. "Seeing as you seem to be something of a star student, we'll let you take the wheel. You can transport us out of here. Just think of somewhere you really want to be, or someone you have a strong emotional connection to. Think hard, then close your eyes and—if that demo was anything to go by—you should be able to port the three of us off the Empire

State on your own. Lorna and I will travel with you."

They stood on either side of me to be sure we all ported together, making a circle with their arms, one wide enough to encompass but not touch me.

"What if she's hiding in the restroom? Have you checked in there?" security man 2 was asking. "They're fast, teenagers. My grandson managed to sneak out to a bar when he came to stay with me last month. You can imagine how mad his mother was at me about that. Honestly, blink and they're gone."

They had *no* idea. I looked at Nancy, then at Lorna. Nancy nodded, silently willing me to give it a go. Just as quickly as I could, please. I shut my eyes. Think of somewhere I really want to be. Or someone I have a strong connection with . . .

I couldn't help it. Much as I tried not to, of course I thought of him. The dizziness started, and I tried not to imagine the world around me whirling, spinning out of my control.

Then it stopped. I opened my eyes. And there we were. Me and my new dead friends.

In David's bedroom.

Chapter 6

"WHERE ARE *WE?" LORNA WHISPERED, HER BLUE* eyes wide. "This isn't the Attesa. Where in Manhattan have you brought us to, Charlotte?"

The one place I'd always wanted to see, but had never been allowed to go: my boyfriend's bedroom. So just knowing where something was *did* give you enough information to port there. But while we were here, he—from what I could tell—was not.

Phew?

I sneaked a preliminary peek around. Blue walls. Matching dark blue comforter. Sun-bleached My Chemical Romance poster (of course). Bashed-up iPod charging in its dock. Acoustic guitar proudly displayed on a stand in the corner. Grime gathering on said guitar due to his move into band "management." (Translation: He might have looked cute carrying a Strat, but playing-wise, he sucked.) Half a toy airplane suspended from the ceiling. Dirty sports socks on the floor.

Typical teen-boy room.

I'd imagined this particular one in my head a thousand times—when I'd finally be let in, what I'd say, how cool I'd be, all *I'm not freaking out about this. I go into boys' bedrooms all the time.* It was beyond weird to finally be here. Especially considering all the other places I'd been in the last few hours.

It felt familiar but super-strange too. As if I were standing onstage in the set of a play—and this was how some big-deal Broadway producer had imagined David's room to be. Why was that? It had only been half a day since we'd seen each other—was I that removed from him already? Would I feel this way if I ported into my own home too?

"Wherever it is, they need to fire their maid," Nancy said.

Slightly harsh, I thought. Until I caught sight of not one but three used cereal bowls on the windowsill—each growing various stages of mold. It *was* messy. But then it wasn't like David had been expecting three ghost guests, was it? I'm sure he'd have gotten out the vacuum and thrown away that pizza box under his bed if he'd known.

Oh, who was I kidding? David had never been a poster boy for neat. He always had ink stains on his hand, his shoelaces spent more time trailing on the sidewalk than keeping his sneakers on, and his locker? He'd be lucky to find a book among the wrappers, empty soda cans, and loose paper.

Some days I'd stand down the hallway from his locker, just

before class, watching as he threw book after book out of it—along with bits of paper, soccer shirts, his two-day-old lunch. Out it all went onto the floor, as he manically searched for whatever it was he couldn't find—*that* day. Nine times out of ten, I'd get to class before him. And he'd bounce through the door just as the bell stopped ringing, mouthing apologies at the teacher and asking if he could share my textbook because—even after all of that—he still couldn't find his.

I was a neat freak and David's locker annoyed me so much that I'd even cleaned it up a couple of times—he was the only person who knew my combination and vice versa—but two days later it was back to looking like a dump.

Lorna stepped over a pair of sneakers (which, doing a double take, I was sure were the ones he promised me he'd thrown out a year ago). *Ewww* all over her face.

"This," I said quietly, trying not to sound embarrassed, "is my boyfriend David's bedroom."

Lorna and Nancy looked at me nervously.

"Well, you did tell me to think of someone I had a strong connection to," I mumbled. "I'm connected to him."

Nancy looked out of the window. Probably cursing herself for not having thought the whole Empire exit strategy through a bit more carefully. I could see her mind working overtime—and it worked a lot already. I bet she was thinking, *Why did I let her have the wheel? Look at the close call we've already had this evening. If Charlotte can turn into an apparition up there, where no one knows her, just imagine what damage she can do here.*

"I really think we should go," she said.

"Oh, is this him?" Lorna asked, waving around a picture on David's desk. How she picked it up, I did not know. But if lifting objects was in the lesson plan for Rule 6, looking at Nancy, I didn't get the impression she was all that hot on teaching it to me anytime soon. I was rapidly becoming a liability.

"He's *too* cute," Lorna said. "Tell all: How did you meet him? How long have you been together?"

I ignored her and walked over to the desk to get a better look at the picture. Ouch. It was one David had taken of us on our first almost-date—that May day in Washington Square. I was carrying a red Amoeba Records tote bag my dad had bought as a present from a work trip to LA. David kept telling me how cool it was that I was "into music" too. I remembered him pulling out his camera phone to get a shot of us. He must have printed it off and put it in a frame. Who knew he was such a secret romantic? He must be so devastated now. Maybe that's why he wasn't here. Maybe he'd gone somewhere that reminded him of me—like our rock.

"Guys, seriously, we have to get out of here. It's not helping the investigation progress at all and—"

Slam!

The bedroom door banged shut, cutting Nancy off mid-flow.

Someone was in the room. Someone Living enough to have slammed that door. Which could only mean it was . . . I don't think

I ever got what people meant when they said they were frozen to the spot before. But right then, *frozen* didn't even start to cover it. Behind me, I heard the mattress springs creak. Whoever was in the room had flopped on the bed.

Come on, Charlotte, I told myself. If you're going to investigate your murder—if you're going to have to haunt the people in your life to find out who did this to you—you're going to have to see him at some point. It's like ripping off a Band-Aid. Just turn around. And don't think about the fact that you can never be together now. Unless he goes all Romeo to your Juliet and throws himself under the next F train he sees.

I turned around. And—just as I'd suspected—there, lying facedown on the bed, was the teenage boy whose room we'd invaded. David. Super help.

Lorna wandered over, all casual and hey-I-sneak-up-on-people's-Living-boyfriends-all-the-time. She pointed at David in a totally obvious way.

"Is this *him*?" she whispered. Honestly, here I was dying inside (again), and she was this excited? Time, place, anyone?

I nodded weakly. As always, he'd changed out of his uniform before he even left school. David was wearing the same sky-blue Penguin sweater (with holes in, obv), baggy Levis and white (or they had been when he'd bought them) Pro-Keds that he'd been wearing when I'd kissed him good-bye that afternoon. Before I went down to the subway and . . . I could still feel the texture of the wool on my cheek . . . how it felt when he hugged me and I buried my head in his chest.

I had to get a grip on myself. And fast.

"Cute!" Lorna mouthed, giving me a double thumbs-up. She was loving this. Like, reveling in the opportunity to gossip about boys and relationships and all that stuff. It must have been the closest she'd gotten to girl talk in months. Any second now she'd be asking me if I thought some Z-list celeb couple were over for good.

By the window, Nancy put her head in her hands. She was about as into losing control of the situation as I was into giving Lorna the skinny on my love life.

There was a sniffle from the bed. David, was he . . . crying? I had to really bite down the urge to run over there and try to stroke his arm and tell him it would all be okay. Because I couldn't. And it wouldn't be.

Or would it? Had anyone ever had a cross-dimensional relationship before? You know, a ghost being with one of the Living? Could that work out? There was more than enough (admittedly fictional) evidence to prove that vampires and humans could date (if you ignored the whole potential blood sucking and death angle)—maybe we could be the first ghost-mortal couple? Sure, dating wouldn't be easy, but is it ever? Being invisible to humans, well, it meant David would look weird if he talked to me/air in the street. But then it did have its advantages. For a start I could sneak into his room anytime I liked and his mom would *never* know. Though would he still find me attractive now that I was an apparition? After all, I'd never asked him if "ethereal pink glow" was on his list of must-haves in a girlfriend, along with curly black hair and blue-gray eyes.

David sniffled some more.

Oh no, he *was* crying. He must have just found out about me. Awww! I was totally going to talk to Nancy about this. If I could just find a way to touch him—like Lorna had that photo frame—maybe we had a shot. Maybe there was even some way we could kiss. Feeling brighter than I had since I died, I started to walk over to the bed.

Nancy jumped up from the windowsill and, quick as a cat, blocked my way. Eye to eye, I noticed that hers were a really pretty green color under those black glasses.

"We can't stand here talking. We need to go." Nancy was officially up to her *enough* level now. "Until you've learned all the Rules, this place is no safer than the Empire State turned out to be. Any second now, he could feel your presence, or you could accidentally apparite your left foot or something, then he'll be all freaked out, you'll be all upset, and—unless he's your murderer—none of us will be any closer to getting the Key."

Wow. That was the most wound up I'd seen her. Nancy must be stressed. "We have to go. Lorna, make the circle and—"

"David! Visitor!" a female voice boomed from downstairs. His mom. I recognized it well. Though I wasn't sure she should be shouting at her recently bereaved son when he was in mourning.

David didn't move. Except to sniff a bit.

"Will someone give the boy a tissue or ten?" Lorna rolled her eyes.

"David! I said you have a visitooor!"

David shuffled on the bed and slowly sat up. His eyes were red and puffy. His floppy blond hair stuck to his face. There were little pink wrinkles on his cheek where the pillow had made an impression. His sweater had ridden up, revealing a crumpled Nirvana T-shirt underneath. He was a mess. A cute mess. It killed me to see him this way. It was all my fault. Well, the fault of the psycho who decided to go public-transport-Bundy on my ass.

There was a light knock at the door. It must be the visitooor. Maybe it was one of his friends from band practice. He'd been sort of managing this group of seniors, Camels on the Freeway, and Tom, the drummer, and he were really good friends. He said he was doing it because "managing was where the creative control was at." Though looking over at the unused guitar in the corner, I suspected there may be another reason.

Another knock, more urgent this time.

Nancy and I stared at each other. I hoped she had a plan. I didn't even have an obituary yet, I certainly didn't have a plan.

"David, can I come in?"

That was not Tom. Or Pete (the Camels' bassist). Or even Plectrum (lead singer—go figure). It was a girl's voice. A *girl*. You know, as in *not* a boy.

And, by the way, David's mom did not let him have girls in his bedroom. She didn't even let me upstairs in his town house—

and we had been dating for around a year and a half (okay, exactly seventeen months). In high school years we were pretty much married with two children, a house in Connecticut (yuck), and a dog. But if we were watching TV in the den ("with the door open, kids, or not at all") and I needed to pee, I was allowed to go only in the small downstairs bathroom. Just in case I—I don't know—ran upstairs, got into David's room, and in some way infected it with girl germs that made him like me more than his mother.

So what was his mom doing letting some other girl upstairs? David didn't hang out with any other girls.

The door creaked open. Just a crack. And a professionally blow-dried blond head popped around the wood.

"Hey, I am *so* sorry to hear your news." Somehow she shimmied her way from the door to his duvet in under a second— simultaneously looking concerned and pulling off a killer look-how-Angelina-my-lips-are pout.

Kristen.

Kristen, the Tornadoes' head cheerleader.

Kristen, the prettiest and most popular girl in school.

Kristen, the bitchiest girl I'd ever met.

Who didn't like me.

Who never talked to *us*.

What was *she* doing *here*?

"Jamie, my deputy head cheerleader, she was on her way to Barneys when she saw Jenni, who'd just been to Bloomingdale's, and she told her that a girl from our school had died underground."

She sniffed, like that was the worst place you could possibly go. "Well, we just had to find out who it was right away—"

I bet they did.

"And when we heard it was poor, poor, poor"—okay, enough already—"poor Charlotte, I just had to race over here and see if you were okay."

Get the gossip more like. Apart from earlier today when we'd had the whole me-bumping-into-her/books-falling incident, I didn't think Kristen even knew I was alive. But she certainly knew I was dead. Oh, the irony.

"That's kinda sweet of you," David said. He sat up properly. He still hadn't noticed his sweater was hiked up somewhere around his middle. Kristen kindly pulled it down for him. I started to seethe. And get hot. What the freaking hell did she think she was doing here? Why was she trying to comfort him? He was *my* boyfriend. Mine. She was not having him. Oh no. Over. My. Dead. Body.

Oh.

Hotter. I was so mad, I was feeling even hotter. It was that warm bath feeling. The same one I'd had up the Empire State. Just before I . . . Uh-oh.

"Lorna, Lorna, quick, she's going to apparite, she can't control it." Somewhere behind me Nancy was talking, but all I could see was that . . . ho (and I *hated* that mean-girl word) now stroking my boyfriend's hair. And David? He was clearly so traumatized and upset by my death that he was letting her do it.

Arms. In front of my face were Lorna's and Nancy's arms.

They were circling me now. Trying to get me out. And just as I felt the warm buzzing in my toes and looked down to see them begin to glow, the room spun. And spun. And spun some more.

Until I felt sick. Until we were back in the Hotel Attesa's lobby. And until all I was left with was porting sickness . . .

And the image of the hottest girl in school pushing David's dirty blond hair out of his eyes.

Chapter 7

"I CAN'T DO IT—NOT TO HER. SHE WAS THE LOVE of my life. We were together for too long to disrespect her in this way. It's . . . it's not fair. It's not *me*."

"Oh, but you can. She left you alone. And she'll never be back. You can't be lonely for the rest of your life. You deserve a chance at happiness. She'd want that for you. She loved you—she wouldn't want you to sit here alone, unhappy forever, would she?"

"But this feels so wrong. I can't. I won't. I—I—I— . . . Oh, okay then . . ."

It was the morning after the day I died, and I was standing outside HHQ, the door slightly ajar. And I could hear a weird, muffled conversation going on inside. Between a man and a woman. Who sounded like they had a lot to discuss.

I slowly pushed the door open a few inches more.

I never—if I was stuck in the Attesa for a million years—

expected to see the sight waiting for me on the other side.

"I shouldn't have kissed you," a male voice was saying. "I was upset. It was wrong. You caught me by surprise."

Nancy was sitting with her legs tucked underneath her, as close to the TV screen as she could get, drinking in the conversation taking place between the actors on it like it was the first pumpkin latte of Halloween.

So that's who was talking—some actors in a shitty TV drama. It seemed that, as well as being an ace detectress, Nancy was a soap-opera addict. Surely there was a Rule that forbade that kind of pointless vegging out, when you could be crime fighting?

"Uh-hum!" I coughed loudly. And totally not realistically. Nancy jumped so hard she hit her glasses on the screen. "What are you doing?" I asked sweetly. I was going to enjoy this.

"Um, I'm, I . . . ," she mumbled guiltily.

"It's the, um, new episode of *General Hospital*," she said quietly. "It's sort of my favorite show. I used to watch it every day after I'd finished my homework. I missed it when I came here. I inadvertently discovered this TV and if you, um, twiddle this knob"—she pointed at the largest of the rusty ones below the front of the screen—"it can pick up the Living's daytime TV!"

"When you're not crime solving, of course," I said.

"Oh, of *course*," Nancy echoed solemnly.

"*General Hospital*, hey? I've got some questionable TV habits myself, Nancy." Don't mention *Gilmore Girls*, don't mention *Gilmore Girls*, or the fact it got so bad that in fifth grade you named your teddy Lorelai. "What does someone as smart as you see in a show like this?"

"I think Jason is kind of dreamy—" Nancy admitted.

"Jason? Is he still in it?" I asked, before I could stop myself. "Not that I've ever seen it either." Damn, upper hand destroyed. I needed a subject change. Fast.

"Nancy," I said as assertively as I could. "I'm going out. Alone."

That shocked her out of her soap-induced coma. "Out? Alone? In the city? Charlotte, do you really think that's wise after everything that happened yesterday?"

She pushed her hair behind her ear and her glasses did their wiggle thing. It was totally her nervous habit.

"I mean, first off you over-apparited up the Empire State— and by the way, I've checked the local news and there are no stories about a small dark-haired girl disappearing on top of the Empire State Building, so that's a major relief." Yeah, because it's the kind of story that makes the evening news, right? Whoa, kid skips a line without paying in New York shocker. "Then you mind-pulled us into David's *bedroom*—and you very nearly turned into an apparition there too. Imagine if he and that blond girl had seen you as a spirit! They'd be shouting about ghosts all over New York. And that wouldn't help our investigation, would it? Rule Five: We can appear to the Living when it *helps* our investigation. Not just because we feel like it. And not when . . ."

Blah blah blah. I'd stopped listening to her. I was really starting to like Nancy but sometimes she could drone on more than the previews before a new movie. My brain had skidded onto another subject already. And it was Nancy's fault. "That blond girl." Kristen. Eww. Even thinking her name made me want to punch a wall. Which would have been pointless seeing as my hand would just have gone straight through it.

I got that ghosts don't sleep. But even if I was still alive, there was no way I would have gotten three seconds of shut-eye last night. I'd had something of "a day," as my grandmother would say. If you triple "a day" by a trillion billion percent. And that does not lead to calm thoughts when the sun goes down.

Death, haunting lessons, extreme dizziness, the Empire incident. I'm not saying they paled in insignificance at the sight of that heinous head cheerleader preying on David in his moment of weakness and need, but it did not help. And that was before I even let myself miss my mom and dad.

I had a horrible feeling death was about to get worse before it got better.

All night I lay on my new bed in the Hotel Attesa and thought way too much. Not about what was going to happen to me now or how I'd get my Key but about everything—and everyone—I'd lost. Who hated me enough to commit murder? To push me in front of a speeding subway train, just to get me out of the way?

And out of the way for what?

By the time I heard the morning cabs honking outside, I still had no answers. It wasn't like I was the kind of girl who made enemies—or friends—easily. Who was bothered enough about me to want me dead? All I knew was that I had to get out of the Attesa and do something. And when I said "out" what I meant was "check up on David and the evil cheerwhore."

"Basically, Charlotte, it's a bad idea. I know you're new, but even you can see that." Nancy was pleading now. Her green eyes all big and *pleeease* at me. Despite the fact that the *General Hospital* couple on-screen were now having a major fight—oh! another male character had come in brandishing a gun—Nancy hadn't even noticed. That's how serious she was about my stay-put-iness.

Whatever. I was serious too. My mind was made up.

"Look, the way I see it," I said, "I may be here for some time, so the sooner I get a handle on the Rules, the better." I patted my blazer pocket where my copy was kept, as if somehow having it on my person meant the wisdom would seep into my body and make me Nancy-smart. "And that includes when to apparite and when not to."

One look at her face told me my argument was going nowhere. It was a shame Nancy would never have kids. If her daughter had ever tried the I-only-missed-my-ten-p.m.-curfew-because-I-was-studying-at-Carly's-house line, Nancy would have seen right through it.

Time to change tack.

"I thought a lot during the night and I've realized what the trigger is that makes me apparite: It's thinking about how much I miss David," I said.

Nancy gave me her special mom-face again. Man, did she have

it down. Did she practice it in the mirror before every new ghost came in for instruction?

"Like, on the observation deck," I said, "I was thinking about David and *boom!* I went all pink and visible and glowy. Then in his bedroom, when I wanted to tell him that he didn't need to be upset about me? Glow city."

"Yes, that's very perceptive of you, Charlotte," Nancy said, going to pat my hand. I pulled mine away. "But with the greatest respect, you may know what your trigger is, but unless you can control it—control thinking about David in that way—then it's no help." She sighed. "Look, you haven't even been dead for twenty-four hours yet." I might not have known the difference between a proton and an electron in the chemistry quiz yesterday, but, like, I'd forgotten how long I'd left the Living for.

"It's amazing that you can apparite already—it takes some new ghosts weeks to learn what you can do already. You have a real talent." Cue: big, encouraging smile. "But why don't you practice some more with me and Lorna, first? Even Tess can be helpful, if you get her in the right mood." As if. "Then, in time, when everything you're feeling about your death is less raw, then I'm sure you'll be able to control your powers better. Or maybe you'll be out of here so quickly that you never have to master them."

Nancy looked at me kindly. "That's just what I think anyway." She had a point.

It was just that I didn't want to hear it. Not in the least.

"But—but—but—," I said, "you've taught me the most important lesson I need to know."

Nancy looked at me blankly.

"How to unapparite." Was that even a word? "How to stop myself appearing to the Living as an apparition." That sounded better. Well, a bit. I went on. "If I start to app . . . to become an *apparition*, all I have to do is blow. That's what you said, right? Then all of my energy goes out and I'm back to being an invisible dead girl. No one is freaked out. All good."

"Yes . . ."

"So, really, you have nothing to worry about." I beamed. Smile and she will believe you. "So I'll head out, do some preliminary investigations . . ." Phew, she was nodding. "And if I, you know, feel the glow, I'll just blow my energy out and think myself right back here. I promise. No drama."

Nancy blinked. Was this good? Bad? A sign I'd talked her into a coma? Was she just thinking about what she was missing on TV?

"Okay," she said finally.

"Okay?" Really?

"Okay," she said. "You're right. You know the basics. I've taught you well. You seem to be one of the fastest learners who's ever come through these doors. As long as you promise me, PROMISE,"—oh, Harsh Nancy look—"that if you start to apparite you will either think yourself back here or become invisible again, then okay. Go."

Result!

"So, where are you off to first?" Nancy asked.

"Back to my high school. If we're ever going to solve my murder, I need to figure out why someone wanted me dead. Maybe if I watch the kids there for a while, I'll get some clues as to who that could be. I dunno, maybe I annoyed someone without realizing it? Though I have no idea who. I guess it's as good a place to start as any."

"I think that's an excellent plan," Nancy said. "We need to be getting out in the field."

The field. This girl really had watched too many cop shows. Maybe she was addicted to them as well as daytime soap operas?

"Lorna and I will stay here, see if there are any similar cases in old files, do more research, check for leads. When you're back we'll talk about what you discovered, and plan the investigation from there."

"And Tess? Edison?" Much as they were, like, not even qualifying for the bottom two places on my favorite-four-dead-people-I-know list, I was still super-curious as to how they fitted into Nancy's operation.

"They . . . Well, Tess helps out when she can. And Mr. Edison Hayes . . . he does his own thing," she said diplomatically.

Hmmm . . . It seemed that I needed to do some investigation into what went on with the ghosts inside the Attesa.

"Okay, well, I'll be off then," I said, trying to sound confident. Now there was nothing standing in my way, I kind of wished there was. Did I really want to go out there—out among the Living—alone? What if I saw something I didn't like? And let's face it, what with me having been murdered yesterday, that was pretty darn probable.

"Great. See you soon," Nancy said, turning back to her soaps, all nonchalant.

Damn her. Was she playing me? Was this like the time when I was seven and Mom said, "Yes, honey, of course you can drop out of school to audition for *Zoey 101*" because she knew if she said I could, I'd totally forget the idea?

"See you," Nancy said again, retuning the TV screen.

Fine. Let Nancy try and pull her mind games. I was not going to be played. I was sixteen. I was dead. What was the worst that could happen?

I looked up at the clock in HHQ. Five thirty a.m. Right about now, most of my classmates would be asleep. I still wasn't in a place to see how my parents were doing. But there was something—well, some*one*—I needed to see before I headed to school. Without looking at Nancy again, I walked out of HHQ, quietly shutting the door behind me.

But as I started up the Attesa stairs, something made me stop. Maybe I'd developed some weird, spooky sixth sense since I'd been here, but I definitely felt someone behind me. Standing in the shadows. Watching. Someone who'd probably been listening to Nancy and me too. And it totally creeped me out.

I whipped around—the hallway was dark anyway, but with the door to HHQ shut, just a few shafts of light from the lobby illuminated the corridor. Nancy couldn't have gotten out of the office without me seeing, and Lorna was hardly the boo!-surprise! type. Which—unless some other dead teen had shown up in the night and no one thought to mention it—left only two dead people it could be.

"Hello?" I said into the darkness. "Who's there?"

A small orange light appeared in answer. Glowing faintly at first, then strengthening, and fading again. I squinted. Whoever was holding the light took a step closer to me. The ember glowed again. Suddenly I realized it was the tip of a cigarette; its lit end burning more brightly every time someone inhaled.

And—as he walked toward me like a guy who had never ever been in a hurry—I could see that someone was Edison.

He stopped an arm's reach from my spot, his head cocked to one side, like he was trying to figure me out, then took another draw. I guess when you're dead you don't worry what the surgeon general says those things do to your lungs. Edison wet his lips, opening his mouth a crack, and slowly blew the smoke right at me. I desperately tried not to dissolve into a coughing fit. Yep, Edison was just the kind of guy to be skulking in the shadows.

Standing one step up the Attesa stairs, I was almost tall enough to be on eye level with him. It should have made me feel more confident, but it didn't. Edison kept on looking down at me, way too intently. His green eyes seemed to pop like fireflies in the darkness—his all-black getup making the rest of his tall, thin body blend in with the darkness. I stared back, trying not to let on he was scaring me. God, would he just say something?

"All that stuff about the Rules? It's BS," he said, finally releasing me from his gaze and taking another deep drag. Edison's breath must really reek. Kissing him would be horrible. Like licking a stale, ghostly ashtray.

Not that kissing him was something I was thinking about. At all.

"They were made up by the Goody Two-Shoes who was here before that one." He pointed his thumb at the door to HHQ. His mouth rose into a grin, one that made me want to run and find my mom. "The Rules are only there to keep newbies under control. To make sure you don't do too much thinking for yourself. Or draw attention to us."

What? I was sure Nancy wouldn't—*couldn't*—lie. She was too logical for that. Even with Tess around.

"So here's the news flash, angel." He leaned in and whispered in my ear; his lips in danger of grazing my skin, "you've got nothing to lose by breaking them. And a whole lot more to gain—some of it *seriously* fun." Edison leaned back and raised an eyebrow. "When you want to know what you're *really* capable of now, you come find me," he said. "Or maybe I'll come find you . . ."

He turned and walked back into the darkness. Leaving a small plume of smoke behind him. And me staring like a tool.

Agh! What was the point of that? Didn't he think I'd been through enough already?

What I was *really* capable of? Sorry, but being able to apparite and port myself anywhere in the city just by thinking about it seemed pretty "capable" to me. And what was all that mumbo jumbo about the Rules not being entirely true? I didn't want to think that, because right now they—Nancy and Lorna—were the only things keeping me sort of sane.

No, screw Edison, I thought. He'd done nothing to prove he had my best—or any of my—interests at heart so far. How did I know I could trust Lucky Strikes breath, anyway? I shut my eyes and focused. Focused on what I knew and where I wanted to be. Not on what some pretentious dead boy with gorgeous green eyes, a nicotine habit, and a James Dean complex had to say about the afterlife.

I focused. Just as I had in Washington Square Park. Just as I had up the Empire State Building. And waited for the familiar sick feeling to wash over me.

For the second time in twenty-four hours, David's bedroom here I come. . . .

Chapter 8

IN DAWN'S STARTER LIGHT, DAVID'S ROOM looked like something from a washed-out dream. Pale fingers of light stretched from the gaps between the curtains across his bed, giving everything a tired white glow. Except, by now, I was pretty sure this wasn't a dream, washed out or not.

My boyfriend was lying asleep on his bed. All five feet eight inches of him curled up in an old shirt and boxer shorts. I stared at David, as if he were an animal in the city zoo. With his mop of messy hair and faded blue tee, he looked almost happy. Like there were no worries inside his head. I'd never seen David asleep before. You'd think after all the months we'd dated, all the hours we'd spent talking and planning and learning everything about each other, I'd have seen him like this: properly relaxed. But I hadn't. Nice Charlotte was glad he'd found some peace after everything he went through yesterday. Nasty Charlotte was kinda pissed he'd taken a few hours off mourning her to crash out.

My plan had been to come here—to train myself not to apparite around him, my trigger—but then I saw it. Curled up in his right hand. The square of pink paper. An old movie ticket. The memento he'd joked he'd keep forever. I couldn't believe he actually had.

As soon as I saw the crumpled piece of pink paper, I was back there: back in the movie theater, back nervously folding and unfolding my own ticket as the lights of the movie flashed on the screen in front of me. Back where it was last spring—a week after that afternoon in Washington Square—and I'd somehow ended up at the movies sandwiched between David and Leon Clark, the meathead captain of the lacrosse team. Watching some *truly* terrible rom-com.

"Dude, this is lay-ay-ame," Leon said, throwing popcorn into his mouth, but more onto the floor. If he wasn't so generally ripped (if ripped was your thing) and in charge of the most successful sports team in our school, would Leon ever score one date? Let alone be a prom king shoo-in? I double doubted it.

Leon turned, burping popcorn breath at me.

Actually scratch that. Even if he were fitter than ARod *and* a multi-multi-and-then-some-millionaire, you would not get me on a date with Leon Clark.

I still hadn't figured out how I ended up here.

Earlier that afternoon, I'd been leaving school with Ali, when I walked past David and Leon in the corridor. Leon hadn't said more than three words to me since, like, sixth grade when I got some spinach stuck in my braces at lunchtime and he called me Charlotte Boogerman for the rest of the semester. But now David was calling me over and persuading me to go see this pathetic film with him and Leon "to say sorry for running off the other day."

Ali raised her eyebrows and made her excuses, but I didn't know how to say no. So there I was, sitting between the hot new boy who was totally my type and Leon the jerk who so was not, trying to concentrate on Cameron Diaz's latest love dilemma. Which obviously called for her to run around in a short skirt.

Seeing as Leon had shotgunned both the armrests on his chair, David and I were kinda sharing one. Every time he laughed at the movie (which was, thankfully, not all that often) the hairs on our arms touched. I wished he'd notice and move his arm away, because just sitting next to him was making my stomach do all kinds of belly flips. Which I kept telling it there was no point in its doing, after what I'd seen with David and the redhead the week before.

Halfway through the movie, Leon's cell started going crazy with this insanely stupid Yankees' ringtone. "Way-hey-hey!" He didn't bother to try to talk quietly, even though he was getting death stares from everyone in the theater. "Dude, I have to *jet*. It seems there's a young lady who needs my attention. If you know what I mean."

Ew. He actually winked before he sprinted up the aisle. Leaving me and David—holy crap—alone.

David stared after him, then turned to me and shrugged. He

put his arm back on the rest next to mine, accidentally tickling my skin as he did.

My heart was pounding so loud, I was pretty sure everyone in a two-row radius could hear it. Now that Leon had gone, why didn't he just move? I felt my palms start sweating. Get a grip, Charlotte, I told myself. He's only here because he felt bad ditching you for his hot girlfriend. Or maybe he wants help with his art project—he knows that's your best subject. If Ali had come with you, you could drag her into the restroom and she'd tell you to stop being so pathetic. When Cameron finally got her man and he pulled her in for a slow movie kiss, I thought I was going to lose it. I wasn't even interested in the stupid film, but sitting this close to a guy I liked, who was totally attached, while we watched movie stars make out was just too weird. I wished the credits would roll already.

"So, can I walk you home?" David asked when they finally did. I felt too dizzy to make up an excuse.

We took a shortcut across the park, talking about the lameness of the film and the greatness of the Drums' new album.

"Sorry, I had to run off the other day," David said. "I wanted to stay and talk some more, but—"

"No, it's fine, I get it," I said, cutting him off. Who needed to hear a whole lot more of oh-I'm-part-of-an-insanely-hot-couple? "You needed to go catch up with your girlfriend. It's cool."

"My *what*?" David stopped and looked at me with his eyebrows raised. His nose wrinkled as his brows disappeared under his bangs.

"Your girlfriend," I said. Why was he dragging this out? "You know, the pretty redhead who came to the square when we were talking last week? The one whose hand you grabbed as you walked across the road?"

Oh God, shut up, Charlotte. You are one sentence away from being filed under *stalker* in his girlectory.

David pulled his iPhone out of his pocket, wiping the screen on his combats. He touched some keys. "You mean this redhead?" he asked, showing me a picture of Square girl. I nodded. He laughed.

"What?" I asked. This was beyond humiliating.

"This would be Taylor. As in my cousin. My aunt's daughter. She's in town to check out colleges. That's why she was down by NYU. We're close, but she's not my girlfriend. I'm pretty sure that's illegal. Well, in most states." He smiled.

Oh.

"So why did you look so jumpy when she caught you talking to me?" I asked.

He looked at me, and sighed. "Probably because . . . I don't want my entire family to know I like a girl," he said, dropping his eyes and concentrating hard on putting his cell back in his pocket, "before I've had the chance to tell her so myself."

My skin prickled and my face flushed. I hoped he was telling the truth. I hoped this wasn't some stupid initiation dare Leon and the lax guys had set for the new kid: make spinach-teeth Charlotte think you like her, and we'll introduce you to the properly hot girls later.

There was a low rumble overhead. Baby thunder echoed off the trees. David looked up at the sky, which had turned from blue to black faster than a bad baseball bruise.

"Got an umbrella in there?" he asked with a crooked smile, patting my flimsy shirt pocket. I shook my head. "Thought not. Then let's go hide in there until this passes." David pointed in the direction of the tunnel under the mall's steps. "Come on, it's going to get biblical on our asses in a minute." He grabbed my hand. "Run!"

It got biblical faster than that. Within five seconds to be precise. The rain came down so hard and fast that I couldn't raise my head to see David running in front of me. I just held on to his warm, wet hand and let him guide me through, as I sploshed into puddles that weren't there seconds before.

We reached the shelter of the arches and stood panting.

I looked out at the park. Water was flooding the fountain and bungeeing off the marble stairs. But weirdly, apart from the sound of the clouds lightening their load, it was suddenly kinda quiet. The tourists had run for cabs. The smarter-than-us New Yorkers had come out ready for rain. So there was just us, under the arches, dripping on our own.

An enormous raindrop fell through a leak in the curved stone roof and landed on my nose. I yelped like a little kid and clumsily jumped backward, right onto David's sneakers.

"Shit!" I spun around, trying to simultaneously get off the poor guy's feet and apologize, but instead I landed right in front of him. So close I could feel his warm breath on the top of my head and see it turn into white, spiraling clouds in the cool evening air.

"I . . . um, I'm sorry about your Converse, but then I guess they were pretty wet already and I . . ."

David smiled and brushed a lock of wet, matted hair off my forehead. *Way to impress, Charlotte,* I thought. *Guys always put "drowned rat" at their top of must-have qualities in a girlfriend.* Chances were my mascara was heading in the direction of Tennessee too. So now I was wet, clumsy, *and* ungroomed. I had it *all* going on. Whatever he said, he so could not like me. Not now. Not like this.

I ducked my head down, concentrating on the puddles of rain splashing and growing on the concrete next to me.

David took my face in his hands. I jerked at the action, too scared to misread or overthink what might happen next. He raised my chin, until suddenly there was nowhere else I could look. Apart from straight at him, as he leaned down and kissed me.

Softly at first, like he was scared I was going to pull away, but when I didn't, he dropped his hands from my face to my waist and pulled me close. As I reached my arms up behind his neck, his shirt was damp against me. His skin was cold—I could feel beads of rain on his cheeks—but his lips were warm. And all I could think as this buzz I'd never felt before flooded out from the bottom of my stomach, taking all the energy out of my legs, before it shot down to my toes, was that I was kissing the hottest guy I'd ever met in the middle of a crazy storm, and that I would do pretty much anything if someone could promise me the summer rain would keep beating down forever so that we never had any reason to leave the arch.

I screwed up my eyes and made myself click out of the memory and back to the now. The now, where I wasn't in a park. Or wet. Or even breathing.

The now where I was dead.

I looked down. David was still sleeping soundly. The way I'd felt then—that day and all the other days when he'd pulled me close and kissed me—could I ever feel like that again? Have that kind of physical reaction when I didn't have a body anymore?

I reached out my hand and put it against his, which was still holding the messed-up ancient ticket, spreading my fingers and hoping his would feel me, twitch awake, and curl around mine. But David simply shivered, pulling his hand away as if swatting a fly and tucking it under his pillow. I'd only been gone a day, couldn't he sense it was me?

Slowly I bent down and brushed my lips in the air above his. I willed that familiar feeling to be there: his warm breath, the pressure of his lips.

But all I felt was nothing. I may as well have been blowing a kiss into the air.

I felt something inside me stir, then drop. But I knew it was nothing to do with David—how he made me feel—and everything to do with me, and the realization of what I'd become.

Chapter 9

"AN AFTERNOON? *IS THAT ALL?*" KRISTEN SAID, acting shocked. "If anything ever happens to me, the school better give us the whole day off. Anything less is plain *embarrassing*."

Yep, I sure was glad I'd ported back to my high school.

The gray school steps had been weirdly quiet. No one was running, no music was blaring out. Everyone looked kind of somber.

I ducked inside to find a load of kids crowding around something on the wall. With Kristen and her surgically attached crew—the four next-prettiest members of Saint Bartholomew High's cheerleading squad, the Tornadoes—standing right at the front of the throng (obv), staring at whatever the piece of paper was.

It couldn't be the notice for who had made the play this semester because that had gone up last week. And it couldn't be the lacrosse team list either; that got decided in September.

I walked over for a better look, but kids were blocking my way. "Excuse me," I said loudly. Like that had worked when I was alive. I tapped my foot, wondering whether it was worth porting the couple of steps to the front of the crowd. Then I remembered I didn't have to do that. I could just bust through my classmates.

I took a few steps back—totally unnecessary but I felt like I should get a running start on my first try; I didn't want to get stuck in any of them, after all—and ran. Whoa! Weird. Unlike apparating, running through the Living didn't make me want to reexamine my breakfast, but it did kinda tickle. In the way a blast of AC does. I guess some of them must have felt it too, because the last one I bounced through, Alanna Acland, a girl from my homeroom, shuddered.

What was that expression my grandma used when I shivered for no reason? Like someone had just walked over your grave. Or *through* you more like.

From my new vantage point, I could see what Kristen was bitching about: a piece of paper. A formal school notice. But it wasn't about sports or the play or extra activities. Alongside the words was a massive picture—of me.

"In memory of Charlotte Feldman," it read, "who sadly passed away yesterday, school will finish at one p.m. today. Please take this time away from your studies to remember an outstanding pupil"—nice, but a lie—"who will be very much missed by all those who knew her."

I took a step back and looked around. Parker and Kari—friends from my homeroom—looked red-eyed. Mina Anderson, this quiet kid from my photography club, was sniffing. But everyone else? Not so much. It wasn't like I was some major social misfit. I had a group of friends I'd been close to since junior high, but I doubted three-quarters of the student body would spend their afternoon off looking as teary as Parker and Kari. They'd need to know who I was to do that. The free afternoon was more likely to lead to a rise in students spotted goofing around drunkenly in the park than sales of Kleenex.

If high school worked like *America's Next Top Model*, I'd have been voted off on week three on account of not being part of the right cliques. I liked it that way, but it meant I was never going to be voted Most anything. And (I cringed to think about it) certainly not Most Loyal Friend recently. I'd known Ali forever—well, since kindergarten, which is practically the same thing—but despite growing up together and seeing each other pretty much every day for ten years, we hadn't been as tight lately. Not since I'd started dating David. At first I tried to get her to hang out with us—like that afternoon at the movies. But more often than not she said no and after a while I gave up asking. I felt bad about it. We'd always said a guy would never come between us. But somehow, without either of us really noticing, one slowly had. I'd hoped things would get back to normal. Now they'd never have a chance.

"So, what shall we do?" Kaitlynnn, a blond cheerleader who always had the expression of someone who'd just eaten bad sushi, asked Kristen.

I always thought it was kinda ironic that Kaitlynnn's mom could earn enough as a high-powered lawyer to afford more plastic surgery than Heidi Montag, but she couldn't give her only daughter a name that was spelled correctly. What was with the *i* and the *y* and that extra *n*?

"Barneys or Bloomie's?" Kaitlynnn asked. "Oh, or we could really mix it up and get my mom's driver to take us to Century Twenty-One—there's supposed to be an even more major sale on today."

"A *discount* store?" Kristen looked as sick as I felt post-porting. "I am not buying clothes that are going for a marked-down price because other people do not want them. Who do you think I am?" She threw a French-manicured hand in the air in disgust. It went right through my chest. Tickle.

Kaitlynnn shrugged. "Just thought it might be a good use of some dead time, that's all."

"Dead time! Ha!" said Jamie, Kristen's deputy, who I always figured was picked for the job because it made Kristen look like she had brains as well as beauty. "You accidentally made a joke! You are sooo funny! *Dead* time!"

Was there a factory somewhere off Manhattan where they churned these girls out, I wondered, watching as the other two members of the posse—who everyone secretly just called Blondes Four and Five because they were so Identi-Kit—joined in the giggling. If one cheerleader left, there always seemed to be a brighter, newer one to take her place.

"Whatever," Kaitlynnn said. "Homeroom. Let's go see if anyone is crying over the dead girl in there." She reread the poster. "Charlotte Feldman. I mean, who *was* she anyway?"

"Curly hair, criminally cute boyfriend," Kristen said. "Always wore way old Converse. Would have been pretty if she'd made something of herself and not always looked so sulky."

Seriously? Even when I was in another dimension I was still getting grief from these people. Wasn't there supposed to be a no-bitch zone around the dead? And, hello, I was wearing DVF boots when I'd died. There was nothing "way old" about these babies. Though there would be if I really was stuck in them forever.

The bell rang. The Tornadoes flipped their blond hair in unison and strutted down the hall.

As I looked around I noticed that a few teachers and a couple of kids I knew—oh, Ali included, there she was—were wearing black. Was it because of me? I kinda hoped so. And I totally wished I could still talk to Ali about everything.

The corridors cleared. I realized I better get going before a teacher came along and caught me out here when I should be someplace else and . . .

Suddenly it dawned on me. I didn't have to go to class. Ever again. I was invisible. In my high school. I could go anywhere I wanted to. Listen in on the most private of conversations all day long. And the best thing? No one would know. For the first time since I'd died, I was going to have some fun.

I spent the morning spying on my classmates. Eavesdropping

on their gossip. Snooping as they got their books out of their lockers. Watching when they thought no one else was.

I sat on the restroom sink while the Tornadoes reapplied their lip gloss. (FYI: barring the ultracompetitive part when they tried to out-first-kiss-story each other, their conversation was *just* as inane as you'd think.) I watched while Drew, the drama club captain, secretly cut lines from the latest script so that he'd have a bigger role than this other, way more talented kid, Martin Forde. I saw Massie Jones, the smartest girl in school, cheat on her English quiz by looking at notes she'd copied on her arm. I watched the teachers be late for class because they were finishing their cigarettes. And the janitor deliberately making more scuffs on the floor, so he could complain to the principal about "those messy kids."

I heard Leon Clark actually tell one of the lax guys that it was a "bummer" I'd died because I was "pretty hot for a muso chick." Kari burst into tears again mid–math class and had to go see the nurse. Mina offered to clean out my locker, neatly putting everything in a bag for my parents to pick up. And, in the staff room, Mr. Millington told the substitute it was terrible to see "such promise extinguished so young" and that my chem was "really coming along." I guess it's true what they say: People (well, the decent ones) remember you way more favorably when you're not around to remind them of the truth.

Fascinating as it was, after some comprehensive investigation (which would have made Nancy full of pride and given Lorna at least a week's worth of gossip), I came to one conclusion: The kids at Saint Bart's had three theories about my death.

"Charlotte was high at the time," Drew said when Martin came into the rehearsal room, asked what he was doing and Drew tried to create a diversion to cover his tracks. "She always looked totally out of it." Martin nodded fervently, which made me feel way happier about those cut lines of his. "Charlotte was a total pothead. Why else didn't she get more involved with school activities? Seriously, dude, did you ever see her outside of this place? Hailie, the junior who does our set design, said she knows someone who was on the platform when Charlotte tripped and it was because she'd smoked something so strong it would have knocked out the quarterback."

"My sources—and of course I am not revealing who—say that she and that cute boyfriend of hers were on the rocks," Kristen said, touching up her Urban Decay sparkle pout gloss in the bathroom mirror. "She clearly knew he was going to break up with her, so she threw herself under the F train in some fit of, like, desperation. She knew he was too hot for her—and it was only a matter of time before he realized that too."

"I heard that David and Charlotte were on the rocks," Massie told her BFF Vicky as she handed in her 100 percent correct, 100 percent cheated-on English test, "because he caught her making out with Mr. Millington, our chem teacher. Come on, why else would she still be able to take that class after she'd flunked every test she took last year? And why she took all those 'science tutoring sessions' with Mr. Millington over the summer?" Massie lowered her voice. "I bet David had threatened to tell the principal, and she knew the affair was coming out any day soon. Think about it: committing actual suicide was preferable to the social suicide that would ensue when everyone at school heard about that little indiscretion."

It was all bull. Ridiculous, stupid BS that, if I hadn't been having the kind of crappy week I was, I might have actually found funny. But death seemed to have dulled my sense of humor.

The one thing no one was saying was that I'd been murdered. Which, for a load of city kids, was surprisingly PG.

Why did no one suspect the truth? How had my murderer covered any tracks so cleverly that no one had any idea I'd been pushed. I guess it was crowded on the platform. And no one ever looks anyone else in the eye down there in case somebody's a psycho. It's the law of the subway. It's actually kinda the perfect place for a genuine psycho to commit a murder unseen.

Whatever. Feeling confused and needing some space, I ported over to the library, which—next to the photography room— happened to be my favorite place in the whole sorry school. It wasn't like I was a Nancy bookworm. More that, it was always quiet. Which meant I could come here to think. Or to gossip with Ali and Parker. Or, occasionally, do some work.

I walked through the door, resisting the urge to giggle as the wood tickled my body, and made my way over to the classics section—the most private place in the library because kids seldom read them, so they never went back there. I slumped at the table in front of Homer and Virgil. In school at least, David and I hung out here a lot. We'd sit here and talk about our day—not too loudly of course, or Library Girl, this geeky little sophomore who seemed to be the student body's self-appointed *shhhh!* policewoman, would come over and tell us to be quiet. One time, she caught us kissing—I know, but it was a *whole* lot classier than eating each other's faces off on the school lawn in full view of every other student and the occasional passing tourist bus—and she actually threatened to report me to the principal. Would David ever be able to study here again without thinking of me? I doubted it. It was probably too painful.

"It's okay, D, it's going to take time before you're over this," said a female voice, muffled by the aisles and aisles of shelves.

Someone was coming? Oh, crap. I pushed myself against the bookshelves, right between the *Iliad* and the *Odyssey*. Then remembered that whoever was coming back here couldn't see me anyway, so I straightened up.

David rounded the aisle. Ohmigod. Maybe he was trying to get over his trauma by spending time somewhere he felt close to me?

"Thank you so much for being here for me," he said, walking right by me and sitting down in his usual seat. Even if he couldn't see me, did he not feel me here? Who was he talking to anyway?

A blonde in a cheerleading uniform rounded the corner and sat beside him. Like, so beside him she was almost on his lap. For a second I thought it was Kristen. Then I looked more closely. It wasn't her at all—but Jamie.

What was with these girls? Why were they all so desperate to comfort my boyfriend? They were supposed to be off in their locker room nursing their eating disorders or learning to hold a pom-pom. Not this.

"Maybe we should talk about her?" Jamie said in a voice so sugary it would have given an Olympic athlete diabetes. "I didn't know Charlotte all that well . . ." You mean *at all*. "But she was someone I always wished I'd had time to get close to."

Oh, AS IF.

"Why don't you tell me a little more about her? About why you loved her? It really might help." Jamie's face was now a whole three centimeters from David's. If she got any closer he'd be able to feel her eyelashes fluttering on his cheek.

"Charlotte was just . . ."

Amazing, brilliant, generally the best girlfriend in the world ever?

"Charlotte." David shrugged. Erm, thanks for the glowing obituary. I knew David was not a boy of many words, but they were usually better ones than that. He'd gone to sleep holding our movie ticket—wasn't he missing me as much as I was missing him?

"That's lovely," Jamie simpered. Oh, *puhlease*, it was not. Any fool could see through her act. It was as transparent as me.

Any fool, but my fool, it seemed.

"Why don't you tell me some more? It might help." Jamie was in serious danger of convincing me that she wasn't as stupid as she looked. Her greatest academic achievement might be being

94

able to read her schedule, but her Boy-Q was off the chart.

"We were both going to study in the city after graduation—her at Columbia and me at NYU—so we could, you know, still see each other most days. She was going to do art history and I was . . . Well, it doesn't matter. I just . . . I'm going to miss her so much." David sniffled, looking down at the wooden table where he'd once drawn our initials in a little heart with the compass from his math set. Jamie stroked his hair. Seriously, she actually TOUCHED and STROKED my boyfriend's HAIR.

The nerve of this girl. And I'd thought Kristen was trouble.

Jamie rubbed David's arm reassuringly, as he put his head in his hands. She leaned in to give him a hug.

I had to stop this. Stop this now before David was taken advantage of by this . . . this . . . Torna*ho*.

Suddenly I knew what to do. I could apparite! Just a little bit. Just my hand or something. I'd wave it at her, in a really menacing way—in a fist!—distract her a bit, then get out of here before I scared David or anyone else who could possibly want to be in here on such a sunny day. Okay, so *technically* it wasn't an apparition that would help to solve my murder, but it would only be a teensy one. That couldn't be breaking the Rules, right?

Okay, apparition. I'd done this before. Twice. All I had to do was close my eyes and think about David and how much I missed him, and how unfair this entire ridiculous scenario was—and then I'd get the glow.

So I concentrated and I thought and I pushed all my pent-up

bitter feelings as hard as I could right down through me to the thick green carpet on the library floor.

But nothing happened. Nothing at all.

I guess it's very difficult to get all overemotional about someone who's sitting right in front of you, allowing another girl to stroke his thigh (seriously, she'd moved on to that) and not looking totally upset that she was doing it.

Come on, glow. *Glow.*

But the more I wanted it to happen, the more invisible I felt.

Brrrrrrrinnnnnnnngggggggg!

I jumped so hard I sprung back and clear through the bookcase. David fell off his chair. Honestly, it was only the bell for next period. I guess after everything we'd been through, we were both feeling jumpy.

"Uh, Jamie . . . ," David said.

"Oh, just call me J. All my friends do," she said.

Urgh, I thought, as I scrambled out of about thirty thousand years of literature.

"*J*, I think I better get to class," David said, pulling himself up too. "It's homeroom next and we're having a memorial for Charlotte before we take the rest of the day off, so I better be there on time. Seeing as I'm the, um, widower and all."

He awkwardly bobbed in front of her and with a "see ya" ran out of the room.

"Yes, you most certainly will see me," Jamie said to herself. "You'll be seeing a *whole* lot more of me."

That was it. Enough. Full-on-scare-the-life-out-of-the-beyatch apparition coming up.

Again, I closed my eyes and concentrated. Hard. But no matter how much I strained and pushed and centered and tried to thrust the power out of me, nothing was moving. I was like a cell without a battery. Totally and frustratingly useless.

Jamie got out her compact and started fixing her face. Not that there was anything to fix. She looked just as perfectly groomed as she did before she started molesting my man. She smiled at herself smugly, snapped it shut, smoothed down her hair, and shimmied out between the stacks.

This was war. I might be dead, but I was not out of the battle. Yet.

I shut my eyes and ported back to the Attesa. Seconds (and a couple of dry heaves) later I was back in the hotel. Back in my new life.

I crept through the lobby and up the stairs. Edison's door was half open. I could see through the gap that he was lying on his bed, reading a beat-up book while he listened to the Doors.

"Edison?" I said, as confidently as I could. "Hey, what are you reading?"

"*Slaughterhouse Nine-Oh-Two-One-Oh,*" he said.

Either he thought I was stupid or he wasn't in a conversational mood. Better get straight to the point.

"You know that lesson you promised me? To show me what I'm really capable of?" I asked, drawing myself up. "Well, I'm ready."

There was rustling. The sound of him turning a page. Here I was freaking out about doing something totally spur of the moment and most definitely not Nancy-approved, and Edison was so not bothered by what I'd just said that he'd not even stopped reading his book.

"Meet me downstairs in an hour then, and we'll get this freak show on the road." He didn't even look up.

I stood there in the doorway, waiting for who-knows-what, and feeling like more and more of a dork with every second that passed.

"That's sixty minutes," Edison said, still refusing to get off the bed and properly acknowledge me.

Which I guessed was my cue to leave. So I did.

Chapter 10

PRECISELY ONE HOUR LATER, I FOUND MYSELF sitting on the Attesa's black couch, bouncing my heels on the floor. Okay, it was more like fifty-one minutes later, but I was always the first one to arrive everywhere. My grandmother said it was one of my "better qualities" (for real). And, even though I knew it was a lame-ass habit, I couldn't make myself act any other way. Even when I was dead, it seemed.

To be honest, I wasn't entirely sure I'd thought the whole call-on-Ed-and-get-down-with-your-dark-side thing through, no matter how upset I'd been in the library. I mean, here I was, only three days off my mortal coil or whatever, and I'd managed to get myself stuck in limbo—if that's what this was—the escaping of which relied heavily on me, Nancy, Lorna, and Tess solving my murder so I could get the hell out of here and move on to wherever came next. Which, with every day that passed, I was reeeally hoping involved unlimited PB and J sandwiches with the crusts off like Mom used to make (but I'd been too cool to take to school for at least, like, five years).

That considered, what was I doing? Not hanging around with the good ghosts, oh no. Instead I was asking the broody-potentially-evil guy to show me how to work against the system— just in case that meant I could maybe talk to my boyfriend again. David. The alive one. Who I was literally dead to now. And who seemed to have become a magnet for perky uniformed blondes. Hmmm...

"It doesn't matter how hard you bite your lip, it won't bleed." I jumped. Ed was standing above me. How did the guy move so quietly? He was sneaky. Even for a ghost. "Sure you're up for this?"

"Absolutely," I said, trying to sound as sure as I totally didn't feel.

"Then let's get out of here. May I?" He held out his hand to pull me up. Like I was the kinda girl to fall for the chivalry act. I made a point of getting off the sofa without Edison's help. Which would have made more of a point had I not nearly toppled off Mom's heels in the process.

Ed smirked. "New, are they? Oh well, at least you have all of eternity to learn to walk in them."

Asshole.

"Come on, let's get out of here before Nancy Drew comes back and persuades you to do some map work or fingerprinting or whatever she has you guys doing in that 'investigation' room of hers."

While anyone who wore as much black as Ed was far too cool to put finger quote marks around the word *investigation*, I could still hear them in his voice. Surprise, surprise, he wasn't about to join the agency.

"Charlotte Feldman, get ready for a lesson you will never forget," he said, making sure I'd had time to get steady and upright, before taking a step toward me.

Oh, hell . . . What was I doing? Edison was taller—and broader—than David, so he must have been over six feet. Even in these heels, my eyes only came up to his chin, which I noticed was covered in dark stubble. Either he hadn't shaved for two days before he died, or he just liked it that way. I'd put money on him being a razor-dodger. It went better with the air of not giving *une merde*. Damn that I'd never get to spend that summer in Europe, wowing David—and any hot Parisians—with my four years of mediocre French. I focused hard on the dimple in the middle of Ed's chin, so I wouldn't have to look up and meet his eyes. If I did, I knew I'd back out.

"Ready?" he asked. Even though we both knew it wasn't a question. He was as close as a person could get without actually touching. I tried hard not to visibly shiver and let him know I wasn't 100 percent cool with any of this.

Edison stretched his arms—for one terrible second I thought

he was going to hug me—and made a wide semicircle about an inch from my body. He was taking no Nancy-style risks here: *He* was going to drive us wherever we were going or not at all. I was just debating whether I kind of liked the fact he'd taken control or hated him for it, when I felt the lobby begin to spin. Uh-oh.

The room blurred from white to black to red to gray. Oh, help, what if this wasn't my best idea?

I looked up to find that the Attesa had melted away. We were standing by a pier on the riverbank. I tried to take a breath.

Dusk was falling, and the lights of New Jersey twinkled on the other side of the Hudson. A sight slightly ruined when an empty plastic cola bottle floated past. White gulls bobbed up and down on the water. Except the lucky ones who'd got prime positions on the wooden poles that poked above the gray ripples. They must be the queen gulls, I thought. That's where Kristen and Just-Call-Me J would be sitting if we'd been reincarnated as birds. I'd be down in the river, bobbing around with all the unwanted crap, and they'd be up there, lauding it over all of us.

Well, enough of that already. It was time to stop being such a wuss. It was time to make some changes. Starting right now. I dropped my shoulders and tried to stand up tall.

Edison was looking at me strangely. He cleared his throat. "So, Charlotte, what are you hoping to get out of our little field trip today?"

Very good question. "I want to find out more about what I, *we*, can do"—no point telling him about David just yet and my whole scare-off-the-cheermonsters plan—"so I can, you know, use all of my powers."

"Your *powers*? Who do you think you are? Ghostgirl?"

I reddened.

"No, I just . . ."

Why? Why was I unable to form a sentence around Edison? I had a boyfriend (kinda), so why did I care what he thought? No matter how green his eyes were and how intently he was looking at me now.

I tried again. "You must remember what it was like when you first died. How you felt like you'd lost so many things. Didn't you want to find out what you were capable of too?"

An emotion flickered across Edison's face. In that instant, I realized I didn't understand him well enough to know if it was hurt or regret. He shrugged and kicked the grass with his sneaker, bringing up lumps of dirt onto the green. (Note to self: Get Ed to teach me how to kick things sometime soon.)

Maybe I needed to try to understand him.

"Just how long *have* you been dead, Edison?"

"Long enough." He lifted his head, but this time there was a smile behind his eyes.

"That's not an answer," I said.

"It is if you don't want interfering young newbies knowing your private business." His eyes really were the deepest green. I laughed, despite myself.

"Seriously though, does it get any easier?" I asked.

"Which part?"

"Any of it, I guess." A couple around my parents' age walked by, enjoying an early evening walk. They looked so content. A wave of loss passed through me so powerfully I shuddered. "Do you ever stop worrying about them?" I asked. "You know, the Living. My parents, I . . . I can't even go there in my mind yet. Think about what all of this has put them through. Does there ever come a time when you don't wonder if the people you left behind are doing okay? Do you ever let them go?"

Ed pulled a packet of cigarettes out of his jeans pocket and tapped the bottom on his palm until one fell out. He rolled it in his hand for a few seconds before shuffling around for a light. He sparked up, inhaling deeply, then sat back on the grass.

"Don't ask easy questions, do you, Ghostgirl?"

"Maybe that's my secret power." Gah, why oh why did I come out with *that*? "Sorry, it's just that I'm not sure even if I asked Nancy and Lorna this, they'd tell me the truth—amazing as they both are. And Tess certainly won't."

He squinted up at me, one eye half shut. "Why do you think that? Don't tell me you've got on the wrong side of Tess already?"

I unsuccessfully tried to stop the answer from showing in my expression.

"Look, I can't really tell you what it's like for 'us,'" Edison said, looking out at the river. "I think it's probably different for every ghost."

"Then how was it for you?" I asked.

He picked some grass off the lawn and threw it in the air, watching as the blades caught on the wind, briefly spiraling in the air before they fell back to earth. "You don't give up, do you?" He brushed his hands on his jeans. I shook my head. "Okay, I'll tell you how it was for me, but I don't know that you'll relate."

I didn't dare say anything or even move, in case he stopped speaking.

"For me, well, the worst happened way before this. My dad, he died suddenly when I was fifteen, and my mom kinda fell apart. Me and my brother, we had to look after her. We both promised we'd always be there for her. And I'm . . . now I'm not. What kills me about this"—he waved his hands at the world around him—"is that people talk about life and death, but they never talk about the moments in between. The ones where you're stuck, just watching and unable to help because you're not really meant to be here."

I thought about my parents. At least they had each other. At least I didn't have to worry about either of them being alone. Or having their heart broken twice.

"But, you know, my brother's done a good job looking after her. He had to. After everything that went down. Aft—" He stopped short, not willing to tell me any more. Emptied of the smug and the wisecracks and cool, Edison's face looked younger now. How old was he? Maybe only a year or so more than me—in Living years at least. In ghost time, I was sure it was a hell of a lot more.

He was on his feet now, clapping his hands on his jeans,

putting back up the barricade, looking annoyed again. "I've got better things to do than sit around riverbanks with newbies, you know?"

"Oh, I'm well aware of that," I said. "But I thought you were going to teach me about the dark arts of ghosting, instead of standing around talking like a sorority girl all night."

He stared at me. For far longer than I can honestly say I was comfortable with.

"Drop dead, Ghostgirl."

"Edison, as you know only too well, I already did." I held his gaze. This time he was the first to look away.

"Right, let's start small," he said, the smirk back at the edges of his mouth. "I don't know yet if you're a fast learner or special ed."

"Can we just get on with the lesson?" I asked.

Over the next hour, Edison calmly and patiently taught me what he considered to be the basics. And, whoa, were they different from Nancy's. First up, I learned the Kick—all you needed to do was focus your energy and pretend you *hated* that grass—then the Jab (most effective if you wanted to poke an unsuspecting member of the Living on the shoulder as they walked by and freak them the hell out). Oh, and not forgetting the Throw (shout some words into your hand, then slam-dunk them into the mouth of a passing human and—hey, presto—they come out as their own). I tried it on a solo jogger first—watching him wonder if he'd gone cuckoo while simultaneously shouting my words, "Faster! Faster!" Ed dared me to Throw "you're not my father!" into a baby's mouth to mess with his parents, but the mom looked kinda sweet and—down with my bad side or not—I didn't want to upset her.

Was I having actual fun with Mr. Oh-So-Serious?

"That's almost enough for today," he said eventually. "We'll wrap up with what I call the Lifesaver."

"Erm, isn't it a little late for that?"

I swear I saw him roll his eyes.

Ed walked over and picked up my right hand.

Pow!

It felt like I'd been shocked by a thousand volts. I jumped back with a jolt and screamed. He dropped my hand immediately. What the hell was that?

"Hey, calm down, it's okay," he said, sounding genuinely concerned. Edison put his hand up and took a step back so I could see he wasn't about to come near me until I was okay with it.

"I'm so sorry, I . . ." Boy, was I embarrassed. I pushed a black curl behind my ear and tried to get ahold of the situation. What *had* just happened? When I'd tried to make contact with David, it felt like running my hand through smoke. But that shock? I'd never felt anything like it before. Edison had only touched my hand. It wasn't as if no one had ever done that before in my last life. But that was different.

"It's just that, well, I think that was the first time anyone's spirit's touched me since I . . . you know," I said quietly. "I guess I've not felt anything since the . . . since the subway train . . . and I guess you, your touch, that was why it made me jump." I was suddenly afraid to meet his gaze.

"Subway train, hey? Well, that's a hell of an act to follow, but I guess some ghost had to do it," Edison said, shaking his head.

He looked back at me, silently asking for permission to try again. What the hell. I needed to get over this somehow. I nodded. Ed picked up my right hand again and this time—even though I still felt a surge of weird rushing through me—I refused to react. It was so strange, freaking out like that just because someone—some*dead*one—had touched me. Maybe being shoved under a speeding train by a psycho killer will do that to a girl.

Sure I wasn't about to go loco on him, Ed raised my hand in the air, putting my thumb and middle finger together. He motioned for me to keep them there, took his hand away and made it into the same shape as mine. "Shhh," he said and winked. He lifted his right hand higher, way above his head, and clicked his fingers.

It took me a couple of seconds to notice what had happened.

The highway, the gulls, the water lapping on the pier: They all went quiet. I couldn't hear a thing—not the bus of tourists being driven by behind us, not the couple walking their Labrador to my right, not the plane overhead making puffy tracks through the clouds on its way out of LaGuardia. Edison had somehow found a way to mute the world. I swear that if my heart was still beating it would have been pounding at that moment, but instead? Just this total silence. Neat.

Ed smiled at me slowly. For the first time since I'd met him he looked somewhere near happy. It suited him way more than the perma-scowl he usually wore. Edison sat on the grass, his long legs neatly crossing under him and patted the spot next to him, silently asking me to do the same. So I did.

And there we sat. For I don't know how long. Just watching the river, and the birds and the lights and not feeling weird about the lack of conversation because, even if we tried, there couldn't be any. For the first time since all the bad stuff, I felt . . . somewhere approaching Charlotte again.

Then Edison took my hand again, put my fingers together, and motioned for me to snap.

Click!

It was like having water in your ears after a swim. The world sounded like it was happening down a long tunnel, not all around me. Then there was a *pop!* And just as quickly the volume turned back up on my life.

"Now, don't get all excited and be trying that trick too much." Edison's voice made me jump. "If you get all on!-off!-on!-off!-on!-off! you will give yourself an earache. Trust me, I speak from experience."

I looked at him, my mouth half open.

"So all of your tricks, are they not breaking the Rules?" I asked.

Edison shook his head. "We'll talk about the so-called Rules next time, but suffice to say I don't think any of what you've learned is technically a Rule break. We're just enhancing your— what did you call them?—*powers*," he said, his eyes laughing at me. "But hey, if you want to stick with the dull stuff, then go back to Nancy Drew, and the world will continue to be all hugs and puppies. Your call." He shrugged.

Now it was my turn to look at the floor and kick the grass. Which—by the way—I could so now do. Which was kinda awesome.

"Nancy's been teaching you basic apparition, right? How to appear to the Living as you did just before you died?"

I nodded.

"Good, well, keep practicing that and the next time we have one of our little tutoring sessions I'll show you some more . . . *intense* materialization tricks. That is if you're man enough?"

"*Girl* enough," I said. "And always." Ed smiled at me again. And for the first time, I felt okay about smiling back.

"Well, until next time then . . ."

Just as before the world swirled. The asphalt gray of the highway, mixing with a yellow taxicab, and the Hudson, which was now almost black. Then suddenly it all stopped and I was back in the Attesa again.

And Edison was nowhere to be seen.

Chapter 11

YOU KNOW WHEN YOU READ THOSE LAME quick-fire interviews with "stars" in gossip magazines? They always ask them the same dumb questions. Like, "What's your diet secret?" "What advice would you give to the teenage you?" or "What song would you want played at your funeral?" As if it'll give us some serious, deep insight into the celebrity's soul. And cover up the fact they're actually about as interesting as waiting for your nail polish to dry.

But there's one thing I know: If I'd lived long enough to get famous and some lamebrain had turned to me and asked, "Charlotte Feldman, what song do you want to be played at your funeral?" I know what I would *never* have said.

"Bring Me to Life" by Evanescence.

"Cool church, but the music sucks," Jamie, dressed in something very tight and very black, said as she strutted past the spot where Nancy, Lorna, and I were watching my friends and family walk down the aisle and take their seats for the big event. My funeral.

So I'd been in limbo for, like, almost three days now (I figured) and, porting aside, there weren't a whole lot of upsides to it. But getting to watch your own funeral? That seemed kinda neat. To see who turned up, how upset they were, find out who really cared for me and who was faking it . . .

Of course the downside was that I had nothing to do with the planning. Which meant my parents had been allowed to include Evan-freaking-escence on the playlist.

I mean, really? Could they have come up with more of a teen funeral cliché? *This* was the song that everyone here was going to associate me with forevermore? Like, if in twenty years' time, one of the guys from my math class was old, married, and on vacation with his kids in Cabo—if this pumped out of a passing car stereo, he'd think, "Ah yes, 'Bring Me to Life' . . . . this reminds me of Charlotte Feldman, that girl from school who fell under a train." Then he'd give his children a lecture on platform safety and say, "Charlotte; She always lent me a pen if I forgot mine, but she did have the *worst* taste in music."

What an epitaph. I may have actually preferred Avril Lavigne.

"This was her favorite song. Her *favorite*," Mom told my grandparents, who were sniffling in the front pew. Yeah, like FIVE YEARS AGO. "Charlotte played it constantly in her bedroom. She loved it. I was always asking her to turn the volume down."

Jeez. You'd think David could have gotten involved and made this entire event sound less like something from the soundtrack of a substandard vampire movie. This is the kind of thing you should talk about with a guy before you start dating them. Like, "Do you promise to love, honor, and respect me. And, just in case I die in a freakish subway accident while we're together, can you make sure that my musical taste is fairly represented at the funeral?"

"Guyliner music aside, your parents have done a good job," Nancy said cheerfully, like she'd been to a million of these things before and oh! aren't they just so much fun.

Looking around, I kinda had to admit she was right. Mom and Dad had chosen the church just around the corner from our apartment. It was a beautiful gray building with spires and buttresses—which make it Gothic in a good way. It wasn't too big, so I looked more popular than I'd been.

Bunches of flowers in my favorite colors—blue and purple— spilled off the windows and were arranged in neat clumps down the aisle. My coffin was black and so shiny that, when she apparited, Lorna could see her reflection in it. (I totally caught her checking out her hair before the guests arrived.) Even the picture of me that Mom had picked to put at the altar wasn't too shabby. It was taken on my sixteenth birthday. Before I danced like a mad woman at a Killers concert and Mom shook her head at me and said, "Oh, Charlotte, what have you done? You looked so . . . neat." I was wearing my favorite American Apparel navy T-shirt dress, my eyeliner was on my eyes and not heading cheek-ward for once.

And my straggly dark hair had been tamed into smooth waves by Mom. I was smiling because I knew I had a whole night ahead where Mom and Dad were taking me for a fancy meal in the Village, before letting me and David go and see a band (even if they were going to wait in the bar while the show was on—the shame). I looked happy. Like I had everything to live for.

Would I have done anything differently if I'd known then what I did now?

"And even though you don't have as many people at your funeral as I had at mine, it's not a *bad* turnout. Better than at Nancy's anyway," Lorna said, a teasing glint in her eye. "There were more empty seats than full ones at that, weren't there, Nance?"

Nancy rolled her eyes. "We're not here to talk about the turnout, we're here to look for clues. Clues about who killed you. Charlotte, your murderer could be in this very room."

That made me stop goofing around.

"Guys, I'm serious," Nancy said. As if she was ever anything but. "We need to stay alert."

Everyone was seated. Evanescence stopped. Thank God, my eardrums said. And the vicar guy at the altar started to speak.

If you've ever seen a funeral in a movie, you pretty much know the score. There was lots of stuff about how sad it was that I'd "passed away so young" but how everything "happens for a reason" even if, right now, we didn't understand "God's great plan." But, hey, on the bright side, everyone could rest assured I'd be with "the Lord now" and "in peace at his side and in his kingdom."

As if. I wanted to apparite there and then and tell them that, no, actually, there were no kingdoms or plans going on here. Kingdoms, I'd be happy with. This, not so much.

"And now," said Vicar Dude, "one of the people closest to Charlotte would like to say a few words."

Uh-oh. Who? Mom hated public speaking and Dad always said he was better on paper than in real life. Which was why he'd become a sports journalist. That, and all the guaranteed tickets to games. My grandparents weren't getting up on that lectern without a crane to help them. Who else could it be?

"David?" Vicar Dude looked down to the front row, where David was nestled between Mom and Kristen.

Wait a second. Mom and . . . Kristen? Erm, *hello*, what was *she* doing here? Stroking David's arm in a "there, there" way. Kristen wasn't even my friend on Facebook, so how had she gotten herself on the front row at my funeral? This was not Fashion Week. She might be Miss Popularity, but she didn't deserve one of the best seats in the house. Especially not when Ali and her parents were crammed into row three.

David walked up to the lectern. He wobbled on the steps and swallowed awkwardly, like he was going to throw up, but was trying super-hard to keep it down. His eyes were red and puffy. I didn't know who he'd borrowed the black suit he was wearing from—because it was most definitely not his—but it was about half a size too small. The trousers were way too tight and the jacket too slim fit for such a "somber occasion" (as Vicar Dude called it).

On any other boy it would have been what Lorna called a fashion faux pas, but David didn't look stupid. He looked hot. Seriously hot. Like he was the newest, blondest member of the Strokes. All ready to rock a sweaty room in some bar in Brooklyn, rather than make a speech in a dusty old church.

"Whoa, *he* was your boyfriend?" a sarcastic voice said.

I turned to my right to see that Tess had ported beside us. What was she doing here? First Jamie, then Kristen, now Tess? I thought funerals were meant to be for loved ones only? Instead, there seemed to be an open-door policy for mean girls.

"Yes, we dated for a year and a half," I snapped back. Why was I trying to defend my relationship? I knew Tess was just messing with me. And that David loved me completely—get a load of the eye puffiness. If I was going to be stuck with Tess for who knows how long, I really had to learn to ignore her when she put her Queen Bitch crown on.

"Er, I'm not very good at standing up and talking to people," David said nervously. The mic screeched and he took a step back from it, eyeing it suspiciously. "In fact the last time I did, it was when I, erm, played Joseph in the fourth grade Christmas nativity . . . Those of you who were there that day will remember it didn't go so well."

David dropped "Jesus" (some other kid's rag doll) on the floor and its head rolled off. I wasn't there, but I knew it had gone down in elementary school history because the story had even reached my school downtown. It was the reason that, after that, every Joseph in the city had Jesus attached to their hand with some string and tape.

Some of the kids in the congregation giggled. David's shoulders unhunched a little and he carried on. This time with more confidence in his voice.

"I don't hang around a lot of churches," he said. "But I hoped that one day I would be hanging around one with Charlotte. Well, not hanging around as such . . . That didn't come out right. I . . . let me try again."

Tess sniggered. I shot her my best Nancy stop-being-sooo-immature look.

"What I meant was that—I know we're only sixteen and have a lot of growing up to do . . ." He looked down at the lectern as if hoping to find someone else had left a speech there that he could read out. "But I sort of thought that if I was ever in a church in a suit with Charlotte, it would be for a reason that would make my mom happy—like getting married one day. Years and years away, of course."

He looked down at my coffin. "Not like this. Not with her in there." He sighed unevenly. "I can't even begin to tell you what a hole Charlotte has left in my life. I'm just going to miss her so much." He looked over at my parents, who were properly sobbing now, then Ali, who'd fixed her stare on the flowers at the end of her pew. "We all are . . . I don't know how I'll get through this. That's . . . that's all I wanted to say."

Wow. Forget what he said about me to Jamie in the library, *that* was amazing.

The church was totally silent. I think every single person was a little bit in love with David at that second. Except for my dad and the vicar. Because that would just be weird.

"That," said Lorna, who was quietly making sobbing noises next to me, "was *the* most beautiful thing I have ever, ever heard. Beat my eulogy hands, feet, and elbows down."

"It wasn't half bad," Tess admitted, refusing to make eye contact with me.

Wow. She actually said something not nasty.

David stepped off the lectern and went back to his seat hiccuping with a little sob. Even Nancy gave me a he's-very-lovely, lucky-living-you look.

Kristen stroked his arm fondly, gently running her nails over his skin. Mom gave her a stare so evil Kristen actually took her hand off David's and put it back on her electric purple Mulberry Alexa bag (could she not have found a black one, just for today?). I had to admit that, even though I'd probably never get a chance to tell her, my mom could be pretty cool.

After a couple more hymns and some readings, Vicar Dude dismissed everyone. The choir behind him sang some kum-by-ya-yas and everyone filed out. It still wasn't my kind of music, but at least it wasn't you-know-who.

"How are you holding up?" Nancy gave my arm a supportive squeeze. I jumped a little—not as badly as I had when Ed touched my hand, but still enough to hope Tess hadn't noticed—and tried to smile.

"Okay, I'm sure I should make some it's-my-funeral joke, but I'm feeling kind of beat," I said. "Shall we get out of here? I didn't see anyone acting weird, did you?"

Nancy's face went all detectress again. Of course.

"We need to look out for anything strange. Is there anyone here who you're surprised to see? Anyone you weren't friends with in life?"

"Nancy has this theory that murderers always turn up at their victim's funerals," Lorna explained. "She saw it on some Agatha Christie drama on the I'm-Pretty-Much-Geriatric Channel once."

Nancy sighed. I scanned the crowd. Aside from my family, it was pretty much all the people I'd expect. Kids from my school, most—like Ali, Parker, and Kari—I'd known since kindergarten, others—like Alanna and Mina—weren't my BFFs, but we talked, a few of my teachers who probably thought being here was preferable to grading the mountain of essays they had sitting at home, Mr. Millington (excellent—so that did very little to disprove Why Charlotte Died Rumor 3, then), the Tornadoes, and . . .

"Actually there is someone who shouldn't be here. Well, three someones actually," I said. And one of them—the one I was most worried about—was nowhere to be seen.

"Who?" Nancy asked, pulling out her little spiral notepad.

"The cheerleaders: I wasn't friends with them at school, I wasn't even allowed to stand next to them in the lunch line, but now three of them are taking time out of their hectic preening and self-tanning schedule to be here. Do you think it could simply be because they know they look good in black?"

Lorna nodded sagely. "Yes, that does sound strange!" Nancy smiled excitedly.

"In fact I can't see the head cheerleader now." I looked around some more. Most people had left, but—unlike Jamie and Kaitlynnn—she hadn't walked past us. "Kristen—she was the sickeningly pretty blonde who sat in the front row during the service. I didn't see her leave."

"That's because she disappeared into the vicar's private room with your boyfriend about ten minutes ago," Tess said. "I wonder if she's comforting him in there?"

A sick feeling, much worse than porting sickness, started bubbling up in my throat. If this was one of Nancy's stupid soap operas, I would storm in there and find something bad going on.

But it wasn't. This was real death. Kristen might be the über-bitch, but David was my loyal boyfriend—the guy who'd just given the cutest speech ever. He'd been talking about *marrying* me some day. What sixteen-year-old boy says crap like that—especially to a girl who is dead so he's got nothing to gain from it? He wouldn't be fooling around with another girl already. Not after that.

"Let's go see what's going on then," Nancy said, trying to calm things down. She must have been terrified I was going to get overemotional again and apparite at my own funeral. While we hadn't covered that as a specific Rule no-no, I was pretty sure spooking everyone you've ever met right after your wake was in there under "really, don't do."

Nancy, Lorna, and I walked across the aisle to the small wooden door Tess had pointed to. We all looked at one another expectantly. Nancy was hoping for a breakthrough. I was just hoping I wouldn't see anything that would break my heart.

We walked through the shut door. Tickle. David was standing by the window, looking out at the busy street outside. Kristen hovered beside him. Now that Mom was out of sight, she was back on arm-stroking duty. Grrrr . . .

"It's not even been three whole days, but I miss Charlotte so much already," David said quietly, his voice shaking. "Is this empty feeling ever going to get better?"

"Of course it will," Kristen said brightly. "Look at Brad and Jen. Okay, she didn't die—unless you count the career suicide that was *The Breakup*—but Brad was back in the game and dating again within *weeks*. And dating someone who was way more on his social and attractiveness scale." Bitch. "Your Angelina could be just around the corner!"

I was pretty sure David had no idea who she was talking about. But he smiled anyway.

"I tell you what, how about we think of some of the things you *didn't* like about Charlotte," Kristen said.

Um, how about we don't?

"That's what I always do when I want to get over a guy," she said. Like *she* had ever been ditched by any man. "It helps me realize he wasn't perfect and that I can live through this and find someone better."

Kristen pouted, waiting for David to speak. She'd somehow found time to reapply her lip gloss between the front pew and here. If I wasn't so mad, I'd be impressed by such stealth styling.

"Charlotte was . . . she was amazing," David said. "She was everything I ever wanted from a girlfriend: She was kind and smart and cute and she got me."

More pouting—this was not what Kristen wanted to hear.

"Though she could be kinda controlling at times, I guess," he said quietly, ducking down his head.

WTF? Controlling? *Controlling?* The only thing I ever tried to control was the frizz level of my hair.

"Oh, and . . . ," he started.

Oh and *what*, precisely? For someone who thought I was "amazing" three seconds ago, David seemed to be warming to his subject now.

"Once, when I wanted to have a Brooklyn bands day on my iPod, she pressed shuffle because it was making her depressed and that meant I had to listen to music from all over the world, which was really not the point of what I was doing. That kinda annoyed me."

Give me strength.

"See! She wasn't totally perfect after all." David nodded. "You know what I think? I think the way through this pain is for you to try to forget about Charlotte," Kristen said. "This is a new time in your life now. A new start for you. And I'd"—*muchos* eyelash batting and shy floor-staring—"really like to be part of that."

"I cannot believe he is falling for this," Lorna whispered.

"That was ridiculous," Nancy agreed, nodding.

"Will you guys just shhhh!" I pleaded. "He's not falling for it. Not David—you heard what he said out there. He loves me. He'd never go for this blowup Barbie, he—"

Then the blowup Barbie did the worst thing imaginable. She looked up, tilted her head, and slowly gave David a kiss. ON THE LIPS.

"Noooooo!" Lorna and Nancy said in unison behind me.

And then, an even more unimaginably worse thing happened. David didn't pull away. In fact, for one long horrible second, it looked like he was kissing her back.

"I'm sorry, Kristen. I can't do this," David said, as he *finally* managed to tear his lips away from hers.

My boyfriend, my supposed soul mate, the guy I was pretty sure I'd lost my best friend for had just kissed a hideous cheermonster. At my *funeral*? My body might have been cold, but I hadn't even been buried yet. He should have pulled away faster. Ducked. What was he doing?

Much as I wanted to, especially with Tess there, I couldn't hide how I felt. I was devastated. Sure, I had allowed a teeny tiny, like, 0.000000001 percent of my brain to think that maybe one day David would move on. But I thought that would be *years* away. And by then I would have found my Key, gone through the Big Red Door, and whatever was on the Other Side would hopefully have been so awesome I could have forgotten about David until he came through it to join me. That would have been okay. That was the plan. Even if he'd lived until he was really old and got all Regis-wrinkly, I could have taken it. As long as he didn't have an elderly wife in tow.

I didn't expect *this*. He hated cheerleaders. He hated cliques and gangs and popularity contests. He hated high school. Now he was sucking face with its queen bee?

"Oh, dear," Tess said behind me. "Guess lover boy wasn't so keen on you after all."

I turned around. Why was she here only during the bad times in my afterlife? I wished I had some smart remark, the kind of comeback that Lorna and Nancy would be quoting back to me later on. But I didn't. I didn't have anything. Apart from a massive lump in my throat, and a prize view of David getting over me by getting under another girl.

I had to get out of there. To somewhere else. Somewhere that always made me feel safe. Somewhere I knew, where I could try to erase the image in front of me, and just pretend that my funeral had ended when he gave that lovely, beautiful speech.

Which was clearly a crock.

I closed my eyes, ignored the nausea, and thought my way out of there. Blocks and blocks away.

To Central Park. To our favorite rock. The place where David and I had last been in love. Eternal soul mates. Or so I stupidly, stupidly thought.

Chapter 12

I LAY ON OUR ROCK, WATCHING THE EARLY evening sun duck behind the trees all around me and draw long shadows across the grass of Central Park, like a silent alarm telling everyone to go home and start the evening instead.

I'd always loved sitting up here—ever since I'd discovered it as a kid. I guess I used the rock in the same way Holly Golightly used Tiffany's. It was a place I could head for if things weren't going my way. Nothing bad could happen to me here.

If you sat on the rock and looked around, it felt like you were in a forest, surrounded by trees. As a kid, I'd pretend they were enchanted and that, when night fell, they came to life and swallowed up anyone stupid enough to be in Central Park after dark. But if you stood up and looked above you, New York's skyscrapers loomed above their leaves. It was like two worlds had been messily glued together. I loved both of them. That was one of the reasons why this was my favorite place in the city and why—even though I totally wanted to travel—I couldn't imagine living anywhere in the world but New York. Even after we started dating, I didn't bring David here for months, because it was *my* place. I didn't want us to break up and feel like it was tainted by memories of him. But sitting here now was weirdly comforting.

Somewhere, not that far away, I could hear a group of kids giggling in delight. Whatever they were doing, they sounded happy, while for the second time in as many days, my world had fallen apart. First I died. Then I was dumped.

"Shhh! I've found her. Here she is!" Was Lorna ever going to learn about volume control? Her attempts at a whisper were anything but. At least she was never going to be able to sneak up on me. Unlike Edison. Or Tess.

I pushed my body—not that you could even call it that anymore—up by my hands and sat up straight. Just as I expected, out of the corner of my eye I could see Lorna and Nancy on the other side of my rock. Half crouching, half kneeling, so as not to ambush me: the poor, fragile cheatee. They must be here to check I was okay. As if okay were something I was ever going to be again.

All I needed now was for Tess to show up, say something sarcastic, and make me wish someone would kill me all over again. Not that I'd even managed to *die* properly. Who messes that up? Was it any wonder David had upgraded me for some perfect, perky, popular blonde whose life line was still visible on her hand?

Kristen was six foot in heels. I was six feet under. What did I have to offer a relationship anyhow?

"So I know that looked bad—what we just saw in the church—but maybe Kristen and David were just . . ." Even Nancy was struggling to see the positive here. "Maybe he was thinking of you and he got caught up in the moment? And he did pull away eventually." She grimaced.

"The only thing he was thinking of was himself," Lorna said, fuming. "I'm sorry to speak ill of the Living, but David totally deserves it. That was beyond disgraceful. Has he not heard of the time-date continuum?"

Despite myself and my twenty-stories-deep depression, I managed an *eh?*

"The time-date continuum," she repeated. "The rules for when you can and can't do things in a relationship?" No, Nancy and I clearly did not know them. Lorna sighed at our ineptitude, like she couldn't believe we'd made it to our sixteenth birthdays while still being *this* clueless. "When it comes to how you behave in a relationship, it's what governs everything," she said. "For example, after a guy texts you for the first time, you can't reply for at least three hours or you look desperate." Okay, fine, even I knew that. "And, after you actually go out with a boy, you need to make him wait a *week* between dates." She fluffed up her hair. "It's called playing hard to get."

Lorna was rattling this off at an alarmingly well-versed rate. Though I wasn't quite sure what first datetiquette had to do with kissing someone else during your girlfriend's memorial service.

"Likewise," Lorna said, "though this is not something that happens, like, all that often, if you do happen to die while you're dating someone, he definitely, definitely, definitely is not allowed to suck face with anyone else until at least a month after your funeral. It just looks bad. Like he never cared about you in the first place."

Ouch.

Lorna realized what she'd said and stopped. Fast. "Not that David didn't love you—I mean, we all heard his eulogy—of course he did. I think he just got confused and did something bad."

"I just don't get why he did it," I said. "Right now, David's supposed to be mourning me, not proving he's got no morals and even less taste. I just didn't think I'd die to see him behave like this. There are some guys you know—pretty much the second you meet them—are total creeps who will make out with another girl when your back is turned. I didn't think he was like that. I guess Kristen *did* take advantage of him when he was having a moment of weakness. And that grief makes you do crazy things. So I should be more annoyed at her than him, right?"

Lorna and Nancy wouldn't meet my stare.

I looked down off the rock, at the grass below. It didn't seem to have any magic here's-what-to-do-when-your-soul-mate-turns-out-to-be-a-sniveling-worm advice either. Bummer.

Nancy tried to change tack. "You know what this is?" No. "It's a classic case of post-mortal depression. That's why you're feeling so bad." She gave Lorna a help-me-out-here look.

"Yeah, like, after I died, I felt weird about it for the first few weeks too." Lorna gently sat down next to me, which was super-sweet of her because I could see that she was totally hating the thought that the rock might somehow get a speck of dirt on her skirt. "But it soon passed. And your blue feeling will too."

"And after my town house went up in the explosion . . . ," Nancy said. "Oh, don't look at me like that, Charlotte. It's okay—and it could have been so much worse. My parents were out so I was the only one hurt. Thankfully." She touched my arm and took a second. "Anyway, afterward . . . well, I'm glad I had Lorna here to help me through. Just adjusting to being here was hard enough, so I can't imagine how you're feeling."

Poor Nancy, I thought.

"You've had a lot to deal with," Nancy added kindly. "Murder *and* a double-crossing boyfriend? Well, that's every girl's worst nightmare."

"Apart from the never-getting-to-wear-different-clothes thing," Lorna said and smiled in her attempt to cheer me up. She clapped her hands. "You know what you need?"

A time machine to go back seventy-two hours, so I wasn't in this mess?

"You need cheering up!" she said, punching the air.

My face fell. I didn't need "cheer" anything.

"Sorry, you need a *treat*!" Lorna said. "Don't mention the 'cheer' word," she mouthed at Nancy.

"Great idea!" Nancy said.

"Now, what can we do to chee—to make you *happy*?" Nancy asked. "How do we fix a broken heart?"

"When I was alive, and a guy love-ratted on a friend, I'd take her for a mani," Lorna said. Her face fell as she remembered that was not an option. "Oh, or . . ." I dreaded to think what was about to come out of Lorna's mouth. "I'd let her do whatever she wanted. No matter how silly. Anything! Come on, Nancy, I think this is one of Charlotte's Nine Times."

Nine Times?

"One of the Nine Times when you can break the Rules and Miss Goody Two-Shoes here won't go mad at you," Lorna explained.

"Break the Rules?" I asked.

"Charlotte, have you even read the red book I gave you?" Nancy said with a playful scowl.

"You know what, I kinda haven't. I've been too booked up with death, burial, and betrayal to fit it in," I said.

"I know, sorry." Wow, Nancy just apologized when I was clearly in the wrong. She must feel bad for me.

"How about you get it out now and turn to page thirty?" she said kindly.

I pulled it out of my blazer pocket and thumbed through the pages until I got to one headed "Your Nine Times."

"So it explains there that every ghost knows that death is a tricky time, especially for teens," Nancy said. "So that's why we have the Nine Times. It's kinda like nine hall passes—nine opportunities to break the Rules on nine separate occasions, just for fun, repercussion-free."

"It's basically in here to cut us some slack," Lorna said.

"To make the transition from livinghood to ghostdom a little easier," Nancy explained.

Says who?

"So the big question I've been meaning to ask," I said, "is where do the Rules come from? Like, I get that Lyndsay gave you guys the book and you've passed it on to me, but who wrote it originally?"

And is it really, as Edison hinted, just a load of crock to keep us in control?

Nancy and Lorna exchanged a look. "All we know is what I told you, Charlotte," Nancy said quietly.

"But tell her your theory," Lorna said, her blue eyes pleading.

Nancy looked at her hard, then back at me. She slowly nodded. "Okay, so here's the thing: Soon after I first got here, there was kinda this . . . *incident*," she said. This sounded interesting. "This new kid, Jimmy, he arrived and, well, he was kinda annoyed to be dead."

"Which is, like, the most *major* understatement ever," Lorna whispered to me, sitting closer.

"According to the information we got from our preliminary investigations, we found out that he'd gotten in with the wrong crowd at his school and got into some *bad stuff*"—Nancy said the words in a tone that let me know she'd not be elaborating on what the "bad stuff" was anytime soon—"and one of his supposed friends ran him down with a car."

"Whoa."

"Exactly," Lorna said.

"Well, when he arrived at the Attesa, I explained that Tess, Lorna, and I had formed the Agency and decided to use what we'd learned to help newbies solve their murders," Nancy continued. "We taught him how to apparite and port, but after that he wasn't interested. He said he knew who'd killed him already—and all he wanted was revenge."

Revenge?

"We didn't see much of him after that," Lorna said. "He was always out. Especially at night."

"I hoped he was making his own investigations"—Nancy shook her head sadly—"but then *they* arrived and we realized he hadn't been using his new skills wisely."

"They?" I asked.

"The adults," Nancy said. "Murdered teens come to the Attesa, adults to another hotel uptown, remember?"

"I told you that," Lorna said.

"I'd never met any of them before," Nancy continued, "just heard from Lyndsay that was how it worked. But that day two of them turned up—a man and a woman—who explained that Jimmy had been drawing attention to himself."

"Apparently he thought he knew who his murderer was, but instead of trying to prove it and get his Key, he'd been haunting

the guy—like, scary, nasty, taunting haunting—to make him pay."
Lorna shuddered. "To get your Key, you need your murderer to
confess out loud, but he didn't care about that. It was only a matter
of time before the news spread. The adults were worried he'd ruin
it for us all."

"They waited for Jimmy to come back, then they took him
away," Nancy said quietly. "We never saw him again."

"What happened? Do the adults have a Door in their hotel
too? Do you think they helped him get his Key and he went
through that?" I asked.

"We don't know," Nancy said. "All we know is that's what
happens when you break the Rules. So who cares who they were
written by—a ghost before us, one of the adults—it's better to
obey them."

I thought back to Edison and the river. He'd said everything
he'd taught me was fine, just tricks and loopholes rather than Rule
breaks. I *really* hoped he was telling the truth.

"Anyway, you still have all of your Nine Times to go!" Nancy
said brightly. "Let's have some fun—and get you to put your
breakup behind you."

Breakup? It sounded so final when someone else said it out
loud instead of me just running it around in my head. But—if
there was one thing my funeral had proved—it was that David
and I were officially over, even if I wasn't sure I wanted us to be.

"Seeing as you're dead there are certain traditional girl
heartbreak remedies that we can't use," Lorna said.

"Like, we can't feed you ice cream." Nancy shook her head.

Or get me drunk, I thought.

"Or give you a break-over new look," Lorna added, "or rent *Titanic* so you can get some perspective on the whole situation." Because that's what watching Leonardo DiCaprio die did for a girl. "But we do have the whole city to play in—and you can *really* play when you're dead. Especially when you have porting and invisibility on your side."

She turned to Nancy. "Let's get the smile back on Charlotte's face. I'll try first."

Their arms circled me. I really appreciated their attempts to happy me up, but I wasn't sure they had this right. Making me want to puke my guts up from another bout of porting sickness was not about to make me forget David. No matter how badly I wanted to hurl.

But there was no point complaining. Before I could even say, *Actually, I'd kinda rather mope on my own*, Lorna winked at Nancy and the world whirled. Urgh.

The nausea didn't last long this time (was I getting used to it?) and the next thing I knew we were in a very smart apartment, overlooking the park. I peered out of one of the huge floor-to-ceiling windows, thinking how weird it was to be all the way up here, when we'd just been down there, then started to look around.

There were gold discs covering the walls and what looked like a recording studio in the corner. On the table in front of me was a picture of a couple posing. On a red carpet. They looked like they were. No, it couldn't be. It was . . .

"This is Jay-Z and Beyoncé's apartment!" Lorna screamed. "Would. You. Check. It. Out. They're soooo totally private that no one knows what it looks like in here." She lowered her voice. "Even if you work at *Us Weekly*."

"Lorna, are you sure this is the way to beat the breakup blues? Charlotte doesn't look like the kind of girl who was into Destiny's Child." Nancy's brow was fully furrowed. "Maybe we should have taken her to see those Evan people?"

"Destiny's Child split up *years* ago, Nancy. Where have you been?" Lorna said. "And I think Charlotte's had more than enough of Evanescence for one day. Plus everyone likes to be nosy where celebrities are concerned. Whatever, I'm just trying to prove my point." She turned to me. "Which is this: Charlotte, forget the we-can-only-port-to-solve-your-murder Rule. Tonight, for one night only, we're going to break it and port all over the city as many times as you like. We can go backstage, behind closed doors, into VIP sections. Anywhere you want—as long as we get you smiling and forget about dumb-boy back there."

Dumb-boy. Must forget about dumb-boy. And break lots of Rules. Okay, so maybe this could be kinda cool.

"So, where do you want to go?" Lorna asked, momentarily distracted by a pile of Prada shopping bags by the front door. Nancy dragged her back to my side. "Maybe you'd like to see what it's really like inside the hippest bar in the city?"

Arms raised, sick, whoosh.

Suddenly we were out of the popocracy apartment and in some cave of a bar with low lighting, crazy art prints, and a *Balearic Sunset* soundtrack. All the women around us—and there were plenty—were so rail thin, so pretty, and so beautifully dressed they made Lorna look plain. They were sipping colored cocktails (too many calories, surely?) while guys in perfect suits straight out of a Dior ad stood chatting to them. If this was the hippest-bar-land, I could not have hated it more. Even if I raided all the cheermonsters' closets and spent my entire traveling fund in Aveda, I'd never fit in here.

"Too sophisticated?" Lorna read my get-me-out-of-here look instantly. "Then how would you like to be a guest on *Letterman . . . ?*"

Um, wait a minute—well, more like two seconds—and give me a chance to think. Their arms went around me, the room blurred, and . . . the three of us were sitting on David Letterman's sofa. Next to Robert Pattinson, who was talking (well, stuttering a bit) about his new movie. He was totally not as hot as I hoped up close.

"Or . . ." Lorna jumped up on the sofa next to R. Pattz and bounced around a bit. He and his hair didn't even move.

She and Nancy armed me again and a second of spinning later, we were in some store. With a lot of dresses and stuff. It looked super-expensive and so not me. Lorna meanwhile was pretty much genuflecting in front of one rail.

"Prada," she breathed. "The biggest Prada store in the city. As soon as I saw those bags in Beyoncé's place, I knew I had to bring you here. And it's after closing time, so no one is here but us. Just look"—she waved her arms at the pricey outfits around her—"look at *all* this. It's like your own private store opening. It's, it's—"

"More like your idea of heaven than Charlotte's?" Nancy butted in.

Lorna reluctantly came to. "Okay, okay. So what do you want to do, Charlotte? Where do you want to see? Where have you never been allowed to go? The city is your lobster."

"Oyster," Nancy said.

"What?" Lorna wiggled her nose.

"The city is her *oyster*. No city can be a lobster."

"Oh. Whatevs. Where do you want to go?"

I knew my answer. But Lorna was so not going to be impressed. Not after the Knowles-Carter apartment or the Letterman sofa or the private Prada view.

"Could we go and see a band?"

"A band?" Lorna blinked.

"Yeah, I'd love to go and see a band at the Bowery Ballroom," I said. "It's just that Mom never let me get tickets—except one time on my sixteenth—because she'd never been allowed to see bands on her own until she was seventeen. It was a stupid rule, but if we're breaking them, can we break that one?"

Lorna looked properly dumbstruck. Nancy stepped in. "If

that's what makes you happy, Charlotte, of course. Let's make sure you get a ringside seat."

Before I knew it, I was feeling slightly sick—and standing next to Alex Turner.

As in Alex Turner, the lead singer from the Arctic Monkeys. Every one of whose albums I'd downloaded and listened to a trillion times. Onstage. At the Bowery. As hundreds of fangirls screamed below me. Whoa. Stick that in your pipe and smoke it, David You-Weren't-That-Good-a-Kisser-Anyway Maher.

"This sure beats ice cream and bitching about your ex, right?" Nancy managed, stepping out of the way just as Alex swung his guitar around and almost put it right through her stomach.

She was right. For my first proper, no-parents concert, I couldn't have had a more perfect view: the band, the guys crowd-surfing over the fangirls' heads, Lorna sitting on an amp, the moment the Arctics struck up the chords of my favorite song, and the encores they came back for three times.

It would have been perfect if it wasn't so painful too. The problem with dating someone for as long as I'd been with David is that, much as you hate the idea, your tastes merge. You kinda forget who liked which book first and who introduced who to what film. So the more I tried to forget him and the traitor kiss, with every chord I heard, the more a bit of me wished he was here—because he would beyond love this. Even though I couldn't hold his hand if he was. Even though he was a cheating, cheerleader-kissing idiot who I never wanted to see again and would soon be totally over. I hoped.

"Feel any better?" Nancy gave me a small smile as the band packed up.

"You know what," I said, lying my unapparited ass off. "I think I do."

The whole trying-to-cheer-Charlotte-up plan, it was actually kinda nice. It felt good to know they were on my side. Even if they were borderline insane.

"Um, Charlotte." Lorna grimaced as a massive, sweaty roadie walked straight through her. "Can we get out of here now?"

"Yes, enough with the distractions," Nancy said, switching speed. "Your funeral didn't throw up any leads, so tomorrow—when the Living are awake again—we need to begin the investigation into your murder properly."

I watched as my friends ported away, each disappearing into the air with a small *pop!* Much as murder investigations weren't my idea of a pull point, I guessed I better get back to the Attesa too.

I swung around to take one last look at the stage—and crashed straight into a tall guy. I was so unprepared for the force of banging into someone instead of walking through them, I lost my balance and tumbled backward toward the wooden stage.

"Whoa!" The guy grabbed me back up with such force, I found my face momentarily buried in his hard chest. Firm, not as permeable as smoke. One thing was for sure: Tall guy wasn't alive either.

"Still haven't learned to walk in those heels, Feldman?" he

said. I knew who it was even before I had time to smooth down my hair and lift my head.

"Edison, what are you doing here?" I asked, my words tumbling out in a rush.

"Shock, horror, just like you, I happen to like watching bands. Though I should ask how you got Tweedledum and Tweedledee to take a break from sleuthin' 'n' shoppin' to attend something as downtown as a gig." He lifted his green eyes from mine and scanned the room. "Where did they port off to in such a hurry, anyway?"

"Back to the hotel. They were trying to snap me out of my funk. I kinda had a bad day," I said, my voice breaking.

"Hey, as everyone who's had one knows, the 'fun' in 'funeral' is something of a misnomer." He looked down at me with a crooked smile, but his eyes were serious. He was still holding my shoulders tightly, as if I might fall again at any moment. If he let go, I wasn't sure that I wouldn't.

"Do you just sit around at night coming up with these lines? Waiting for new dead girls to show up so you can try them out?" I asked.

"No. I made that one up just for you," he said.

There was a low click and the lights in the Bowery shut off. Suddenly I was aware of just how close Ed and I were standing.

"I guess that means they're not going to do another encore then," I said unnecessarily. Hell, was I glad it was dark in here. I was pretty sure my face was flushed and I had no idea where to look or what to do next.

Edison gently dropped his arms from my shoulders to my waist, resting his fingers on the small of my back. "Then I guess we better take this party someplace more lively," he said quietly in my ear.

All I could manage was an uh-huh.

He tightened his grip, pulling me closer. OMG. I'd only known for sure that David and I were broken up today, and already I was alone in the dark, with the dead guy next door, my body feeling more alive than it had in days. Did this make me as bad as David? And if so, why didn't I want to pull away?

"Shhh . . . Close your eyes," Ed whispered.

I mentally calculated my chances of breaking away and porting back to the hotel before he caught up with me. He had me pretty tight. They weren't good. Broken, I did as I was told and shut my eyes tight.

As he pushed his fingers harder on my back, my shoulders stiffened. Was he going to make a move? What if, any second now, I felt the pressure of his lips, that pressure I'd wanted to feel when I tried to kiss David in his room? What would I do? Would I let him? Or push away? Suddenly I felt really faint, sick even. Somewhere inside my head, there seemed to be lights.

"Open up," I heard him say.

I did. But Ed wasn't holding me anymore. And I wasn't on the stage in the Bowery either.

No, he'd taken me somewhere else—somewhere low and dark and dank. So that was what the nausea meant, it wasn't because he was touching me; we'd ported here. And those lights I'd seen—they weren't in my mind. Oh no, now my eyes were open, I could see they were real. Very real.

Staring ahead, two yellow lights were coming toward me. Blinding through the darkness. The kind on the front of a subway train.

My brain clicked into gear, and I realized I was standing on a track. And the lights were hurtling right toward me at an incredible speed.

Chapter 13

I DON'T REMEMBER HOW IT FELT THE FIRST TIME the train ran over me. But now my senses were in overdrive, as if they were under someone else's control and determined I'd experience every sensation. As the lights got closer, a scream stuck in my throat. Then the metal cut through my being, jolting me, as car by car rolled over track after track. There was no pain. No hurt. No actual damage this time. Just confusion and fear, as my upper body skimmed above the train's floors, and I saw into every car, took in every sitting passenger, as the train screeched by.

It was late and the subway was almost empty, but—even as I willed my open eyes to shut until this was through—I saw the sleeping businessman who would miss his stop, the college kids drinking beer out of brown paper bags, the security guard on the way to his night shift. Normal commuters, with no idea a ghost was trapped somewhere between where they sat and the track beneath them and was watching them all speed by in a blur.

Then when it was over and the train had gone, I stood motionless on the tracks, wishing I could cry and the tears would come.

"Hurts a little less the second time around, huh?"

Edison was standing on the subway platform above me, blowing cigarette smoke out of his nose. Under the artificial lights, he looked like a black fire-breathing dragon.

"Why am I . . . ? How did I get down *here*?" I asked, my voice raspy. I was standing down in the middle of the subway tracks. And as much as New Yorkers complain about the city's shitty public transportation system, as one of them, I was pretty sure another train would be coming in any minute. I had to get out. If I could get it together enough to move. Or port.

"I guess I owe you an explanation." Edison squatted down on the platform, so he was almost on my eye level, and grinned. "So here's the thing: After our last lesson, I was thinking that maybe I was a little too easy on you. Like, the tricks you learned, sure they're fun, but would they really help if you found yourself in a death-and-death situation?" He tilted his head, like he was pondering the hardest math problem in the quiz. "I think not."

Two guys pushed through the turnstile above me and took their place on the platform next to Edison.

"You've been a good pupil. You can Kick, you can Jab, you have apparition down pat—honestly, I've never seen a newbie pick that up as fast as you, Charlotte—but your porting skills . . . from what

I've seen, they're kinda crappy." His grin had turned to a scowl now. I was beginning to wonder exactly how sane Edison was. Hot? Definitely. Unhinged? With every passing second, more than possibly.

Another guy arrived on the platform. When was the next train coming?

Ed continued. "It seems to me that, when it comes to porting, Nancy and Lorna are carrying you—*literally* today—and every time you port, you want to puke your guts up. Not that you have any guts anymore, right?" He laughed. "So I figured— surprise!—why not make our next lesson more practical? Why not put you somewhere where speed was of the *essence*. Why not take you down here and show you that porting quickly is a piece of cake. If you just try hard enough. If you know you really *have* to do it."

The rumble. I knew that sound. Low. Really low. I could feel it vibrating under my feet and down the concrete tunnel. It was far off, but it still meant one thing: Another train was totally coming. I had to get out of here. Fast.

But not before I'd done one little thing.

I turned to face Edison.

"You *what*, Edison?" I shouted. "You are completely crazy." I knew I was being loud, but I didn't care. It wasn't like anyone down here could hear me anyhow. "You saw me having a perfectly nice night watching a band and you thought, 'Oh, I know, what poor recently murdered Charlotte needs is to be kidnapped and have the life scared out of her—again—that'll make her a better ghost!'—is that it?"

Ed stared at me. His expression neutral. Like he was a mom letting her toddler get it all out before she decided to reason with it. Or spank its butt.

"Who gave you the right to do this to me?" I was ranting now. "What? You didn't think I'd had a bad enough day with the funeral and the crying and the total lack of my Key, so you thought you'd freak me out some more, under the guise of 'teaching me how to apparite quickly'?"

The rumble was building now.

"For your information, Edison, you do not have any hold over me—"

"Er, Charlotte?" he said, his forehead wrinkling.

"Shut up! I've heard just about enough from you with your 'shhh . . . close your eyes' and your 'let's take this party someplace more lively.' You might think you're *it*, but you, Edison Hayes, are the most pretentious, irritating, smug, conceited, senseless doofus I have *ever* laid eyes on—"

"Charlotte, I think you should . . ." Edison was pointing down the track. Actually looking nervous now. Whatever.

"I said, SHUT UP!" I shouted. "I am doing fine without your lessons, thank you very much. So fine, that if I never saw your dead ass again, it would be too soon. So fine, that—"

My words didn't seem to be having any effect. Instead Edison stood up and slowly crossed his arms across his chest in a don't-say-I-didn't-warn-you way.

Idiot.

I turned back to the tunnel. Crap—there they were. The lights. The two lights. Speeding at me. Ohforgodsake. I was not being run down *three* times. Once is careless, twice is stupid, but three times, well . . . Concentrate, Charlotte, I told myself. You can do this. Just close your eyes and port and . . .

Bang! I landed on the platform in record time—right on top of Edison, just as the train sped past.

"See, I said this would help your porting skills," Edison said, the grin firmly back in place. "Though if you'd wanted to get me horizontal, all you had to do was ask."

Right at that moment, I wasn't sure if I was in more danger up here, sprawled all over Mr. Tough Love, than I was down there, in the path of a careering train.

"Well, looky what we have here . . . ," a voice said.

I unsuccessfully tried to pull myself off Edison's lap, and saw Tess standing on the platform in front of us, with her hands on her hips and a quizzical expression on her face. She looked like a girl who'd just walked into her closet to find her little sister stealing her new clothes. Which was weird. Seeing as there could not be less going on between me and Edison—not now anyway—and, as far as I knew, Tess didn't like anyone but herself (and sometimes Lorna/Nancy when they behaved).

"Um, Tess, what are you doing down here?" I asked, doing my best to sound casual, like getting caught lying on top of Edison on an empty platform after dark was no biggie.

"Nancy was worried when you didn't port straight back to the hotel after her and Shop-a-lot," Tess said. "She seems to think your porting skills aren't up to snuff yet." I tried to ignore Edison as he smugly poked me in the ribs. "Seems like you're not that green in other areas though, doesn't it? Is this your new tactic for holding on to guys now, Charlotte? Don't worry, honey, we've had cheerghosts in the Attesa before—they weren't Edison's type then, so I doubt they would be now."

Ouch. Could she just give me a minute while I pulled that knife out of my back?

Edison lifted me off his lap and onto the concrete beside us. For someone who looked like a dead poet, he was strong. He gracefully stood up, then reached a hand down, pulling me up too. This time I didn't end up with my face in his chest, thank God.

"Thank you," I said, before I could help it. Gah! Why was I thanking the strong mad boy? It was his fault I was in this mess in the first place.

Ed smirked. I half wanted to punch him and half wanted to kiss his self-satisfied grin away. Except, no, I didn't want to do the last one. I so didn't want to do any of that. I wanted to . . . ? Ohmigod.

"Look, Tess," I said, carefully taking a step away from Edison to show our total not-an-item-ness. "This is *not* how it looks."

"That's a shame, because it looks kinda interesting," she said, pretending to look down at her nails. I couldn't help but notice that her face looked—as my grandmother would have said—like thunder.

"No, sorry, it's not interesting *at all,*" I said, trying to keep my voice even as Edison took a massive step toward me, and casually slung his arm around my shoulders, making my whole right side buzz. He smiled encouragingly, as if to say, *Go on, please finish your story.*

I straightened up, trying to take control.

"So it turned out that Edison was also at the Arctics' show but when I bumped into him Lorna and Nancy had already ported back to the hotel so I couldn't tell them he was there and then he suggested that we come here because he knew I was afraid of the subway after everything that happened and I'd not had the best day with my funeral and the dying and so you can see there is less going on here than you think."

Tess looked from me to Edison, then back again. He gave my shoulder a deliberately obvious squeeze. Tess's jaw tightened.

"What's up, Tess, you look stressed out? Want to bum a smoke?" Edison offered her a cigarette and blinked at her innocently.

"No thanks, you know what those things do for your health," she said evenly. "Now, Edison, if I can just have one second of your time on our own, that would be very helpful."

"Oh, come on, Tess, it's kinda late, I'm beat, and . . ."

Pop!

Talk about avoiding the issue. Edison was gone. Leaving nothing but a burning cigarette behind him. He'd ported off the platform to who knows where, leaving me with an angry Tess and a whole load of questions about what the bejesus had just happened. Could I actually be crushing on a guy who was dead, hot, *and* the object of Tess's . . . what? Irritation? *Affection?* Jeez, the way my luck was going, I wouldn't be surprised to learn she and Edison had dated at some point and, thanks to tonight, she now had even more reason for giving me the scowl.

Tess slowly and very deliberately walked down the platform toward me, stopping right in front of my face. For one horrible second, I thought she was going to push me on the tracks for a third time, but instead she pursed her lips into a small hard line, then focused on the burning butt on the concrete beside her.

"Look, Charlotte, I don't know what went on tonight, and to be perfectly honest with you, I have no desire to hear the details. But I do know this," she said, stamping out the cigarette, "the more time you spend getting distracted by Edison, the longer it's going to take to solve your murder"—she put her arms around me, ready to port us home together, and looked me hard in the eyes—"and the longer I have to put up with you in my afterlife."

I tried to hold her gaze as the platform melted and the Attesa lobby appeared.

As soon as she could, Tess dropped her arms.

"I think we'll both agree that neither of us want that to be too long," she said. Her eyes were harsh again now, there was no mistaking the flecks of hatred being fired at me. Just what had I done to annoy her this much? Was it *really* that I was another newbie who had the chance of a way out of here that it seemed she'd lost? "If I were you," she said, "I'd stay away from Edison, get investigating hard, and then, let's hope, everything around here will go back to normal."

Tess turned on her heel and started up the stairs. "And I can forget you ever existed."

Chapter 14

THE TITLE NANCY HAD SCRAWLED ON THE blackboard wasn't her most subtle effort, but it did the trick: *Murder Suspects*. Then underneath in smaller letters—as if to clarify anything Lorna, Tess, or I may not have *fully* understood: *People who might have killed Charlotte*.

Nancy stood by the board, chalk in hand, like some expectant teacher who'd just asked her class a tricky algebra problem. Lorna and I sat on small swivel chairs opposite her. Tess—typically—was slouching on the table to her right with her feet dangerously close to a pile of ancient case files. There was no way she could see Nancy's board from that position. But I doubted she cared. Even her legs were pointing away from us, as if to say, *Yeah, whatever, I may be here, but don't expect me to be into it*. Edison, who I'd not seen since what-the-hell-happened-last-night, was, as usual, sitting this one out.

"Let's start then, shall we?" Nancy tapped her chalk on the board. White dust swirled and whirled in a shaft of morning light. "We'll go through what we know and make some lists."

Lists. Woo.

"First off, from observing your friends at the funeral and the high school, no one seems to suspect you were killed in suspicious circumstances, Charlotte," Nancy said, walking back and forth in front of the board. "And the police don't think that either."

"Which means they either think you were a total clumsy-head who tripped onto the tracks or a jumper," Lorna clarified.

"Thanks," I said. Man, this was shaping up to be about as fun as a root canal.

"But"—Nancy raised an eyebrow—"we know that both of those conclusions are not true. If you'd killed yourself or just stumbled, you wouldn't be here with us. Someone pushed you and meant to do it. That's why you're in the Attesa."

Yes, the push, the heat, yada yada, I remembered all that. Way too clearly after Edison's actions last night. Could we move it along?

"What about security cameras?" I asked. "There must have been cameras down on the subway platform. They must have seen something? Someone standing close to me, the moment I"—nope, still no easier talking about this out loud—"went under the F train?"

"Yes, we checked out the security footage while we were waiting for you to arrive," Nancy said. "Well, Lorna ported to the nearest

NYPD station and she watched over the officers' shoulders while they looked at the tapes. Unfortunately there was a problem with the way the cameras had been set up, so they weren't much help."

"The cameras were pointing in the opposite direction to the tracks—to focus on the turnstiles," Lorna said. "So there's no footage of the platform or you being pushed under the train."

Figures.

"So seeing as we don't really have any evidence from the crime scene—because the police didn't think a 'crime' had been committed—and there's no Living investigation in progress, we'll have to solve this case on our own," Nancy said. Awesome. "I guess the first big question we have to ask is, who wanted you dead?"

Who wanted me dead? I looked blankly at the others. Sorry, no lightbulbs were about to ping anytime here.

"No obvious suspects, then?" I got the impression this was really not going the way Nancy wanted, but I'd been thinking this over since I'd arrived and I hadn't come up with anyone.

"Okay, let's think about things differently," Nancy said, tucking her hair behind her ear. "Did you go home via that route every day?"

"Yes," I said. Every day after school let out, at three thirty p.m., I caught the F train at Rockefeller Center, before getting out at Lexington and Sixty-Third. It might not have been the most direct route, but it meant I could walk home through the park, which gave me alone-time to think.

"So if someone wanted to push you under a train, for anyone

who knew you, it would have been a pretty safe bet that you would have been on the F train platform at about three forty p.m. on a school day."

Yessss. Where was Nancy going with this?

"My point is that ninety-five percent of murders are committed by someone the victim knew." Nancy was *way* too knowledgeable on this stuff. "So, seeing as you were killed somewhere you went every day at pretty much the same time, I think we can surmise that whoever did this was someone you were at least on first name terms with."

Lorna's eyes were wide. "Or"—she was so about to come up with something classic—"it was an evil stranger who stalked you for weeks and weeks until he knew your routine."

Eww, not a thought to dwell on.

Nancy wrote *random madman/woman* on the blackboard in round, neat letters.

I visibly shuddered. Nancy shot Lorna one of her pipe-down looks. Tess over-yawned.

"But that is really unlikely," Nancy reassured me. "There's much more chance that your murderer was one of your friends or family." She smiled as if that were a comfort.

Scratch that. A crazed random stalker sounded way better than someone I knew hating me enough to take my life.

"I get your logic, Nancy, really I do," I said. "It's just that, well, I can't think of anyone who'd want me dead."

Tess snorted loudly behind me. Who did she think she was?

I got it: She had something against me for whatever reason, and catching me sitting on Edison didn't seem to have helped our relationship, but I was getting so bored of the Cruella act.

"Think again, think hard," Nancy said. "There must have been someone who stands out as not liking you."

So I thought. But I couldn't come up with a name. Not one. It wasn't like I stood out in my high school. Don't get me wrong, I wasn't one of those weird kids who is so quiet and shy she practically merges into her locker and you only notice her when, one day, your lab partner is ill (or at least pretending to be) and the teacher pairs you up and you think, "Oh, were you here all along?"

I wasn't invisible. I just wasn't very . . . well, anything really. I was into music and photography. I loved art. I wanted to see the world and go to college—who didn't? High school sucked. Everyone knew that. But if the Tornadoes and the lacrosse team wanted to pretend like it was all some big preparation for the rest of their lives, I knew better. David knew better. Which was why we kept our heads down and waited until graduation called, when we could get the hell out and socialize with people who didn't think Joan Jett was a kind of airplane.

I was just your average sixteen-year-old. Who would have the time, energy, or inclination to bother killing me?

"Let's just do the motives test." Lorna was getting as bored of this as I was.

"Yes, the motives test." Nancy drew a line down the middle of her blackboard and wrote *Possible Motives* as a header on the right-hand side. Tess pretended to stifle another yawn.

"Okay, motive number one," she said, writing a large number one. "Revenge—was anyone mad at you?"

Nope, it appeared only mean girls like Tess were mad at me now that I was dead.

"Number two: jealousy. Did you have anything someone else at your school would have wanted?"

"That's always a good motive," Lorna said.

Noooo. My grade-point average was so not enough to threaten Massie Jones or any of the nerds. I could paint and take pictures a little, but I hadn't won one scholastic prize since I was the only member of my class who colored Santa Claus within the lines in first grade. Mom always said I was good at "making stuff," but no one gets murdered for being able to customize an old shirt. And it wasn't as if I was up for prom queen.

I shook my head again.

"Motives three, four, and five aren't really that helpful to us," Nancy said. "Number three being that there is no motive, just that your murderer was a loony. Number four being that they didn't mean to do it, they just killed you in the heat of the moment."

"And five is that it was mistaken identity." Lorna had obviously sat through this little brainstorm so many times even she knew what was coming. "And while you do look like a lot of other teenage girls, I don't buy that for one second. If you're going to commit teenicide, you're going to get the right girl."

Duh.

This was going nowhere. At this rate, I was going to be stuck in this stupid hotel, in these stupid boots I could not for the death of me walk in forever. I'd spend my days watching Edison try to smoke himself back to life. While my friends grew up. My parents got old. Ali went to college. David and Kristen fell in love, got married in the church where I'd just been buried, and had a soccer team of perfect little blond-haired babies.

"So we don't have a suspect or a motive?" I asked.

"What about lover boy?" Tess asked.

We all turned to stare at her in shock.

"What, David?" I eventually managed. "Are you insane?"

"Not clinically. But let's look at the evidence, shall we?" She swung her legs off the desk, narrowly missing pushing the case files onto the floor. Not that she cared. "Ever since you checked in here, who has been having the time of his life? Blondie." I cringed. Tess stood up, looking down at me. "Maybe that little speech he made to the cheerleader wasn't so far off the mark, Charlotte. Maybe he felt suffocated, so he found a way to get himself some breathing space—forever?"

Right. After everything that had happened on the subway platform, I was already at my enough limit, and now she'd tipped me clear over.

"Tess, I don't know what you have against me—maybe you're like this with every newbie who comes through the door—but you've been a grade-A bitch ever since I checked in here," I said.

"As far as I know, I've been nothing but nice to you. But for some reason that doesn't seem to be enough. Whatever. I'm tired of trying to work it out. Because believe it or not, I don't want to be here spending time with you, any more than you want to be spending time with me. But guess what? There's not much I can do about it."

Lorna tried to hide behind Nancy's back.

"You might have these two convinced that the Big Red Door is the worst idea since exorcism, but I am not as easily fooled," I continued. "If you hadn't been scaring them with all this mumbo jumbo about the 'bad things' on the Other Side, maybe they'd have tried to find their Keys and gone through it by now. Instead of staying here with you just because you don't want to be lonely. Because that's the real problem, isn't it? You know you're stuck here forever so you don't want to be left alone. And you don't like anyone new coming around who might convince your friends that they need to leave you behind—for their own sakes."

I stopped. From the look on Nancy's face I could tell I was about one sentence away from saying something I'd really regret.

"There. I'm done," I said. "Sorry for the outburst, but at least I feel like now I've given you a concrete reason to have a beef with me."

Instead of fighting back, Tess stared at the floor.

Lorna was the first to speak. She came out from behind Nancy and patted my arm. "Charlotte, no one is making anyone stay here. It's really nice that you're looking out for us, but really, you don't have to."

She turned to Tess. "And Tess, you're not funny. Charlotte might be new, but anyone can see that she really loved David. I may not be the sharpest ghost in the box, but I know people, and I can see Charlotte was not the kind of girlfriend a boy would want to murder."

That made one of them. I smiled a thank-you at her. Just as Nancy wrote *David* on the Suspects side of her board. Right under madman/woman.

"What?" She shrugged. "I don't think he did either, but we can't cross off suspects without investigating all the leads first."

"What about your friend? Ali, was it?" Lorna asked, desperately trying to change the subject. "Didn't you say you weren't getting along as well with her as you had been recently?"

"Yes, she could feel like you dumped her for David and wanted revenge." Nancy wrote Ali's name below David's. "So there, we have two suspects. I'm ignoring madman/woman for the moment, because those kind of random psychos are notoriously hard to find."

Excellent. "Two suspects who I am one hundred and one percent sure are innocent," I said.

"There is no such thing as one hundred and one percent," Nancy said. "Let's check Ali out first, then David next." She looked at the clock. "Nine a.m. They'll be in school now. Let's make a move."

My (sort of ex) best friend and my (sort of ex) boyfriend? No way. But even if we just crossed them off the list at least it was better than sitting here. Watching Tess come up with stupid theories when she knew zero about my life.

Nancy looked out of the hotel window, onto Washington Square. "Charlotte, we have to get a move on. Because somewhere out there is the person who killed you—a person who thinks he or she is getting away with murder. And I, for one, am going to make sure that is not the case."

Chapter 15

"WHO CAN TELL ME WHAT THE ATOMIC NUMBER
of oxygen is?" Mr. Millington asked, briefly taking off his horn-
rimmed glasses, cleaning them on his dull-as-gray sweater, then
repositioning them neatly on his thin face.

Able to see the class again clearly, he smiled encouragingly.
"Anyone?"

His question was met with complete and utter silence. Only
broken by the sound of Alanna Acland accidentally knocking her
pink gel pen off her desk and it bouncing twice on the tiled floor.

"Nobody?" More silence.

"Okay, then let's take things back a step—recap on the ground
we covered last week to refresh your memories." Mr. Millington
looked around the class.

"What *is* an atomic number?" Even though he'd suffered
eighteen years teaching high school science, he had still not lost

the optimism that maybe, someday, he would ask a question like this and one—just one—of the kids in his class would stop daydreaming about last night's TV, the opposite sex, or what they were going to eat for lunch and actually answer.

The class kept their eyes firmly on the floor. The eleventh grade chem students may not know what oxygen's atomic number was, but they did know that if they made eye contact with Mr. Millington, he'd take that as a sign of *intelligence* and they'd be asked the question directly.

"No one remembers? It's on page seventeen of your textbooks. How about we all get them out?"

Eighteen books were slowly and very begrudgingly pulled out of backpacks and messenger bags.

"Everyone there? Great. Now as it says so succinctly on page seventeen, 'Every single element has its own unique number that tells how many protons are in one atom of that element. The atomic number is the number of protons in the nucleus of an atom of a particular element.' Is everyone remembering this? Yes? No questions? Okay then, so if an oxygen atom has eight protons— can anyone tell me what the atomic number of oxygen is now?"

Eugh. Was it possible to die of boredom when you'd already had your funeral, like, yesterday? It sure felt like it, if the numbness spreading through my brain was anything to go by.

I wiggled around in my seat and shuddered. Chem class. I never thought I'd be back here again. Sitting in my old seat. Leaning on my old desk. Listening to poor Mr. Millington.

But seeing as Dead Girls' Chief Detective Nancy had decided that I needed to cross Ali and David off my most-likely-to-have-murdered-me list before we could investigate anyone else, I had to be here. Chem class was where they were both supposed to be.

Supposed being the operative word.

When I ported in, I'd found my chair empty. Which I totally got. I mean, it was pretty much still warm from when my body last sat on it. Nobody was going to be going there anytime soon in case it was cursed, or the kid caught a case of the Charlotte clumsys and accidentally fell under the nearest fast-moving mode of transportation too.

But what I didn't get was where David was. He should have been sitting next to me in his usual seat. As he had every Wednesday.

Though, just in case I hadn't noticed the absence of my dirty, cheating, no-longer boyfriend, I kept being reminded of it by Kristen—who was sitting three rows in front—turning around to stare at the empty chair every couple of minutes. Like, just by doing that, she was going to will David to appear.

Well, everything else in life went her way, so I guessed she couldn't understand why David wasn't there holding her hand, stroking her hair, feeding her grapes or something—seeing as she'd deigned to kiss him and all.

Even though Nancy and Lorna had done their best to make me feel better about things, I still couldn't get the image of David and Kristen kissing out of my head. I could only hope David wasn't showing his sorry ass around Saint Bart's today because he was beyond ashamed about sucking face with *that* yesterday.

Hopefully he was somewhere far away—like the Bronx—in an inner ring of tortured mental hell, wishing he had access to a time machine so he could honor my memory properly instead of stomping all over it in his size 11s, like good boyfriends are meant to do.

Or maybe he'd just slept in.

Whatever. He was so not worth another second of my time.

"All hydrogen atoms contain one proton and have an atomic number of one, and all other atoms' atomic number is also determined by . . ." Mr. Millington was still droning on.

Enough. I clicked my fingers, activating the Lifesaver trick Edison had taught me. Mr. Millington's blah instantly went on mute. His mouth still popped open and closed, open and closed, like a possessed puppet's—which was kinda eerie to watch, but way better than what I'd previously had to listen to.

I stood up from my seat. Even though I knew, as a ghost, I was invisible, I kinda expected the M-man to shout and tell me to sit down and concentrate. But he didn't. I walked between the desks and to the front of the class.

Next to the board, Mr. Millington had pinned up a picture of Rachel McAdams and Ryan Gosling in *The Notebook*. Underneath he'd written, "They have chemistry, so can you!"

I stood in front of Mr. Millington's face as he talked silently on and wrote about isotopes and potassium and positions in the periodic table on the whiteboard. Since I wasn't getting any leads on who'd killed me here, would a little light haunting to stop the monotony be wrong? It was hardly Jimmy territory. What Nancy didn't see, she'd never know about. And couldn't take off my Nine Times.

I tried my first solo Jab, *sans* Edison. Really lightly on Mr. M's left shoulder. He flinched and rolled his shoulder back. Like a horse batting off a fly with its tail, then carried on teaching. Yet another guy I didn't need to waste any more of my kinetic energy on.

I walked over to Ali's desk instead. May as well concentrate on her for a bit so I could take her off the list. I sat on top of the desk of the kid next to her, and leaned in for a better look at my friend.

I hadn't been this close to Ali since I'd been killed. That second day when I was in the school hall, she sort of wandered past without me noticing her until she was a bit blurry. And at my funeral, I guess I'd been too focused on slut boy to pay her attention. But now, centimeters away from her, I realized that Ali looked . . . bad.

Her normally shiny straight brown hair was kinda greasy, she wore zero makeup, and there were bags under her eyes.

Ali stared at a spot on the floor, somewhere in front of her. Unlike the rest of my class, it didn't look like she'd zoned out because of Mr. Millington's scintillating teacher style. It looked more like she was miles and miles away and . . . upset?

A tear welled up in the corner of her eye. Ali silently wiped it away. Then looked around to check that no one had noticed.

What was wrong with her?

Suddenly Ali seemed to snap out of her trance. She wiped a second tear off her cheek and swiveled in her chair, staring hard at Kristen and Jamie. What on earth had they said? I clicked my fingers to turn the volume back up on the world. *Pop!*

"I have chemistry with David too—so you can't just say he belongs to you, Kristen!" Jamie was ranting in an angry voice. "Just because you've been trying to cozy up to him ever since that girl died, that doesn't mean I'm not allowed a chance with him too."

I looked down at Ali. She was bolt upright now. Her eyes looked as wild as mine felt.

"Let's not get into this here, shall we?" Kristen was trying to be all upper-handy. "It's really not the time or the place. Aren't we supposed to be here to learn, J?"

"Learn? As if! And *you* brought it up!?"

"Girls! Is there a problem here?" Mr. Millington asked from the board.

Ali slowly stood up and turned around to face the Bicker Squad.

"Oh, be serious. I've seen you, following David into the library, talking to him after class and I—" Kristen started.

"STOP!" Ali shouted.

This time there was a silence so harsh, no one even noticed when Alanna dropped her gel pen for a second time in shock.

Everyone turned from Kristen to Ali, like the crowd at a tennis match watching the ball bounce from player to player.

"You two are *disgusting*." Ali walked toward them, straightening up as she did. She'd grown a couple of inches over the holidays—now she was taller than I had been. How come I hadn't noticed? That made me feel so, so bad. "Charlotte—that is 'that girl's' *name*—has not even been dead for three full days and you are fighting over her boyfriend? What is wrong with you? You're like . . . vultures."

Kristen looked totally thrown. She was not used to people standing up to her. Especially girls she wouldn't even put on the B-squad. How dare Ali question her? In public. She blinked uncomprehendingly, then her expression hardened. Uh-oh. She was back.

Kristen's chair scraped on the floor as she pushed it back. "What's wrong with us?" she asked, her eyebrows high. "What's wrong with you? Why are you getting involved? Why are you all boo hoo over some girl who dumped you as soon as she got a boyfriend anyway?"

Ali flushed. Kristen carried on. "I may not pay much attention to who you people sit with in the lunch hall, but I do know that you and Miss Feldman were like some badly dressed Siamese twins. Until hot David came along and noticed she wasn't entirely unfortunate looking. Then she was always with him. And you were always on your own. In the library. After every single class. So why are you so desperate to stick up for Charlotte when she wasn't that great to you anyway? Don't you think that makes you a little"—Kristen looked Ali up and down and back again slowly—"*pathetic.*"

Ali opened her mouth to speak. I willed her with every bit of my dead body to come out with a brilliant line. If I'd have been able to think of one myself, I'd have tried a Throw and put the words into her mouth, just like Edison taught me.

But I couldn't. And neither could she.

Ali gave a little sob and ran out of the room, slamming the door behind her. Kristen turned and confidently strode back to her seat, Jamie slumped next to her.

"Er, class?" Mr. Millington said, looking nearly as distraught as Ali. "Can we stop this now and get back to the matter at hand? We've not covered RAMs yet, so we're in danger of getting behind on lesson plans and . . ."

I bounced through the door—so desperate to find Ali, that I hardly even noticed the tickle of the wood. Where would she go? Where did she always go when she was upset?

I looked at the clock. Nine forty-five a.m.: fifteen minutes before class ended and everyone piled out into the halls. Which meant there was one place that was nearby and safe right now: the girls' restroom.

I pushed myself through the wall (yep, definitely getting used to the tickle) and heard a snuffling noise coming from under the door of the cubicle farthest from me.

"Ali?" I asked, out of habit.

But of course, she couldn't hear me. She had no idea I was here.

"I'm sorry, Charlotte." Ali sniffed. "I know it's crazy to talk to you when you aren't around anymore, but I don't know what else to do."

It wasn't crazy. For a while after my grandfather had died last year, I'd talked to him. Maybe not out loud, but . . .

"I should have been there for you. Even if our lives were changing and there were new people in them," she said.

I pushed my head through the metal toilet door—Ali sat on the floor, hugging her knees to her chest and crying quietly. "Maybe if I'd been a better friend, you'd still be here," she cried. "I mean, if I'd gotten the subway after school with you that day like I always, always used to, then maybe you wouldn't have tripped and fallen under that train. You were always the clumsiest person I knew. Remember that time when we were eleven and we were practicing kissing on pillows and you fell off my top bunk and broke your arm? If I'd been there on the subway, maybe I could have grabbed you, held you back, and everything would be different."

I pulled the rest of my body through the door and crouched on the floor beside my friend.

"It's okay," I said, even though she couldn't hear my words. "You couldn't have done anything. I didn't trip. I was pushed. I'm the one who's sorry. Sorry for letting a stupid guy come between us."

"Or if you really did have to die—if it really was your time—I wish you hadn't gone when things weren't good with us," Ali said, her sob turning into a hiccup. "I should have been less jealous of you and David. Hung out with you guys more when you asked me to, instead of being weird about it. Now I'll never get to tell you how much I'll miss you."

"I'm so, so sorry," I said.

I forgot myself—forgot the train and the push and the Rules and Kristen the hell bitch—and leaned over to give Ali a hug. I put my arms around her, being careful not to touch her body in case I passed into it. Instead I surrounded her and listened as she quietly cried.

"Charlotte?" she said. "Are you . . . ? Oh, stop being stupid, Ali," she told herself.

I wasn't sure quite what just happened—maybe I needed her to feel my presence as badly as she needed a sign that I'd heard her. Whatever, I didn't move.

As we sat there in silence, neither of us certain the other knew we were there, I was a hundred percent sure about one thing: Ali hadn't killed me. There was no way.

She was the only one who had stood up for me. The only one. I wished I could tell her that I knew that—and how I'd do the same for her if things had gone another way. I wished I could go back to the time when we were best friends. The time before everything got so messed up. I thought David had my back, but after everything I'd seen since I'd died? Well, I didn't for a second think he'd killed me either, but he wasn't who I thought he was. No matter how much I tried to justify that kiss, I just couldn't.

Down the hallway the bell rang. Ali pulled herself up off the floor and started rummaging in her blue Gap satchel for her makeup bag to fix her blotchy face. She always looked terrible when she cried.

I went out of the cubicle and found a chair to the side of the restroom door. I concentrated hard and Jabbed it three times, until it was nestled under the bathroom door's handle. There, now no one would be able to get in until Ali had had time to get herself back together. I owed her that much at least.

And so, so much more.

Chapter 16

"SO YOU JUST LEFT HER, LIKE, SITTING ON THE grimy bathroom floor, crying her eyes out?"

"Well, no, not exactly. Ali was pretty much okay by the time I ported back here—there wasn't much I could do, was there? If I'd apparited while she'd been reapplying her eyeliner, she may have been scarred for life. And I feel like I've been a shitty enough friend without doing that to her too."

Back in HHQ, I waited until Tess was out of the way before I filled Nancy and Lorna in on what had happened at school.

"Wow," Lorna said. "Ali sounds really cool. A real girl's girl. Not like Kristen."

Nancy walked over to the blackboard and neatly drew a red line through Ali's name. Of course she had a whole different color chalk to do the cross-throughs. I wondered what color she had to draw a big old check when we figured out who my killer was.

Or maybe I wouldn't be here to see that part.

"Knock, knock!" Edison poked his head around the door, making me almost fall off my swivel chair. I did my best to act like it hadn't happened. "Afternoon, ladies, just thought I'd stop by and see how the investigation is going."

"Good," Nancy said. "Thank you for asking, Edison. It's nice to see you getting involved in a case. It's not often we see you down here." She peered at him suspiciously over the top of her black frames.

"Well, sometimes, Miss Radley, even busy guys like me have a moment to spare." He jumped up and sat on the table next to me. "And I thought, what better way to spend it than by dropping in on you and Lorna." He looked down, his bright green eyes serious and focused intently on me. "And how are you, Charlotte?"

Edison's face was a picture of concern. He bent down and gave my shoulder a supportive squeeze. Even though I was sitting down and I really, really, really hated him, my legs still felt weak. Bad legs. "Hang in there," he said. "If anyone can find your Key, it's Nancy. She's the best detective the Attesa's ever seen." He gave her his most winning grin.

I smiled in spite of myself.

"So, we know one person definitely didn't kill me. Now what?" I asked, moving out of squeeze distance of Edison's arm and trying my best to ignore him.

"Well, we've been spying on the Living for days now and we haven't turned up any decent leads," Nancy admitted. "Despite the uninventive nature of your death, your murderer is clearly very clever. You were killed in a majorly public place, yet everyone thinks you jumped or clumsily slipped. And ever since the night you died, your murderer has done nothing to give us a clue."

Awesome.

"So, basically, what you're saying is that we're fresh out of ideas and I'm going to be stuck here for eternity?"

"Wouldn't be such a bad thing," Ed said, under his breath so only I could hear.

"No," Nancy sighed. "What I'm saying is that light haunting isn't working. I think it's time we went to Dead-Com Two." She paused dramatically. "We need to start possessing the Living to really find out what they're up to."

"Possession? Eugh, like, again, Nancy?" Lorna wrinkled up her perfect little button nose as if she'd just smelled some especially potent trash. "You know I HATE possession more than jeggings. It's just sooo gross getting in other people's bodies. It's like wearing someone's dirty underwear. You don't know where the people have been. Or if they've taken care of themselves when they were there."

Ed was swinging his feet so they occasionally bounced off my chair. He was way too close for comfort.

Right, focus. Possession. Possession sounded . . . exciting. I'd seen *The Exorcist*. Okay, so I hadn't actually seen it because when I borrowed it from Drama Club Drew in ninth grade Mom confiscated it on account of the fact, as she put it, it "messed me up for months when I saw it and no daughter of mine is having sleepless nights." But I had seen the *Simpsons* episode where Maggie's head spins around. And the trailer for *The Exorcism of Emily Rose*. So I sort of knew what we were talking about here. Jumping into human's bodies, so we could control them. Cool.

"Come on then, Nancy, tell me the possession rules. There are bound to be a gazillion of them," I said, pulling my still-unread Rules book out of my blazer pocket.

"Oh, Rule time," Ed said, standing up and dusting some invisible dirt off his skinny jeans. "This would be my cue to go. Good luck with it all today," he said to Lorna and Nancy.

He turned to face me and dropped his voice. "Hey, don't go running through that Door just yet, will you, Ghostgirl?" And walked out.

I listened as the door clicked shut. Bad boy, nice guy, flirt: Edison was one big sandwich of contradiction, with a side order of WTF? And I was not wasting any more of my time trying to figure him out.

"There are actually only two Rules for possession," Nancy was saying. "One: Get in quick, and two: As soon as you're done, get out quicker."

"Really?" I asked.

"Really," Nancy said. "It's easy. But there's no point hanging around the Living's bodies any longer than we need to. That's just weird. So let's go show you how it's done." She closed her eyes. By now, I knew what they meant. "Everyone think 'Times Square' and on the count of three, port. One . . . two . . . three!"

I opened my eyes and there I was in Times Square, feeling less sick than I ever had after a port. Standing in among all the brightly lit billboards was kinda claustrophobic. Like being trapped in a gigantic pinball machine.

"Oh, for goodness' sake," Nancy said, beside me.

"What?" I asked, as she disappeared again, porting back a second later with her hand firmly on Lorna's wrist.

"I know you don't like it," Nancy was ranting, "but we need to help Charlotte out, right now. And get back on schedule."

Lorna snapped her arm out of Nancy's grasp with an elaborate *tut!* and straightened up her dress.

"I hate this place," she spat. "It's so full of . . . tourists. And dirt. And smells. And there is not one decent clothes shop within five blocks. It's stupid."

"Yes, but it's also the busiest place in the city," Nancy said, "and the one thing we need right now is lots and lots of members of the Living to jump intooooooooooo . . ."

As she spoke, Nancy started running at a girl of about our age who was taking pictures of the mega-scrapers and McDonald's signs, just a few feet away. When she got to her, Nancy jumped— right into the girl's body. And disappeared. The girl shook, then straightened up.

"That's the really gross part," Lorna whispered. "It's like jumping into a swimming pool that you doubt has been cleaned properly. Only, like, one million times worse."

I stared at the Nancy-Possessed Girl. Really slowly she raised her right arm and waved it at the place where Lorna and I were standing. Nancy was moving her! She raised the other arm and did a double wave, just to make sure we were paying attention. How weird. The girl's mouth opened.

"See what I'm doing, Charlotte?" she yelled at me. The voice wasn't Nancy's. It was lower and kinda croaky, like she smoked ten cigarettes a day. "It's easy," she said with a rasp. "I'll get out of here, then you can have a go."

Smoker Girl's arms dropped, then she shuddered slightly— shivering at a blast of cold air only she could feel—and took a massive step forward.

Nancy fell out of the back of her body, almost tripped over her own feet, then quickly righted herself and smiled.

"See! Easy! All you need to do is run, jump, then when you're ready to leave just wiggle yourself out and take a step backward. The Living people who've been possessed usually feel a bit weird and quivery—but only for a second—so they shiver themselves, which helps you to pop out the back."

"I can't get stuck?" I asked. Because that would be (a) gross, and (b) exactly the kinda thing I'd do.

"Honestly, in three years of possessions, I've never seen any ghost do that," Nancy reassured me.

"And that includes that dumb stoner jock we lost for two days in Central Park," Lorna added. "Even *he* managed to get out of his football coach. And you are so much smarter than him."

Thanks.

I looked around. Did I just run at some stranger I liked the look of? Did it matter if I went for a guy over a girl? Was it better to get one who was standing still so I didn't miss them and fall over like Nancy almost did? Or was this actually a time when I should go for a moving target—because there was more momentum and stuff?

"Start off with someone who's sort of the same size as you," Nancy said encouragingly. "That makes it easier. I guess because you don't have to try so hard when you're controlling them— because you remember what it was like to be alive and move someone of that weight."

Right. Good advice.

"It's like when my driver's ed teacher started us off with our first lessons, we all took turns in his teeny Mini before we were allowed to move on to our own Jeeps and BMWs," Lorna added.

Yep, I imagined it was *just* like that.

Right. I scanned the crowd. I needed a shortish, size 4-ish girl then. Who didn't look like her insides were somewhere I didn't want to be.

How hard could this be in the most hectic place in town?

"Oh, this one! Try her!" Nancy shouted, pointing at a small red-haired girl in a camel-colored coat and matching boots, who was walking toward me. "Run at her, before she gets to you. Go on! Run!"

I geared up to run, really I did, but I just wasn't quick enough. The girl was walking straight at me. Fast. I lifted my right heel, ready to go like an athlete on the starting block, but I couldn't move. I chickened out.

She walked right through me without my moving a muscle. Tickle.

"What about this one over here?" Lorna said, nodding at a seriously tall office worker in her thirties. She looked a little big for me. What if I couldn't even lift her leg to make her walk?

"Or this one?" Nancy shouted, motioning to a smaller pink-haired girl with piercings.

OMG, this was like that time my parents took me on vacation to Hawaii and I tried to surf and I didn't stand up once. Every time I saw a good wave coming and knew I was supposed to paddle, I totally panicked, then froze, and got my timings all wrong, wiped out and nearly drowned while still lying down.

Then I saw her. Standing right between the glowing T.G.I. Friday's sign and the neon red steps in the middle of the square, looking at a map. She was about my age (check), my height (check), my weight (check), looked like she'd showered in the last twenty-four hours (check, check), and seemed to be on her own so no one would notice if she acted weird for a couple of minutes. That was my girl.

"Okay, I'm going in," I yelled. "If I am the first ghost to ever get stuck in a human, I hope there is some supernatural emergency service you can call to come and get me out."

This was it. I started running at the girl. As fast as I could. She was getting closer. And closer. So close now, that I could see her hair was tied back with a cool purple-and-silver band.

I closed my eyes and jumped.

My feet landed hard on the ground with a thud.

Was I in?

I did feel a bit different. Heavier than before. It reminded me of that time in kindergarten when Mom made me a pumpkin suit to go and watch the Thanksgiving parade because she thought it would be cute, but actually it was just hot and clunky and kinda hard to see any of the balloons through. But I couldn't complain, because even at six years old, I knew she'd spent far too long putting it together for me to be a brat about it.

I guessed this meant Operation Possession had been successful.

"Charlotte, wave to let us know you're safe," I heard Nancy call. It was like hearing her voice through earmuffs.

I picked up my arm and waved. I felt like I was operating a puppet—a very well-behaved, Living puppet—but a puppet nonetheless.

I wiggled the other arm. Then made Girl I'd Possessed jump up and down. You know what? If you didn't think about it too much, this was actually fun.

"Hey, Charlotte, how are you doing?" I felt a tap on the GIP's shoulder and turned to see a gorgeous woman in her early twenties talking to me. She was wearing a beautiful purple silk dress with futuristic pink-and-green-patterned flowers on it and matching green pumps. Her hair was the kind of Penelope Cruz brunette I always wished mine would be. It fell in perfect waves around her face. The kind of waves that said, *This hair? Oh, I just got up late and pulled a brush through it this morning.* But actually meant, *This hair? I was up at five a.m. with my blow dryer, a hundred dollars' worth of products, and the skill of John Frieda.*

Crap. Who was she? Maybe the GIP wasn't alone after all. Was this her older sister or aunt or something? And was GIP freakily called Charlotte too?

Too scared to say anything, I just smiled fakely unless I gave the game away.

"It's me! I'm inside here! Me! Lorna!" the woman said.

"Lorna?" I heard myself ask. The GIP had a Southern accent. Not totally *True Blood*, but she wasn't from around here either. "What are you doing in *her*?" I motioned at the perfect woman in front of me. "I thought you hated possession."

"OMG, I doooo," Lorna said. "But have you seen what this woman is wearing? It's next year's Spring/Summer Erdem. As in *Erdem*." I had no idea what she was talking about. But for Lorna, this was clearly A Big Deal. "Not even Michelle Obama can get on the waiting list for this yet! She must work in fashion or—" Lorna reached into the GSP's red Mulberry purse and pulled out a business card. "OMG! OMG! She has Anna Wintour's third assistant's details in here! Like, of course she does. You do not get an outfit like this without knowing some seriously stylish people."

"Um, guys?" Nancy said. She hadn't possessed anyone again, and was standing beside us, looking paler than ever next to our Living bodies.

The fact I could still see her must mean that, even though I was looking through the GIP's eyes, I could use my ghost powers too.

"Charlotte, it's only your first go at possession, so want to try to get out of there now? And Lorna?" Nancy scowled and went to say something. Then decided it was so not worth it. She turned back to me. "Like I said, wiggle your shoulders a bit, then take a step backward—and out you should come."

I turned back to Lorna. "Well, it was lovely to meet you, Ms. Erdem," I said, holding out my hand.

Lorna shook it. It was so weird to feel human skin again. It felt . . . less soft than I remembered. "You too, Miss Unspecified Blue Sweater and One Size Too Big Jeans," Lorna said. "I'll be out of here in a minute. I just want to enjoy this dress for one second longer. And check out my reflection in that window over there."

I turned back to Nancy. Wiggle, step back. Wiggle, step back. That sounded fine.

"Come on," Nancy said. "It's as easy as taking a wet swimsuit off." She smiled.

Hmm . . . which wasn't that easy from what I remembered. Still. I wiggled. It was as if I were moving in a really tight winter coat. One more go. A really big wiggle this time, then I did as Nancy said and threw myself backward.

A little too hard, as it turned out.

I found myself sitting on the concrete next to an overflowing trash can and a half-eaten hamburger.

"Oh, so that's the famous Feldman grace I keep hearing about," Nancy said with a smile. "*Now* I get why your whole class thinks you were clumsy enough to trip to your death instead of being pushed."

Hil-ar-ious.

I pulled myself up. The GIP was still standing in front of me. She looked around slowly, then down at the map in her hand, and carried on walking in the direction of Broadway.

"She doesn't seem to have noticed I was even there," I said. "Does she have no memory of it? None at all?"

It seemed bizarre that I'd done something as major as possessed her—even though it was for less than a minute—and she hadn't known. As far as she knew, she'd seen the world-famous Times Square and now she was off to the next attraction on her itinerary.

"Have you ever had déjà vu?" Nancy asked. "You know, when you've been standing somewhere and you suddenly feel like you've so been there before? Or when you're having a conversation with someone, and you know you've already had it?"

"Yesssss," I said, intrigued.

"It's a side effect of possession," Nancy said.

What?!

"Déjà vu is just the Living's brains trying to readjust after a ghost's been in the driving seat for a while. That's why the Living feel like they've been somewhere before—because they have, just a few seconds earlier, it's just that, at that moment, someone else was in charge of their body so they weren't really able to take notice of it. Same with conversations—they end up having the same one over, because they can't remember having it the first time around."

"Ghosts go around possessing the Living so often, it's become a common phenomenon? Comforting thought," I said.

Nancy laughed. "Come on, let's go find Lorna. We need to stop her treating that woman like her own personal doll. *Invasion of the Body Snatchers* wasn't entirely fictional, you know . . ."

Chapter 17

"THIS IS SOOOO EXCITING!" NANCY BOUNCED up and down on the spot three times, her curls flying and looking redder than usual in the light. "I know you guys might be under the impression that, when I was alive, I was some bookish super-serious type . . ."

It took massive reserves of self-control not to catch Lorna's eye and make a face.

"But ever since I saw *Bring It On* when I was having a study break from my Latin lessons, I have always wanted to try on a cheerleading uniform and wave pom-poms," Nancy said, bouncing twice more. "Just for a day! It looks so . . . mindless and silly. Which must mean it's fun. And now I get to try it! Do they still say, 'Goooooooooooo, team'? Or is that just in the movies?"

No question about it, this was up there on the most-disturbing-sights-of-my-death-so-far list: Nancy Radley standing in the cheerleaders' inner sanctum, their changing room, and seriously loving it.

"Don't you mean you, like, have totally always wanted to, like, be a cheerleader and, O to the M to the G? you could not be hearting this more?" Tess asked, in her best airhead voice.

"Oh, puhlease," Lorna rolled her blue eyes. "You guys are so, like, totally stereotyping popular kids. As if anyone talks like that in real life."

"So can we just go over the Plan: Stage One one more time, please?" I asked, trying to get things back on track.

"Quick on the uptake, aren't you, Feldman?" Tess said. "With lightning intellect skills that good, you'd never be the kind of girl whose boyfriend could cheat on her in front of her face and *still* think she had a chance to get him back." Tess paused. "Oh, hang on . . ."

Bitch.

"Nancy, the Plan, *please*?" I said, trying my hardest not to glare at Tess.

"Good idea, Charlotte," Nancy said. "You can never recap a plan too many times, I always say."

"Really?" Lorna asked. "Because even I am up with this one. Do we really need another play-by-play?"

Last night, after my possession lesson, we'd gone back to Lorna's room (she said it had better feng shui than HHQ's, and even though I had no idea what that meant, I agreed with her) and talked about where we needed to take the investigation next.

Ali was off the list, none of us (bar Tess and least of all me) seriously believed that David should be on it—so we needed some new suspects to look into. And after that little incident in chem yesterday, Kristen and Jamie had shown they were more than happy to fall out with each other to get what they wanted—what I used to have: David.

"I wonder if one of them was willing to commit murder to get him too?" Nancy had asked.

I knew Kristen wasn't going to become New York's newest Girl Scout leader anytime soon, but was she really capable of pushing me under the F train? Come on, if she'd been that into David, wouldn't she have just asked him on a date? He clearly wasn't as cheerphobic as he'd always pretended. And shitty as it was to admit, either Kristen or Jamie could probably have stolen him from me if they'd just put their minds, lip gloss, and a couple of low-cut tops to it. How could I compete with that? He was a guy after all.

Then again, maybe Kristen didn't believe she should have to *steal* anyone. She was the prettiest, most popular girl in school, so guys should come to her—even if it took their girlfriend dying to figure that out. Plus the way she'd turned on Ali in chem class was pretty brutal. And, in a lot of ways, she had the perfect alibi: No one would ever believe that she'd set foot on public transport, let alone killed someone on the subway. It was the kind of low rent she would never do.

So Nancy wrote Kristen's and Jamie's names on the suspect

list on the board. Had we been underestimating them all along? Had one of them wanted me out of the picture enough to kill me? And have all the excuses for "comforting" David they'd ever need?

That's when Nancy came up with the Plan. And why we were here—in the cheerleaders' locker room—waiting for the squad to arrive.

"So the Plan is this," Nancy said. "Kristen and Jamie are fighting over David. Kristen's the head cheerleader, but it seems like her second in command, Jamie, wants to be queen bee. We need to find out what those two are *really* thinking. But we can't do that by simply possessing them."

"Because then they'll just become our vessels and do what we want?" I asked.

"Exactly." Nancy smiled. "We can't find out what they're up to if we're controlling them. So, instead, Lorna, Tess, and I will possess the other three—the people closest to them—and interrogate Kristen and Jamie from there. Blonde Four, Blonde Five, and . . . what's the one with the ridiculous name again?"

"Kaitlynnn," Lorna said. "I get to be her because her hair's cut in a really cute bob, so I want to see how that feels."

"*Kaitlynnn*," Nancy said, ignoring her. "Then when we're inside them, we will be the eyes and ears of the inner circle. We can talk to Kristen and Jamie through Kaitlynnn, Blondes Four and Five, ask them questions about David and basically figure out if they killed Charlotte or not."

Comprende loud and clear.

Tess made a this-is-so-stupid noise. "Nancy, as you know I have gone along with many of your plans in the past. And I said I'd help you out today, so I will." She walked over to Nancy, who'd finally stopped bouncing now she was in plan mode. "But honestly? Do you really think this is going to work? Even if Kristen and Jamie aren't the sharpest pencils in the drawer, they're not just suddenly going to admit to murder just because one of their equally dumb friends asks nicely if they killed Charlotte, are they?"

Good point. Even though I would never agree with Tess out loud.

"Maybe, but that's where Charlotte comes in." Nancy turned to me. "You know what you have to do if we're not getting anywhere, right?" Nancy asked.

I nodded. Unfortunately, I did. I just hoped it wasn't going to come to that.

"OMFG! Have you seen what Jessica West is wearing today?" Five pushed the locker room door open so hard it slammed into the wall. A cheer trophy on a shelf next to me wobbled, but stayed upright.

"OMFG? Like, what?" Four asked. I wondered if they knew that no one ever bothered to learn their names. "Was she double denim-ing her jeans with her jacket *again*?" Four gasped.

"No, it was waaaaayyyyy worse than that. She was actually ..." Five leaned forward to deliver her fashion bomb.

"Ladies, *please*, a little decorum before we practice." Kristen strutted through the door with Jamie and Kaitlynnn following close behind. "If we're ever going to perfect the K pyramid, we need to focus and stop jabbering on about irrelevant people in the preparation area."

"Preparation area?" Tess said. "Who is Miss Fancy Pants trying to kid? Can I possess her? Please? I could take her down to one of those budget beauty salons off Canal Street and get her a haircut she'll never forget."

Finally a Tess suggestion I could get on board with.

"Tess! We need your help and that suggestion is firmly in the hindrance bracket," Nancy scolded her. "Let's wait for them to get into their uniforms, then we can possess them and move on with the plan."

Behind us, the Tornadoes were getting ready. We all silently turned away to protect their modesty.

"Can we just get this over with?" Lorna asked. "Charlotte, you know these girls, who should get who?"

I looked around. The Tornadoes were all uniformed up and having an argument about whether Jamie had the first stages of cellulite on her thighs or not.

"Well, Kaitlynnn's dumb, but she's also feisty, so I guess she should be yours, Tess. That way if you say something bitchy, no one will think it's wildly out of character for her."

"Whatever do you mean?" Tess actually grinned at me. Then dived into Kaitlynnn, who shuddered, then stood perfectly upright. Tess made Kaitlynnn turn to us and smile. "I'm not bitchy," Possessed Kaitlynnn said. One down, two to go.

"Nancy and Lorna, you get Blondes Four and Five," I instructed. "I'd love to give you advice on which one to take, but honestly I cannot tell them apart. All I can say is that you should probe Kristen and Jamie gently. Remember Four and Five are usually their puppets, so they're not likely to talk out of turn a lot."

"No problem. Let's hope this is quick," Lorna said, making a must-I-do-this? face before jumping into Four.

Nancy turned to me. "Okay, so we'll see you out on the field?" I nodded. "And remember what I told you—stay by the stands, then if we need you, Lorna or I will give you the signal. Then all you have to do is . . . well, you know what you need to do. I'll leave you to it."

Nancy looked at Blonde Five with slight trepidation.

"Oh, come on," I said. "One jump and you're a bona fide cheergirl—it'll be high kicks and splits all the way—and you'll be in a body that can do all that." Nancy gulped. "Gimme an N. A. N. C. Y.—NANCY!" I cheered.

Nancy smiled and ran at Five.

"Everyone ready?" Kristen asked.

In so many ways more than you know, I thought.

"Then let's get out on the field!" Kristen led her squad out of the locker room in popularity order. Head bitch first, Jamie second, Four and Five, then Kaitlynnn last. I followed behind.

I managed to duck through the door before it swung shut and through me. I jumped out of the way of the wood—and almost collided with a Living boy who was standing outside the locker room, up against the wall, so that no one would see him.

David? Since when did he start waiting outside the Tornadoes' room.

He waited until Kristen, Jamie, and the other Blondes had passed by, before grabbing Kaitlynnn's arm.

Possessed Kaitlynnn shrieked.

David put his finger to his mouth, trying to get her to be quiet. "Er, Kaitlynnn, can I have a second, please?" he asked.

Tess-as-Kaitlynnn stopped in her tracks. And smiled like a cat surveying an unfit mouse that she knew she could catch in one jump. Great.

"Of course, David," she simpered. "Now why would you be speaking to little ol' me and what can I do for you?"

Tess-as-Kaitlynnn ruffled his hair. Oh, why did I put Tess in her?

"Tess, don't you dare," I said, knowing full well she could hear me even if David couldn't.

She smiled at the air to David's left, where I was standing. And defiantly mussed up his hair again.

"It's about last night . . ." David smoothed down his man-bangs, then did that nervous thing that I always used to find so unbelievably cute: He tilted his head and looked up at her from under his lashes.

"I was going through a really tough time and it was so great of you to come and meet me like that. A real comfort."

So he was getting Kaitlynnn to "comfort" him now? What

was wrong with Kristen and Just-Call-Me J?

"Hey, anytime." Tess somehow managed to simultaneously flutter Kaitlynnn's eyelashes and look concerned for David's well-being. "Everyone at school feels so terrible about what you're going through. I was more than happy to help out."

I was so about to be sick.

"Oh, and Kaitlynnn? Just one more thing," David said. "I know it sounds kinda weird, but would you mind not talking to the rest of the squad about us meeting up last night? It's just that I'm a very, er, private person and I don't want anyone thinking I can't handle what's happened with Charlotte."

Tess made Kaitlynnn's head nod. "Of course. Actually I'm kinda free now. How about I just blow off cheerleader practice and we go somewhere and talk about Poor Charlotte some more. I—"

"Kaitlynnn! Ah, there you are." Kristen strode over, looking slightly out of breath and uncharacteristically red in the face. "And with David."

I'd never been so glad to see her. Actually, scratch that: I'd never been glad to see her before.

"I was just walking by on my way to the library and Kaitlynnn stopped to talk to me because she noticed that I looked sad." Was David always this convincing a liar? Or was it another talent he'd been hiding, along with his love of organized sports and skanks. "It's because I used to go to the library with Charlotte all the time and the thought of going there on my own . . ."

Man, why had he never auditioned for drama club? Drew

would have snapped him up in a flash. And hadn't he already been to the library? Just a couple of days ago? With J?

"Oh, David, it's okay. Please don't cry." Kristen gave him a massive hug, at the same time managing to elbow Kaitlynnn hard in the ribs and push her out of the way. Tess winced. "It's so hard for you, isn't it?"

She pulled away from him and gave Kaitlynnn a look. Tess got the hint, shrugged, and took her possessed cheerleader out to the sports field where Lorna and Nancy were waiting in Four and Five.

Kristen carefully watched her leave. "Here's some news that will cheer you up," Kristen said, when Kaitlynnn was out of earshot. "You've probably not noticed this because you've been grieving, but the Halloween dance is taking place next Saturday in the school gym."

David nodded in a pained way that seemed to say *No, I haven't had time for such frivolities, what with burying my girlfriend and all, but please do go on.*

"And this year, the dance committee decided to spice things up a bit—do something different instead of just hanging up a few paper skeletons and downloading tracks by bands like the Grateful Dead. This year they're going to have a *Ghostbusters* theme—you know, like, as in that old movie? Whatevs, that's not the exciting bit, they're also going to have . . . a Scream Queen and King!"

David nodded some more. Honestly why did he care? He

hated that kind of thing. We both did. He'd rather have stepped in dog poop than attend a high school dance.

"The nominations are out tomorrow, but . . ." Kristen looked around the hallway, as if she were about to unveil a secret of upmost national security. Like what really happened in Area 51 or where Jimmy Hoffa went. "I happen to know *for a fact* that you are up for Scream King! And everyone is saying you're going to win it. And I'm a shoo-in for Scream Queen."

Man, I really hated her. Like would-have-found-a-way-to-suffocate-her-with-a-pom-pom-if-it-didn't-mean-her-turning-up-at-the-Attesa hated her. But I also wanted to know how she got her hair to be that shiny too. Which made me hate myself almost as much as I hated Kristen.

I looked over at David, expecting to see a horrified expression on his face. King? At a dance? As if! Kids like David, who were going to make it in the music industry managing some incredibly authentic yet lucrative hipster band, did not become Scream Kings. None of Fall Out Boy had that on their CV. And memo to the social-climbing saddo who came up with the whole Halloween concept theme: Scream Queen might (almost) work, but Scream King? It did not even rhyme.

"So I wondered if you'd like to go with me," Kristen asked. Oh, so she *was* the ask-a-boy-out type after all. Did that make her more or less likely to be the murderess type too? "It just seems kinda fitting. You've changed so much since . . . you know . . . Everyone around here looks at you differently now.

Like, without Charlotte, you've become a somebody. We'd be perfect together."

Eww. She was pure evil.

"If you're ready to be seen out with me that is," she said, faux shyly.

"I—I—, well, I . . . ," David stammered. Here it came: the rant explaining why he refused to get involved in a pathetic paranoia-forming popularity contest thinly veiled as a legitimate rite-of-passage ritual, where the only mind-retracting forms of entertainment on offer were bouncing around like a Pavlovian puppy dog to Miley Cyrus's latest piece of auditory turd or groping the nearest member of the opposite sex on the dance floor during the erection section.

"I'd love to go with you." David smiled.

WTF?

"Great!" Kristen beamed. "Well, we'll talk Ts and Os later."

"Ts and Os?"

"Times and outfits," she explained. "If everyone's going all out for the *Ghostbusters'* theme, then we have to make sure our costumes match. Was there, like, a cute boy and a cute girl ghost in it? I'll ask my mom. Anyway, for now I have a state-championship-winning K pyramid to form. I'll see you around."

She squeezed his arm lightly, then breezed out onto the playing field leaving a cloud of vanilla fragrance behind her.

I gawked in her wake.

"Cool," David said out loud.

Cool? Cool? He never said "cool." Especially not about attending a social event that could feature as the climax of a John Hughes movie. If I didn't know better I'd think David, instead of Four, Five, and Kaitlynnn, had been possessed.

David turned and walked down the corridor in the direction of the library. Much as I didn't want to admit it, he didn't look like a man whose soul mate had just died.

As he rounded the corner, I swear I saw him do a little skip.

Chapter 18

"KAITLYNNN! WHAT ON THIS PLANET IS WRONG with you today?" Kristen flipped her long blond hair over her left shoulder and swung around to face her squad mate confrontationally. "You have been off ever since we got here. Either go inside, read a guidance pamphlet on whatever pointless teen turmoil you are currently going through and get over it, or FOCUS on the matter at hand."

Kristen spun around dramatically on the heel of her pristine white sneakers and took a few strides away from the squad so she could appraise her team from a distance. As head cheerleader, if there was so much as a glob of lip gloss out of place, it reflected badly on her. And anything less than perfection was not something Kristen tolerated. She wrinkled her nose as she looked them over. As if on cue, the sixteen girls in front of her straightened up, pointed their left legs forward and swiveled their bodies ever so slightly, like they were posing for a paparazzi camera no one could see.

Actually, only thirteen of the girls struck an insta-pose. Three of them were two beats behind everyone else. Because three of the squad were possessed by my dead friends.

"Okay, let's go for the pyramid!" Kristen shouted, clapping her hands loudly.

This was going to be interesting.

"Oh gawwwd," Blonde Four (Lorna) mouthed at Blonde Five (Nancy). She looked like she was rooted to the spot with cold hard fear. Which was so not a Goooo Team! stance.

Looking at the sports field, I was happy to be away from the action—for now at least. It was much better to be standing on the sidelines (well, over by the bleachers) while Nancy, Lorna, and Tess were forced to take part in cheer practice. In the name of the investigation, of course.

But while Lorna looked like she was about as up for being part of a teen girl pyramid as she was for wearing man-made fibers, from the way Five was bounding over to the rest of the squad like an overexcited Labrador puppy, Nancy was loving this part of the Plan.

"Guys, places, please. You may have all day, but I, quite frankly, have a life, so do not test me," Kristen said.

I scanned the sea of yellow-and-blue uniforms—the "cute" (if your style role models were the girls of the Playboy mansion) pleated micro-skirts and navel-skimming vests. I was so teasing

Her Geekiness about the fact she'd actually enjoyed this the second she unpossessed Five. Still, it seemed that Nancy wasn't the only cheerfan. A few other kids had come out to watch the show too, including Alanna, the gel pen dropper, Photo Club Mina, and Brian, this kinda unpopular kid, who I'd actually dated for about thirty seconds in fourth grade. Back when I thought mud and worms were an acceptable *eau de boy*. Which, past the age of eleven, they are so not.

I focused my attention back on the sports field. Even if no one but their mothers could tell the Blondes apart, knowing who was currently possessing them, it was easy to figure who was who. Five was hanging off Kristen's every word as she explained in detail exactly how the stunts were going to play out today, while Four was looking in disgust at the cheerleader next to her who had just had the gall to accidentally step on her sneaker leaving a dirty black mark.

That was those two accounted for, but where had Tess taken Kaitlynnn's body? Surely she hadn't run straight back to the locker room as soon as she heard the *pyramid* word? And, much as I was getting more over him by the second, I really hoped she'd not run to the library in the hope of finding David again.

Kristen clapped again to signal the end of her briefing—and the squad spread out, ready to start their routine. Kristen motioned for her über-clique—Jamie, Kaitlynnn, and the Blondes—to stand to the side until they were needed. The other girls got into four groups of three, shimmied a little, then simultaneously dipped down, putting their hands together to make four human springboards for the stars of the show to bounce up on.

That meant Tess, Lorna, and Nancy—along with Jamie—were going to have to get their Living bodies up on top of the 'mid. Uh-oh. As enthusiastic as Nancy was in the locker room, I knew she had no acrobatic experience. Lorna would never have joined in any physical activity that could have involved her sweating when she was alive. And Tess? I did not for a second think she was the athletic type. This could so end in tears. Or broken bones. Maybe both.

Just go with it, I silently said to them. *Follow the Living and it'll all be okay.*

And if it's not, in the future, we will think a bit more carefully about the consequences before we possess people.

There was a flash of blue as Jamie ran forward to take her place. She went to her group of three helpers, and lifted up her right foot. She stood on the girls' hands, as they crouched to get more power, then raised their arms, throwing her into the air. She popped up, straightened, and smiled at Kristen. Jamie was up. The first part of the 'mid was in place. Only three more of the top level to go.

Nancy looked at Lorna and smiled. And before I could even hide my eyes, she had mimicked Jamie's movements perfectly, making Five's body run onto the field and—*ping!*—with the other cheerleaders' help there she was, up in the air, being held in place by the three girls below her who were holding on to her feet.

She beamed. "That. Was. The. Coolest! Come on, Lorna, this is so much fun! I can't believe we didn't try this months ago!"

"Lorna? Who's *Lorna*?" Kristen asked.

Lorna had no choice but to go. She looked at me, grimaced, then followed Nancy's lead. I thought she'd panic at the last minute, or refuse to go through with it, but she kept right on moving. Within seconds, she'd jumped and been pushed up there too. Okay, so she wasn't smiling—I didn't get the impression Lorna was loving three strange girls holding on to her feet—even if they weren't actually *her* feet—but she stood tall. I felt Mom-at-sports-day proud.

Only Tess to go. Once she was up there, the Agency would have totally infiltrated the squad—and the major part of Nancy's Plan could really begin. Once they were in, they could start asking questions about me without any of the girls thinking it was super-weird—and see if any of them reacted strangely. If the Dead Girls could do that and keep their balance, that is.

"Kaitlynnn, where are you?" Kristen shouted from her position in front of the triangle of gently swaying girls. Being the captain didn't seem so bad. You got to shout orders and look good, but without doing the tricky stunts. Well, that was how Kristen ran things anyway. "You need to get on top NOW! If this was a competition and it had taken us this long to form the pyramid we would so be getting penalty points."

Even from my position a few meters away, I saw a couple of the squad shudder at the thought. To my right on the benches, Alanna nodded in agreement, as if she were the five boroughs' only judge. Even Brian shook his shaggy-dog head.

Unfortunately Kristen had no idea that the final piece of her pyramid had authority issues and was seriously not impressed that she was being told what to do. Tess walked Kaitlynnn's body over to the others as slowly as she could. So slowly that some of the girls at the base of the 'mid started to sweat. Major squad sin. Suddenly Blonde Four swayed dangerously—any second Lorna was going to cause a cheeralanche—but the girls below her tightened their grip on Four's legs as Nancy held her hand. She stopped wobbling. Phew.

"Kaitlynnn, come onnnnn!" Kristen fumed. "Honestly, I've had relationships that have lasted less time than this."

Kaitlynnn/Tess smirked and took her place. She put her left foot on the human hand trampoline and bounced it up and down, testing how sturdy it was.

"OMFG, Kaitlynnn," Kristen screamed. "Will you just push yourself up here? Jamie and the others will grab your hands and pull you up. If you do not move in the next three seconds, I am replacing you with that fat kid sitting on the benches"—she pointed straight at poor Brian—"because compared to you, he's as fast as Lance Armstrong *avec* bike."

Tess looked at me and shrugged. She took a big step, bounced unenthusiastically, and launched Kaitlynnn's body into the air.

Just not quite hard enough.

Instead of landing up on the same level as Jamie and the Blondes,

Kaitlynnn's body side bounced. Head-butting Jamie right in the ass.

"Wahhhhhh!" Jamie screamed, as three years of hard-practiced cheerleading poise failed her. She wobbled, heroically tried to grab Four to steady herself, then toppled, taking the whole 'mid down with her.

The resulting pileup of blond hair, blue shirts, and toned thighs looked like an explosion in a Barbie factory.

"Mess up much, Kaitlynnn?" Jamie said from somewhere under the heap. "And BTW, if whoever has her foot in my chest does not get off me in the next three seconds, I swear to God this squad will be running one member down."

Kristen looked on, her expression a mix of horror and superiority. One by one, the girls pulled themselves out. Not one helped another up.

"That was *intense*," a tiny brunette who I recognized from my literature class said. "We haven't had a fall like that for, like, days."

"Still, I, um, bet that didn't hurt as badly as it did when Charlotte Feldman went under the F train," Five said, totally out of nowhere.

Subtle, Nancy. A million miles away from subtle.

A couple of the girls nervously giggled, not sure how to respond.

"I heard she hit the track so hard, it took them two *hours* to clean things up," Jamie said, grimacing.

Okay, less with the gnarly details. Been there, got the tombstone ...

"Ladies?" Kristen came over and pulled herself up to her full five foot seven and a half. "You have just performed the worst pyramid I have ever witnessed in five years of cheering and what are you doing—are you running to do it over, this time properly? Are you apologizing for wasting my precious time with your total lame-ility? Or are you standing around, talking about some dead girl that nobody cared about until a week ago?"

Kristen put her hands on her hips, then turned to Four and pulled a piece of grass out of her hair. Whoa, Lorna must be in a state not to have taken care of that by herself.

"We were just—" she started.

"Just what?" Kristen asked.

"What she means is that we were just talking about Charlotte because it's really heartbreaking what happened to her and she's only been dead for a few days, so we're completely entitled to talk about her if we want," Blonde Five said, desperately trying to bait Kristen.

Watch it, Nancy, I thought. I'm not sure Five would use that many words of more than one syllable in a sentence.

"Yeah, I thought Charlotte was cool actually," said lit class brunette. "Her eyes were pretty and she always had the straightest eyeliner ever. And one time, she helped me with a Shakespeare assignment, because I'd just finished reading Harry Potter and I kept getting confused between Hamlet and Hagrid and it was completely messing up my essay on why he had issues."

Sweet. Unfathomably stupid, but still sweet.

Kristen looked around at her squad, balling up her freshly pressed skirt in her right hand. I got the impression that she was imagining it was one of their pretty heads. Was she actually about to . . . blow?

"Charlotte? Will somebody please tell me what is the sudden big obsession with *Charlotte*?" Kristen ranted. "Ever since that idiot girl tripped, I seem to hear her name, like, thirty times a day. First from David, then the teachers, and now you guys? What is with the dead-girl mania? She didn't disturb our practices when she was alive, so why are we talking about her now that she's dead?"

"Because she was smoking hot," a gruff voice next to me said. I turned to see it had come from . . . *Brian*? "I'm sorry I never got to spend enough time with her lately to tell her that."

Well at least someone got what David saw in me. Even if it was my ill-advised fourth grade boyfriend. Mina grabbed her red Amoeba tote bag and scurried away.

Tess sat Kaitlynnn's body on the grass and put her head between her hands. Much as she was not my favorite person, I had to agree with what her body language was saying. This was getting us nowhere. Whoever my murderer might be, she wasn't going to confess just because someone provoked her.

But that didn't stop Nancy.

"That's quite a strong reaction, Kristen." Nancy had clearly watched too many *Columbo* reruns and was taking a page out of his detecting book. "I don't think any of us are *obsessed* with Charlotte. It sounds more like you are."

Kristen narrowed her blue eyes. "Me? Obsessed with *her*? Hello, as if! What is up with you?" She spun around. "In fact, what is up with all of you? Standing around here aimlessly after *that* performance. My housekeeper's ironing board could have put on a better show. It was pathetic. About as pathetic as Charlotte Feldman. Honestly, if you don't improve soon, I'll push you all onto the nearest subway track."

What?

Nancy and Lorna swung the Blondes' bodies around to me as if to say, *See! See!*

That wasn't a confession, was it? If it was, something didn't feel quite right.

"No one said Charlotte was *pushed*, Kristen. Everyone says she tripped. So where did that come from?" Lorna made Four say. "I think you need to be careful when you're talking about the dead." Lorna nudged Five in the ribs. "Because if you have wronged them, you never know when they're going to come back and call you out on it."

"No," Five continued, waving her arm up and down—there it was, the Signal for me to get off the bench and get involved—"you never know *when* they are going to come back, especially if you hurt them. And they want *revenge*."

Right, this was my cue. Kristen was staring at the Blondes like they'd flipped their lids, but according to Nancy's Plan, this was my moment to apparite. Seeing as Lorna's and Nancy's undercover interrogation hadn't got us a full-on confession (yet), it was time to bring out the big guns. I had to make myself appear to Kristen and see if my ghost scared her into saying anything else.

I closed my eyes, concentrated real hard, and tried to make that warm feeling grow.

As usual, it started at my feet. I looked down and watched as the color returned to them. Awesome. Now all I needed to do was make the rest of my body go, haunt Kristen, and we'd know once and for all if she'd killed me or not. I'd scare her into admitting what she really thought of me.

Maybe we'd get a confession. Maybe I'd get my Key.

"Sorry to be a party pooper, Feldman, but you couldn't scare a five-year-old at a sleepover with those moves," said a male voice behind me. I breathed out in frustration and felt my power—and visibility—go. I didn't even have to turn around to see who it was. I recognized that tone. Edison.

"Don't fool yourself, Ghostgirl." Ed jumped down off the bench he'd ported onto from who-knows-which-mysterious-place he hung out in all day, and came to stand by me. His T-shirt really was incredibly tight.

Edison stared out at the field, just in time to see Nancy attempt the splits with Five's body, fail spectacularly, and fall over.

"Nancy Drew seriously thinks one of those vapid rally girls committed your murder?" he asked.

Nancy pulled Five's body up, tripped, and went down again. Smooth.

"Kinda. Well, it is a possibility. After all, the head one did just threaten to push the entire squad under a train—and seeing as that's how someone killed me, maybe she's speaking from experience," I said.

Looking at Kristen now, bossing Jamie and the others around, I knew more than ever that she was capable of a lot of things: blow-drying her own hair to salon standards, making other girls feel hideous about themselves on an hourly basis, and still being seriously thin despite the fact she always seemed to have a full-fat frappuccino in her hand. But was she actually capable of murder? Despite what she'd just blurted out, I wasn't so sure.

"You know Nancy," I said. "She likes to be thorough. We had to cross these suspects off the list before we start investigating the next ones."

"'Thorough,' hey? That's one way of putting it." Edison brushed his hair back off his face and squinted in the lunchtime sun. "Though 'slow' and 'criminally dull' would be another."

I wondered what Edison wore in the summer when he was alive. I couldn't imagine him in anything but lead singer black even if someone made him go to the beach.

Ed gave me a slow smile. "Why does Nancy think one of the pom-pom posse had it in for you anyway?" he asked.

"Look, Nancy seems to know what she's doing," I said, desperately trying to change the subject. I didn't want to get into the David Conversation with him now. Things were WTF? weird enough between us already without bringing David into it. "Without her and Lorna, I wouldn't have even got this far."

"And how far is that?" Edison asked. "Far enough to be one week dead and still Keyless? Far enough to have watched your ex making out with half the school before you've even got one decent lead? Or far enough to be standing here, trying to scare a borderline-anorexic lip-gloss addict into confessing something she doesn't have the brainpower to pull off?"

"How did you know about my ex?" I asked. Calling David that out loud with Edison there made my stomach turn.

Ed turned to look at me, his green eyes searching, but said nothing.

"Isn't a ghost allowed a bit of privacy?" I asked.

"Not around here it seems. That guy is a loser if he didn't know what he had."

For about the ninetieth time, I wished Nancy had given me a book on understanding Edison along with the Rules.

The squad had pulled themselves back up now. Nancy was madly waving Five's arm above her head. She *still* seemed to think that if I apparited it might scare Kristen into saying something more.

"Okay, so I don't know what's going on over there, but Nancy's giving me the Signal that means I really need to apparite now," I said. "Would you mind porting off someplace else so I can concentrate?"

"Got stage fright?" Edison smirked.

"Hardly, it's just that when I apparite and Kristen and the squad see me, they are going to be so scared they're going to run screaming from this field like extras in a B movie—and I don't know if you have the stomach to handle that."

"Clearly," Edison said, raising an eyebrow. He moved toward me, then suddenly stopped, like he thought better of whatever he was about to do. "Look, I know when I'm not wanted. I'll leave you to it."

He climbed back up the bleachers. I couldn't help but notice that his skinny jeans were pretty Ed-hugging too. "Oh and Charlotte? When you want to know how to really scare the bejesus out of someone who might actually need it, you let me know. It won't be as . . . exhilarating as our last lesson. I promise. I'm"— he looked deep in my eyes for a second too long—"well, I'm sorry about that. Maybe it wasn't what you needed after all. But I still have a couple of tricks up my sleeve. All perfectly legal. Just more effective than this." He smiled.

Pop!

Edison was gone.

I turned my attention back to the field. Thrown as I felt, I couldn't focus on Edison and his surprisingly toned arms and his wooo!-check-out-all-the-bad-things-I-can-teach-you speeches right now. Not when I had detecting to do. Lorna and Nancy were waving madly at me now. The cheerleaders were packing up their bags. Practice was over. Either I did this now and found out once and for all what Kristen was really made of, or I stopped trying and just accepted the fact that I might never find my Key.

I forgot about Edison, walked forward, and focused until the warm feeling came. Up my legs, my stomach, my arms, whirling around my head. My body took on that familiar pink glow. I looked back to the field, and while the rest of the squad were too busy chattering away to have noticed me, the Blondes were staring at me with their mouths open. Which I figured meant it had worked.

I was a fully visible-to-the-Living ghostly apparition. And Kristen was walking straight at me. Ohmigod, this was *it*.

She looked at where I was standing, flipped her hair again—urgh, even when I was trying to be scary I could not help but notice that she was like something out of a barf-worthy shampoo commercial—and stopped about five steps in front of me.

Kristen slowly took me in, looking me up and down—twice—before staring straight into my eyes. Her gaze didn't flinch or even flicker. If I hadn't been dead and her immortal enemy, I would have put bets on her launching into an epic put-down about my shoes or my hair right then and there.

Oh God, this was it. She could so see me. Come on, Charlotte, I told myself, haunt her a bit. If she knows anything about your death—if she was the one who pushed you—she'll be so freaked out, it will totally show. Scare her!

But suddenly I had no idea what to do. Wave my arms? Woooo a bit? Instead I stood rooted to the spot. Every bit as pathetic as Edison had predicted. Unable to do anything apart from watch her stare at me. And stare right back.

Kristen opened her mouth. Here it was: the scream. The OMG!-I've-just-seen-Charlotte's-ghost wail.

But there was no scream. No wail. Instead Kristen rolled her eyes. "For God's sake," she said to herself under her breath. "Those idiots have talked about that stupid girl so much, I am actually hallucinating her. It must be the stress. Enough already. I'm not wasting any more of my day on someone dumb enough to trip under a train. I need to go lie down. Or shop."

Kristen stomped off the field, walking right through me.

I meant so little to her that even when I tried to haunt her, she thought I must be a figment of her own imagination.

I was so shocked, I breathed out, quickly making myself invisible again, so that when Kristen slammed the locker room door shut, and the other cheerleaders looked around to see where their captain had gone, I was nothing more than air.

Crap. Edison was right. It was time to admit that Kristen was many things (an uptight-boyfriend-stealing-mental case for a start), but she wasn't a murderer. Not mine, anyway. If she had been, she wouldn't have put me down to a lack of beauty sleep.

Back on the field, I saw Four's and Five's bodies shudder as Lorna and Nancy stepped out of them.

"Whoa, that must have been an intense practice," Four said. "I totally zoned out during the whole thing."

"Ohmigod! I, like, totally did too," said Blonde Five. "Kristen must have worked us way hard. I feel like I'm coming out of a Bikram coma or something."

Out of the cheerleaders' bodies, Lorna and Nancy expectantly ran over to where I was standing.

"Well, what happened? She didn't look like she freaked out," Nancy said. "What did Kristen say?"

"Enough for us to draw one of your red lines through her name on the suspects' list."

Nancy sighed.

"So I've just spent the last thirty minutes taking part in physical education for no good reason?" Lorna asked.

Behind her, I saw Kaitlynnn talking to Brian. His eyes were glowing and she'd somehow persuaded him to give her four candy bars out of his backpack. Now she was stuffing them into her mouth—two at a time.

"Tess, will you get out of that cheerleader already?" Nancy shouted at her.

"Oh, cawm ohn. Ah jusht whanna hahve ohne mohre." She swallowed. "Just let me eat two more. It'll mess her up for weeks when she comes around and realizes she's consumed an empty calorie. Well"—Tess turned over the label of one of the bars— "five hundred of them! In one go. I can put the wrappers in her pocket, so when Kaitlynnn wonders why she's feeling so full she'll find them. She'll think she was sleep-eating or something. It will be excellent."

"Tess . . ." Nancy shot her a look.

"Fun sponge," Tess said, as she stepped backward and left Kaitlynnn's body.

Kaitlynnn shrugged, blinked, and then looked down in shock at the two candy wrappers in her hand. "What the . . . ?" She spun around to check that no one had seen her eating, then dropped them on the ground and ran into the locker room—no doubt already calculating how many squat thrusts she needed to do to work off the calories.

Tess appraised the situation. "Cheerbaiting aside, that," she said, slow clapping, "was what I'd call an *epic* fail. You apparite in front of someone and she doesn't even believe you're a ghost?"

"Well, I guess you're right, Charlotte. It proves that Kristen's not feeling guilty about your death." Man, was Nancy perceptive. "I don't think she pushed you."

"Or any of the rest of them," Lorna added. "They just don't seem that bothered about you. Not even Jamie—unless she is an Emmy-worthy actress and I don't think she's that smart. Sorry, Charlotte." She looked away at the girls walking back across the field.

"So I told Emily, if she buys a party dress from Acne again without checking with me first, we are so no longer lab partners." As if on cue, Jamie pushed through me and shivered.

"Oh, totally." Blonde Four nodded. "Like, you said you were getting an outfit from there for the Halloween dance *weeks* ago. It's off the girl-rules chart if she violates your store."

"But, guys, it's a costume party," Five said, trailing after them. "We have to get costumes that make us look like, like, ghosts or busters or something."

"Oh," Jamie said. "Well, that still doesn't mean I'm letting the Acne go."

We watched as they walked through the locker room door.

"Halloween dance?" Lorna asked. "When's the Halloween dance?"

"Repeat what you just said out loud in your head, think about it, then have the decency to blush," Tess said.

"Oh." Lorna did.

"Saturday then," Nancy said, trying to make Lorna feel less like an idiot.

"And David is going with Kristen," I said. "Which is weird because he hates dances. And the whole popularity BS. But then, he seems to have done a one-eighty on most of these things in the last week. He used to tell me he hated cheerleaders too."

"Charlotte, whatever lies he told you when you were dating, it seems David will now make out with anything with a pulse and, sadly, that removes you from the equation." Trust Tess to drag me down one notch further.

Maybe it was time to stop being so nicey-nicey. Maybe—risk or not—it was time to take another lesson from Ed.

Chapter 19

AS SOON AS PRACTICE FINISHED, TESS SULKILY ported back to the Attesa muttering something about "time wasters" at a volume she knew I could hear. Charm personified.

"Let's port back to HHQ," Nancy said. "I guess the next step is to cross off Kristen and Jamie and reassess the suspects' list. Maybe we could go through some more old case files for inspiration." She smiled hopefully.

Lorna scowled. "I spent most of yesterday in that dungeon," she said. "I'm not really ready to go back yet. Charlotte, how about you and me port part of the way, then walk back to the hotel through the West Village?" She looked at Nancy intently. "It'll give Charlotte a chance to think about everything that's happened today—you know, if there are any major clues we're just not seeing because we're too close to the case." She winked at me. "And it'll give me a chance to look at a couple of new window displays in the shops on Bleecker Street," she whispered.

Typical. Though seeing as my only other option was another episode of *Who Killed Charlotte Feldman?* I might as well just go with it.

"Sure." I smiled.

Outside, it was unseasonably warm, and people had left their coats at home. Bleecker Street was one of my favorite places in the city. I loved the way trees lined parts of the wiggly street, the cute secondhand bookshops and quirky boutiques, and the brownstones where I had hoped I would live one day. The whole neighborhood felt relaxed. None of the buildings down here were more than a few stories high, so you could look up and always see the sky. It was a world away from the madness of midtown. When I graduated college, I'd wanted to run an art gallery here. Or open a really cool coffee shop where photographers could exhibit their work. Maybe I'd even have taken some pictures myself and sold them.

Thanks to the F train, I could kick that stupid dream to the curb.

"So"—Lorna gave me a sideways glance—"what was Edison doing by the bleachers while we were possessing the squad?"

Crap. I thought they'd all been too busy with their cheertricks to notice him. How could I explain it? And why was I even trying to? Tess had seen us together before. It wasn't like I'd *asked* Edison to be there. Or that he wasn't allowed to be. After all, he lived in the Attesa too. It wasn't like him turning up was some big secret I needed to keep from Lorna and Nancy.

So why did it feel that way?

"We were just talking," I said carefully. "I don't know how he knew we were there. Maybe Tess told him. She seems to be his spy. He was just being his usual Ed self." I shrugged, unsuccessfully trying to disguise the fact that I was babbling now. "Shooting me down and saying our plan to interrogate Kristen wasn't going to work. Being all *I'm so cool and you girls have a lot to learn*. Generally making me mad. You know."

"His 'usual Ed self'?" Lorna repeated back at me. She stopped at the junction of Perry Street. To our left, a gang of girl tourists were excitedly having their photo taken in front of Magnolia Bakery. You know, the one that's famous from that episode of *Sex and the City*? Imagine coming hundreds of miles to New York, then just going to see that?

"How do you know so much about what 'Ed' is 'usually' like?" Lorna asked. "Have you guys been hanging out?"

Caught. For someone who seemed so hooked on shopping and shoes and not much else, Lorna could be scary perceptive.

"Not *exactly*," I started. "We've been, well, I, we . . . we talked a little. About how I might get out of here. He had some suggestions about haunting."

When he's not being smug or charming or scaring even more of the life out of me.

"Oh, does he now?" Lorna's expression was—for once—impossible to read. We carried on walking down the street in silence. Maybe she was going to let the subject drop?

The weird thing was that I suddenly realized I didn't want it to.

"Um, Lorna," I asked, "what do you know about Ed . . . Ed*ison*? Like, when did he arrive at the Attesa? How did he get here?"

Lorna stopped walking and looked straight at me. "You seem pretty tight. Why haven't you asked him yourself? During one of your 'talks' . . ."

I felt myself blush, and concentrated very hard on the sidewalk. "Because when I'm around Edison, he makes me feel uncomfortable and I kind of turn into a complete dork." Why was I admitting this? "I guess he's kinda intimidating. Sure, I asked him about his past, but I didn't get very far. I didn't want to push it."

Nope, saying all of that out loud had not helped *at all*. Instead, I officially felt like the afterlife's biggest loser. My soul mate had turned into a school-dance-attending rat—one who, by the way, I was majorly over—and now it looked like I was asking Lorna for the skinny on the dead bad-boy-next-door. She probably thought I was getting myself into some complicated love triangle of me, David, and Ed. Not that you can have a love triangle if two-thirds of it aren't breathing.

Lorna eyed me carefully. "As far as I know, Edison was here before the rest of us," she said. "Then Tess came next. Then me. Then Nancy. Of course there have been others in between, but—apart from a few exceptions, like Jimmy—they've all found their Keys and gone through the Big Red Door. We're the only stuckists."

Nothing I hadn't already figured.

"Well, I guess Nancy and I aren't technically stuck," Lorna said. "I still think we could both get our Keys if we wanted them. But Tess, well, she'll never talk about it of course, but I always get the impression she would have been out of here years ago if she could."

Tess couldn't solve her murder and was stranded? That would be the worst thing *ever*—and could explain a lot.

"And Edison, has he ever talked about what happened to him? What his deal is?" I absentmindedly kicked an empty cigarette packet that someone had dropped on the sidewalk. It bounced off my foot and hit the curb on the opposite side of the street. Lorna's eyes widened and she looked at me questioningly. Uh-oh. She so knew Nancy had not taught me *that* trick. I carried on walking, like I hadn't done a thing.

"No, I don't know what his deal is," she said eventually. "He's pretty guarded about his past, so I never pushed it either."

We walked across Avenue of the Americas. Lorna waited for the lights before she crossed. I don't know if she did it to be kind—while the speeding traffic could no longer kill me, getting mown down by two fast-moving vehicles was enough already—or out of habit. I thought it was sweet.

"Whatever happened to Edison, it's his story to tell," Lorna said as we started up the avenue to Waverly Place, the street that led to the Attesa. "Look, I'm not Nancy," she said. "I'm not going to tell you what to do—unless you start telling me it's okay for women over twenty-five to wear cropped tops—but I do think that, when it comes to Edison, you need to be careful." Lorna kept walking. "I don't know much about him, but I do think that he and Tess . . . they . . ."

My stomach flipped. "They what? They *dated*?" I asked, searching her face for the answer and suspecting it wasn't one I wanted to hear.

Miss Snarky and Ed together? Sure, the thought had entered my head. I mean, he'd told me they talked, and she hadn't looked super-pleased when she found us on the platform that night. But them actually having a proper *relationship*? That was about as likely as David cheating on me with one of the cheerleading squad. And, oh . . . while I found Tess to be one of the least pleasant people on the planet, I supposed she was actually not *bad* looking. She could even be borderline attractive when she stopped scowling. And Edison was . . . well, he wasn't my usual type, but he wasn't someone you'd be embarrassed to say you were seeing either. He was kinda attractive. If you liked the whole dark-mysterious-green-eyed-brooding thing. Which of course I didn't. Tess and Edison being together at some point—the thought was about as appealing as mixing milk and orange juice.

Lorna shook her head so hard, her straight blond hair fanned out around her face. "No! No, I don't think they've ever dated. Well, actually I don't know. Neither of them are exactly the spill-

your-guts types. What I think is different. What I think is that—"
She caught herself and stopped talking. Lorna's perfectly smooth
forehead wrinkled and she looked serious for the first time ever.

"What you think is what?" I asked.

Lorna looked around, as if she were expecting Edison to jump
out from behind the nearest tree or Tess to stomp over and tell her
to keep the hell out of her business.

She lowered her voice. "Okay, don't say this to anyone, not
even Nancy, but I have this theory." She stopped. Jeez, was she
building this up. It better be good.

"Which is?"

"Which is"—Lorna sighed, like I'd got it out of her through
hours of harsh emotional torture—"that Edison and Tess, they
knew each other. Like, before. Before they died."

"They *what*?"

Color me shocked, that was not what I was expecting.

"I think they might have known each other before they died,"
Lorna repeated, just in case I hadn't taken it in.

"How? And how has Nancy, the chief detective, not detected
this most major of all the major facts and you have?" Ouch, that
sounded a lot meaner than I meant it to.

"I'm not totally useless," Lorna huffed. "I've been dead longer
than you and Nancy put together. I do have some experience at it."

"I know, I'm sorry. That came out wrong." I sat on a wall and
motioned for Lorna to sit beside me. "Where did this theory come
from?"

Lorna checked for dirt, then sat.

"It was before Nancy got here. Right about the time when I'd decided I wasn't that into finding my Key and more into making sure my family was okay," she said. "Edison and Tess hadn't exactly been the most welcoming new hotel mates"—understatement of the eon—"don't get me wrong, Tess wasn't as mean to me as she's being to you. She really, really hasn't taken to you for some reason." Great to have *that* confirmed. "I guess she's just seen so many newbies come through the hotel that she can't be bothered to be polite anymore. But with me, well, she wasn't exactly asking me for sleepovers in her room on a nightly basis either. I was lonely. So I decided I should try to make her like me. I'm not sure we would have been friends when we were alive, but I was feeling kinda sad with no one to talk to but Tiger, my kitten—"

"Your *what*?"

"Oh!" Lorna brightened. "So this is a really cool fact! Cats can see us. Like, without us appariting or anything. Nancy thinks it's one of their 'special senses' or something. Have you ever had a cat?" I nodded. Arthur, fifth grade. "You know when they sort of bristle or jump for no reason? Tiger used to do that all the time and I thought he was just being weird, but now I know it was because he was probably seeing something from this world. Look, I'll show you."

Lorna jumped off the wall and walked across the street, where a tiny tabby cat was lying stretched out in the afternoon sun.

"Watch this. Hey, kitty, kitty," she said as she stroked her hand over the cat's belly. It wiggled, like a contented snake. OMG, it could feel her!

"Cool, huh?" Lorna said. "Sometimes they do freak out if they don't know you, but . . ."

Suddenly the kitten opened its eyes, saw Lorna, and sprung up with a terrified *mew!* It ran off down the street.

"Yeah, that one didn't look too ghost friendly to me," I said.

She shook her head and came back to the wall. "It's different if they're used to you," she said. "Now, where were we? Oh yes, the important stuff: how I know about Edison and Tess."

She shuffled. "I was trying to get Tess to talk to me more, so one morning I came down to try to be friendly. But when I got to the lobby, I could hear them talking."

"Them? Tess and Edison?"

Lorna raised her eyebrows at me, telling me to keep up.

"Of course, Tess and Edison. I couldn't really hear what they were saying, but they were talking about one of the Living, and from the way Ed was speaking, it sounded like they both knew this person. And not just from haunting him after they'd died."

Lorna looked down the street. The tabby she'd terrified had found a new spook-free patch of sun and was lying in that.

"And?" I asked.

"And I don't know because they saw me then and stopped." Lorna stood up off the wall again. "Maybe they had friends in common—it wouldn't be that weird, would it? This island's not that big. They're around the same age. I didn't pry. I've got enough of my own stuff to deal with without getting into theirs."

She held out a hand to help me up.

"I may be wrong, I sometimes am, but just be careful with Edison," she said. "If Tess doesn't heart you and they're actually close, she may feel, I don't know, threatened or something. You don't know the real story there."

She was right, I had no clue. But I was sure as hell gonna find out.

Chapter 20

"SO THE SPORTS FIELD TODAY," I SAID. *"I AM* willing to admit that was slightly embarrassing."

"What, the part where the esteemed members of the Dead Girls Detective Agency caused a pretty-girl pileup? Or the part where you tried to haunt that Kristen chick and she just walked straight through you?"

"Er, all of the above," I admitted.

It was a mere three hours since Lorna had warned me off Edison so, clearly, here I was, standing by the river with him alone. I figured he may have a Tess-involved past, but—when he wanted to—Edison also talked a lot of sense. Exhibit A: He was right about the whole cheerbacle today. For a group of supposed detectives, we completely sucked. So as soon as I'd gotten back to the Attesa, I'd gone to find him and asked for the scare-the-bejesus lesson special.

"You would have done things differently, then?" I asked.

"I would not have been down there wasting my time in the first place," he said.

See? Sense.

"Look, if finding your Key is what you really want to do, let me offer some advice from my many years hanging out in the afterlife. Because"—he leaned in like he was going to tell me a secret—"when it comes to dead years, I'm practically at retirement age compared to a freshman like you."

Good point. One that conjured up some unpleasant mental images but still . . .

Edison reached an arm across my body, his eyes firmly trained on mine. Up this close I could see the tiny gray flecks in them. Even though his skin was pale, his lips were still a deep pink.

"Ah, here it is." Fast as a cat, he whipped my copy of the Rules out of my blazer pocket.

"Hey! Paws off," I said, trying to grab it back. "I need that."

Edison held the book high above his head. I tried to jump to snatch it, but he was two heads taller than me, so I didn't stand a chance.

"Fine," I said. I crossed my arms and stood back. "Tell me, oh wise one, why you need the book so badly to get this lesson on the road."

Ed waved the Rules in the air one more time, then—when he was sure I wasn't faking the whole surrender thing—held it in front of his face, and turned to page ten with a flourish.

"The Dos and Don'ts of Apparition: A ghost should apparite when it is only in the interests of solving his/her murder case," he read in a measured, high-pitched voice. For someone who didn't seem to give a lot of airtime to Nancy and what she thought, Edison could mimic her almost perfectly.

"When appearing as an apparition, ghosts will manifest themselves in the form they took in everyday life before they died," he continued. *"In this way, they may scare humans with a little light haunting, but will not upset them irrevocably. This should help them to uncover any extra information they might need, but cannot be discovered by traditional detection methods."*

Ed slammed the book shut and threw it on the grass behind him. He was lucky Nancy was a good ten blocks away. Even she would have flipped out at that.

"You know what page ten is?" he asked. I shook my head. "It's only half the story. Manifesting in the form you took when you were alive? Christ. Where is that gonna get you?"

"Really? Apparition seems like one of the cooler things we can do, is it really so wrong?"

"Not wrong, just a little useless," Edison said. "I'll prove my point. Can you apparite, right now, for me, please?"

Ever since I lost my glow-jo in the library when faced with the heinous sight of David and Just-Call-Me J, I'd been practicing apparition on my own in my room at night. And, even if my little display earlier hadn't affected Kristen in the way I wanted it to, I'd still been able to apparite on demand.

I looked around to check that none of the Living were near, then pushed all the power in my body down to my feet and let it swell up. The warm feeling rose until, limb by limb, I slowly appeared in a pink glow.

I smiled—okay, I'll admit it—a bit smugly and turned to Edison. "There you go."

Edison looked me up and down critically. He walked around me in a circle, inspecting my work.

"I'm sorry, Charlotte, but when I see you now, you are in a slightly paler, more iridescent version of your former Living self." Yeeesss, wasn't that the idea? "And being a typical, attractive high school girl in eleventh grade—"

Attractive? Did Edison just say I was *attractive*?

"You, Miss Feldman, ain't scary to look at, not at all. Even when the Living can see you. Sorry to break it to you, but that's the truth. Sure, if you popped up and clanked a few chains in your parents' living room right now, I imagine they would need to get themselves to the nearest shrink." Edison stopped circling and stood in front of me. "But if I was your murderer, and you materialized one night looking like that . . ."

He raised his arm and traced a line in the air next to my body, from my head to my knees. The space between us seemed to hum.

"Well, being the unbalanced murderer that I am, I would probably just put your appearance down to a little post-kill guilt."

Oh.

"Or if I did believe that you were a ghost and haunting me,

being such an unbalanced murderer, I would be so badass that I wouldn't be scared of you at all."

That put me in my place. I blew my energy out and became invisible again.

"But . . ." Ed took another pace toward me. He was so close now that my hand would brush against his if I just lifted it up. ". . . if you materialized looking like *this* . . ."

There was a loud flash of yellow light, then smoke. I jumped at the noise, putting my hands over my ears. What was with the pyrotechnics? And where had Edison gone?

I looked up to see Ed was floating above me. His feet on a level with my shoulders.

Only it wasn't Ed. Not normal-possibly-attractive-when-he-wasn't-near-a-subway Ed, anyway. It was a big, scary, straight-out-of-*Thriller* (if they *seriously* updated the special FX) *zombie* Ed. He'd somehow managed to turn himself into a hideously scary ghost: His pupils were red and unfocused, his skin was green and glowing—and parts of it looked like they'd fall off if you touched them too hard. He'd expanded, so he was Ed-and-then-some-size. Some gross green slime was dripping off his black Adidas and forming a smoldering puddle on the ground.

So how was he still totally hot?

"Then I'd be scaaaaaaaaredddddddddddddddd." He roared. His voice had all the echo of a bad dance track.

I was so shocked, I tripped over nothing and fell on my butt.

"See, Charlotte," Zombie Ed boomed, "you're used to the

afterlife and its many freak-out moments, but even you're scared of me when I look like thisss."

"I am SO not scared." I tried to get up off the ground, but my legs weren't working the way I wanted them too. I stayed put.

Suddenly I had a bad thought: What if Lorna was right? What if he was Tess's secret BFF and this was part of their plan to get me out of their lives—for good. What if, now that he'd turned into a zombie and trapped me down by the river, they were about to send me off to some alternate as yet-uncharted-hell dimension where I'd live forever until time finally stopped?

Help.

Just as I was wondering how fast I could port out of there, there was another flash of green light and a thunderclap bang. Normal Ed stood in front of me again.

"Neat, huh?" he said, giving me his hand and pulling me up. I carefully moved my feet to the left, trying to avoid the ectoplasm pool, but that—like Edison's flaking skin—had gone too. His eyes were twinkling with excitement.

"Um, you could call it that," I managed.

I looked around expecting to see police cars or fire engines or at least a couple of the Living lying on the sidewalk, having zombie-sighting-induced heart attacks. But there was no one around. Apart from a couple of oblivious, drunk Wall Street guys in suits trying to hail cabs.

"Seriously, don't worry about them," Ed said. "They're too wasted to have seen a thing. That's what three dirty martinis and a round of flaming sambucas will do to your levels of perception. You have been warned."

Wow. I definitely preferred Dark-Arts Ed to Tough-Love Ed. "So you can teach me to do . . . *that*?" I asked. "It's not against the Rules?" Much as I wasn't sure quite when I was going to use my zombieness, it was a "neat" trick. Plus, as Mom always said, it was better to be over- than underprepared.

"Course I can and, no, it's not. Look, like I said the Rules are only half the story," Ed explained. "If you promise to only use this when you really, honestly need to and won't go getting any Zombie Charlottes on CNN, I'll show you how it's done."

I looked at Ed. So far his loopholes had proved a lot more useful than Nancy's book-approved tricks. Right now, Ed didn't look like the incarnation of evil (well, not anymore). Down here, away from the others, he seemed genuine.

Maybe Lorna hadn't heard what she thought she had in the lobby that day. Like she said herself, she had been wrong before. And, if Edison wasn't on my side, why was he taking time out from his exhaustive schedule of brooding and being a smart ass to fit me in?

"How do you know all of this stuff?" I asked.

Edison sat on the grass and took a cigarette out of his pocket. He inspected it, then bounced it up and down on the Lucky Strike box, his forehead crinkling. He took a minute, then stood up to face me.

"Come on, Charlotte, think about it," he said, staring hard

into my eyes. "Everyone in our world—well, they haven't got here through the most pleasant means. You were pushed, Nancy was blown up, Lorna died of head injuries, and—"

He stopped short. "What I'm trying to say is that none of us reached ninety-five years old and died in our sleep after a long life of love and fulfillment and grandkids. We all had our futures stolen. We were all *murdered*. When we were teenagers, forgodsake."

He broke my gaze and looked out to the water. More than anything I wanted to touch his arm and tell him I got it. I got how life could be so, so, so unbelievably unfair. But I was too scared. Too scared to touch his arm in case he pulled away.

"It's a big, bad world out there. We're proof of that." He looked down at the cigarette in his hand, as if remembering it was there, and slowly lit it. "So I figured that one day I might need some extra tricks, ones that aren't in there"—he pointed at the Rules book lying in the grass—"to protect myself. And my family."

His eyes were unfocused. His mind going someplace else. "What happened to you, Edison?" I asked, in a small voice.

He turned and walked away from me, toward the river. "Like I said, after my dad died, things were tough," he said in a tight tone. "Mom wasn't making enough money, so my brother, Matt, and I . . . we got jobs as soon as we were old enough to help out." Edison was still facing the water. Like telling his story to the gulls was easier than telling it to me.

"I worked in the local record store, waited tables, walked the neighbors' dogs—anything I could to make Mom's life easier. But after a while, Matt started bringing home more cash than me, despite being a year younger. Just occasionally at first. Then his 'wage envelopes' became more and more frequent. He told me he was washing dishes at some restaurant downtown, but no busboy ever got paid that much." He shook his head. This was the longest I'd heard Edison talk without making a joke or a jibe.

"I got suspicious. One day I followed him to work. Sure, 'work' was a restaurant—this dirty-looking place out at the wrong end of Soho—but there was no way he was making that kinda cash from cleaning the place up every night. I confronted him about it and he admitted he'd been helping the owner out—delivering packages around town."

"He was a drug dealer?" I shuddered.

"Yeah." Edison took a last drag on his cigarette and ground the butt into the ground. "I didn't want to tell Mom. I couldn't. It would have killed her. So instead I told Matt he had to leave the job—that if he didn't I'd make sure she found out. It was an empty threat but it was enough. The only thing was he had to do one last job before his boss would let him off . . .'"

Edison turned back to me, his eyes finding mine.

"And because he was your little brother, you went in his place," I finished.

Edison shakily put his hands behind his head. "Let's just say things didn't go according to plan." He looked away now. "The next thing I knew I woke up here."

Wow. "Do you have any—"

"Regrets?" he said, finishing my sentence now. "About going in Matt's place? Never. Man, Charlotte, it didn't matter what he'd got himself into. He'd done it for the right reasons. There's no way I'd want him here instead of me. But do I have regrets about that time? Of course I do. I always will have. I should have found a better way to support Mom. One that meant Matt never went near something like that."

"That's why you're still here? To look out for him and your mom?"

"It's the least I can do after I left them like that."

"But, Edison, it wasn't your choice," I said.

"No, but I have a choice now," he semi-shouted.

Ed caught hold of himself, gave me an I'm-sorry look, and went on.

"And I choose to stay here to make sure they're okay. And if that involves working out how to use my . . . what did you call them?" A glimmer of the twinkle was back in his eyes. "*Powers* to put on a scary light show if I ever need to, then those are the breaks."

"Now, enough of this serious talk. Come over here, Feldman," he said, beckoning me with his finger, "and I'll show you how to create Ghostgirl's evil nemesis: Zombiewoman!"

The tension punctured, I allowed myself to giggle. It felt good. I felt good. No, whatever Lorna said, Ed wasn't bad. Not bad at all.

Chapter 21

"GUYS, WHEN I SAID I WAS REALLY INTO MY boyfriend, I did not mean *literally*."

It was eight thirty a.m. and the Dead Girls Detective Agency had gathered in the hallway of Saint Bartholomew's, right in front of the eleventh grade lockers. No students would be here for at least half an hour. (Nancy said even she hadn't got to class this early when she was alive.) Which was a good thing, because Nancy, Lorna, and Tess were looking at me oddly.

Like really, really oddly. Like they didn't recognize me anymore.

Which, to be fair, they didn't. I was in David's body at that point, after all.

"I totally get it," I said. "After the Plan: Stage One, Possession of the Cheerleaders tanked, we need to step it up." I looked at Nancy. "And the Plan: Stage Two makes *mucho* sense. It just feels a bit strange, that's all I'm saying. Possessing my own boyfriend."

"*Ex*-boyfriend," Tess corrected me, smiling a smile that stopped short of her eyes.

"Ex-boyfriend," I repeated. Was David making a screw-you face? Because that was what I was thinking.

"You need to take the mind-over-matter approach," Nancy said, patting my—well, David's—head. "Don't overthink it. Just see him as your vessel."

Hot guy, boyfriend, soul mate, asshole, vessel. Quite the résumé.

"And try not to think about the fact that you've made out with your own face," Lorna said.

I raised my boyf— sorry, *ex*'s hand to his face and touched his lips that were now sort of my lips. Ew. I grimaced at Lorna. "Thanks for that," I said.

"Stop thinking about the fact it's *David's* body you're inside and focus on the Plan." Nancy walked a few steps down the hall, then came back. Pacing helped her think. "He was the person closest to you in life, so if we spend a day in his sneakers, we might spot something new." She smiled optimistically.

"Because, quite frankly, we need a break," Tess said, peering inside David's trash can of a locker. "You've been dead for a whole five days now." She spotted an old tube sock, pretended to hold her nose, and threw it through Nancy. "So I would really like you to find your Key and get the hell out of here."

"At least that's one thing we agree on," I snapped. It was hard to sound angry with David's voice. Tortured, maybe. Angry, not so much.

Harsh as Tess could be, she was right. We weren't getting anywhere. Apart from more and more annoyed by each other. After Ed's lesson last night, I was pretty sure I could pull the zombie trick if I had to, but who should I be zombiing at? We had more kids with alibis than suspects. My vessel session better give us some leads or I was looking at spending infinity here.

"I think Tess has the right idea," Nancy said, ignoring the insult volley between us. "Let's investigate David's locker. There could be a clue in here."

Or more proof we didn't have one.

Nancy poked around inside, moving textbooks about. Hmm . . . so she could touch the Living's stuff too? That was a trick she'd not seen fit to show me. Maybe she only wasted the complicated stuff on lifers like Tess and Lorna.

"Whoa, Nance, sure you want to do that without protective gloves? You might mess up the evidence or put your fingerprint someplace it shouldn't be," Tess said leaning against the wall, crossing her arms and yawning.

"Don't be silly, dummy, ghosts don't have fingerprints," Lorna said. "We lost them when we lost our fingers."

"I think she was being *facetious*, Lorna, but well done for remembering," Nancy said, riffling around in the stacks of papers and other crap for a few seconds more, before picking up a stack of unopened letters in sky-blue envelopes.

"What are these?" Nancy asked, holding one up to the light, like she was on a cop show or something. She looked at them more carefully. "Oh, wait, there's a stamp on each: 'Saint Bartholomew's Library'?"

"Those are late slips they send to warn you you've got books overdue," I explained.

"But there are, like, eleven of them!" Nancy said in disgust. "I can't believe he's this irresponsible."

"Really?" Tess said, stifling another yawn. "Because the rest of the evidence was pointing toward Mr. Charlotte being such a together guy."

"I bet he'll do that with bank statements and bills when he gets older too. You're lucky to be rid of him, Charlotte," Nancy said, shaking her head.

"Forget those, look at *these*!" Lorna pulled a pair of mini hair straighteners out from under the debris. Trust her to discover the one beauty product among all that mess. David's Spanish textbook clattered to the floor, taking a half-eaten, fuzz-covered apple with it. Good to see something had been decomposing for longer than me.

"OMG!" Lorna shrieked. "I'll give him props—he must be very accomplished with these things. I would never in a trillion years have suspected he was fighting the frizz. His hair always looks great."

Lorna stuck her head into a pile of folders and class notes.

"What are you doing?" I asked.

"Just seeing what else he has hidden back here," she said in a muffled voice. "There's no smoke without fire. Or heated irons without leave-in conditioner."

Great, so now David was vain beauty addict? Did I ever know him at all?

"Wow, you were dating a genuine New York metrosexual," Tess said, giving me her special poor-you face.

Despite myself, I really wanted to swing at Tess now. But what was the point? David's arm would go right through her smug face without leaving a mark.

"Actually male grooming is increasingly *en mode*," Lorna said seriously.

"Guys, fascinating as this isn't, can we get on with it before the entire school shows up?" Nancy tried to put the letters and textbooks back neatly on one of the shelves, but they just fell off and joined the rest of the trash. She sighed and pulled David's beat-up schedule off the inside of his locker door instead.

"Now according to this"—Nancy tried to flatten the crumpled piece of paper out, ignoring the coffee stain that made all of Friday's classes illegible. Unless you spoke fluent mocha— "David's first class of the day is, I think this says . . . *chemistry*?"

"Nuh-uh. Hell to the no," I said firmly. "Even if you dig up my dead body and drag it here for me to walk over, there is still no way I am sitting through another blast of that. *Comprende?* David is simply going to have to play hooky from that class today."

Nancy looked at me aghast. She was not the hooky type.

"Which will serve the double purpose of, one, not making me any more brain dead than I already am," I continued. "And two, giving us a chance to walk around the school to see what's going down."

"Jeez, whine much, Charlotte?" Tess dramatically rubbed her ears.

I felt a familiar dry feeling in David's throat—what was it? I hadn't had it for *days*. It may have been all the "whining," but something wasn't quite right. I might be in charge of David's brain, but his body was telling me he wanted something.

I put his fingers in the pocket of his combats and pulled out some coins, a paper clip, and a guitar pick (as if he had any real use for that) and went to get a Coke from the soda machine. I pulled back the ring pull with a *pssst* and downed the whole thing in one.

I belched so loudly Lorna flinched. Even with a girl at the wheel, guys were still gross.

"Hey, Maher, you're here eaaaaarly," a familiar-looking guy in black cords and an Iron Maiden T-shirt yelled.

I looked at the clock on the wall of the arch in front of me. It was 8:59 a.m. The students were arriving.

"Yeah, Ms. Jackson said that if I didn't clean up my locker before lunch she was going to give me detention again." I shrugged.

The guy was carrying a folder with *Camels on the Freeway* scribbled on the front. Okay, so he was one of the band. A quick glance at his frizzy chin confirmed that he was trying to grow a hipster beard. Figured. Tom or Pete or Plectrum? I had no idea.

Even though I'd taken pictures of the Camels play before, it was so hard to recognize them in daylight instead of some dive bar.

"So . . . ," I said. Camel looked at me expectantly. "Soooo . . . ."

Oh help, I was tanking here. I needed the Camel to go leave me to possess my ex alone. Someone distract him please, I thought to myself.

As if on cue, Tess Jabbed an old OJ carton precariously balanced on top of David's gym bag. It tumbled out of his locker and onto the floor, spilling moldy orange grossness on the light gray tiles. Forget what I said about the apple. The OJ had been dead longer.

"Man, I do not normally agree with Ms. Jackson, but that is rancid, my friend," Camel said.

"Rancid," I agreed, trying not to laugh as the citrusy goop slid from tile to tile and right through Lorna's right foot. Of course it didn't stain her immortal Pretty Ballerinas, but she gave Tess a look that clearly said that was not the point.

"So, I guess I'll catch you at band practice tonight then?" Camel mimed an air guitar strum with his hands. "We've got the downstairs room in Arlene's from five to seven. My brother's working the bar, so the manager said we could use it until the support act needs to tune up. We'll be jamming where some of the greats have played."

What, like That Band No One's Ever Heard Of and the One Supporting Them?

"Excellent. Arlene's at five." I strummed back at him. Camel sloped off down the hall. See, pretending to be your ex-boyfriend was a piece of carrot cake. I could totally do convincing guy chat. You just shrugged a lot, repeated back what they said, and tried not to sound like you cared. Easy. Why had I been freaking out?

And why had the world gone black?

"Hey, gorgeous," a female voice drawled in my ear.

Hey, *who*-geous?

"Guess who!" she asked.

Much as I hated to admit it, Mystery Girl Covering David's Eyes could be one of very, very many.

"Um, Kaitlynnn?" I tried.

"No, naughty!" she scolded. The girl removed her hands, so I could see again, and stood in front of David's body. A bit too close actually. Had she not seen *Dirty Dancing*? Was she not aware of the concept of other people's dance space?

I took a step back to let David's eyes focus and get a better look at her. Just-Call-Me J. "It's me!" she trilled.

Even though there were only a handful of kids around, Jamie looked furtively up and down the hallway.

"I know you had to say I was Kaitlynnn out loud just now so that no one gets suspicious. And I know why—she said you told her that you don't think you're emotionally ready to exclusively date me *or* Kristen at the moment . . ."

Oh, had he now?

"But I just wanted to tell you that what happened between us last night"—Jamie leaned in and whispered in David's ear so close that I could feel her warm breath in the part only Q-tips normally go—"it was really special. And when you're in more of a relationship place, I hope you'll give me a call."

"Really special"? I shouldn't have been surprised, but I still cringed. What had happened to David—had his standards died with me? If Jamie caught the weird look on David's face (which was mine and read *what a giant boy slut*), she ignored it. Instead she thrust her number into his hand. OMG, this girl actually had little "call me" cards with lipstick kisses she'd personally puckered on them.

"Oh, cute!" Lorna said, eyeing one.

"Oh, heave!" Tess said.

Ohforgodsake, I thought.

The flirting and the kissing with the other two I could (begrudgingly, seeing as I was dead) take. Well, kinda. But this? This "really special" thing between them? It was the whore that broke the camel's back.

It was time to get even.

I couldn't stop David systematically working his way through every girl on the entire island, but I could ruin his chances with this one—right now.

"Actually, Kaitlynnn," I called after her.

Jamie spun around to me and frowned. "My name's not Kaitlynnn," she pouted. "You do know that, right?"

I had David make a puzzled look. "Oh yeah, sure. *Sure.* It's just that there are so many girls at the moment, I keep forgetting all your names." We shrugged. A proper noncommittal shrug. The kind I imagine George Clooney gives whatever waitress he's dating this week when she asks how he feels about settling down, having kids, and giving up summers in Lake Como.

"That's not very nice, Davey." Jamie brushed an invisible piece of lint off the retro *Rolling Stones Rock and Roll Circus* tee he was illegally wearing under his regulation blazer, and looked up at him from underneath her heavily mascaraed lashes. "But I forgive you."

She batted him on the nose with her forefinger like he was a naughty, but adorable puppy dog. "You have sooo much going on in that cute head of yours right now, even I would have trouble remembering really important details—if I was you." She stroked his man-bangs in sympathy.

Honestly, what was it with these women? They were like the cockroaches of the dating world. Trample on them and they just came back stronger.

"Actually, there's something I've been meaning to tell you," I made David say. "It's kinda hush-hush, but I can trust you, right? I bet you could keep a secret better than Kristen or Kaitlynnn."

"Oh, I can." Jamie practically purred.

"You see, I do like you, but I have this little issue. A health issue."

Jamie visibly paled.

"Sometimes I break out in . . ." David trailed off. Let her guess what it might be. "And, well, I don't wanna go into it, but it's kinda gross."

She took a massive step back and bashed into a sophomore walking behind her.

"Maybe it's the stress of what I've been through recently," I said. "But I am pretty sure it's not contagious. At least it hasn't been in the past. And the doctor said he was thirty percent sure it wouldn't be. But I just wouldn't want you to catch anything that would cause a rash or blemishes on that beautiful face."

I took two steps toward her and ran David's thumb down Jamie's flawless cheek. She jumped back like she'd been touched by a hot poker. A very hot, very unhygienic poker. "You get what I'm saying?" I asked.

Jamie looked at David in disgust. "Of course. That is, like . . . I . . . better get going. See ya."

She bolted down the corridor. Job done.

"Wow, I've never seen anyone in five-inch wedges move that fast," Lorna said, wide-eyed.

"That was a total waste of investigation time, but it was very, very cool," Nancy said, putting her hand on David's shoulder. "He deserved it."

"You do realize that will be all around the cheersquad in about five seconds flat?" Lorna asked.

"Really?" I said. "Damn, I'd hoped they'd all hear it within three."

249

Chapter 22

"MAHER! MAHER! IT'S NINE FIFTEEN A.M.—ISN'T there somewhere you should be?"

While the other kids trailed into their first-period classes, we took David's body for a tour of the school to see what was going on. We were peering in the gym, discussing how pleased we were that phys ed was something that died with your body, when Ms. Jackson, my English teacher, appeared from nowhere. Wasn't she supposed to be in class too? Like, teaching?

"David, why aren't you in homeroom?" she asked. "As far as I know Advanced Hallway Loitering isn't on the Saint Bartholomew's syllabus. At least not this semester."

"Oh, I like her," Nancy said, stepping away from the glass and leaving the ninth grade class to their softball game. "She's funny."

"Though she has *the* worst taste in shoes." Lorna was eyeing Ms. Jackson's flat-booted feet.

"I bet she just walked here in those boots because they're warm, and she's going to change out of them when she has to teach a class." For some reason Nancy had decided she was Ms. Jackson's newest fan. Maybe it had something to do with the fact that Ms. J looked rather like a grown-up version of Her Geekiness: black-rimmed glasses, brown hair that shone red when it hit the light, only a little lip gloss to pass for makeup and a bulging handbag that was big on the practical and small on the likely-to-be-featured-in-*Vogue*.

"In fact . . ." Nancy poked her entire head into the second bag Ms. Jackson was holding. "Lorna, get in here! See! She has some really cute pale-blue sling-backs ready to go!"

Lorna popped her head into Ms. Jackson's green canvas Strand Book Store bag too. "Oh, they *are* lovely. Look at the bows! They match the little one on her belt and . . ."

"Oh, please, if you two don't stop goofing around, I'm going to have to take charge and I think we all agree that is not something we want to happen," Tess said. "Short of old Tree Trunk Legs in there"—she pointed through the gym window to Coach Brock, who was trying to break up a softball-induced fight between two girls who'd gone for the ball at the same time and nearly knocked each other out—"telling us we have to get down and give her twenty. So come on already."

Chastised, they pulled their heads out of the bag and, as they did, Ms. Jackson looked down at it strangely, as if she were half expecting a wild animal to crawl out.

"Look! She's spirit sensitive!" Nancy said in delight. "She felt us. I love it when that happens."

"That happens much?" I asked, thinking back to Ali and the girls' bathroom.

"Only with *really* tuned-in people." Nancy smoothed down her curls.

Ms. Jackson tilted her head and refocused on David with a confused look. She took a second, then seemed to remember what she was doing. Which was giving him hell.

"David, I'm waiting. Shouldn't you be learning something right now?"

"I have a free period," I made David say. "I'm just off to . . ." Quick, look around, find an alibi. Ah, there one was. "I'm heading to the *library*. I need to get ahead with some extra reading for that assignment you gave us last week."

"Really?" Ms. Jackson looked like she believed him as much as my dad did when Mom said she'd "only be five more minutes" getting ready to go out for dinner.

"Course," I said. "You said we should find a Shakespeare character and think who their modern-day pop-culture counterpart would be."

How was I remembering this? I obviously paid way more attention in lit than I thought. I cocked David's head to one side in the hope it made him look less like he was lying. "I have this theory that you can draw some very direct comparisons between the way Shylock is treated in *The Merchant of Venice* and how

Spencer Pratt was in *The Hills*."

She couldn't be buying this. Unless she hadn't watched *The Hills*. Which seeing as she was over thirty, may be the case. I hoped.

Ms. Jackson stared at me intently, like, if she made David uncomfortable enough he might break and say, *Yep, you've got me. I'm a ditcher, hands up. Do your worst.*

I held firm.

"Then I'll wait with great interest for our next class." She hoisted her green bag back up on her shoulder. "Now get in there before I remember who Spencer is, think through properly what you've just said, and have to send you to the principal's office. Okay?"

"Okay," I said . . . and tried to walk through the shut library doors.

I banged David's head, bounced right off them, and fell on the floor at Ms. Jackson's feet.

"You're acting very, very strangely. Even for a teenage boy," she said.

If only she knew.

Behind me I could hear the others giggling.

I pulled David's body up and brushed the dust off his jeans. His head was throbbing. Man, that was going to hurt tomorrow. With any luck he'd have a black eye for the Halloween dance.

"I'm fine. On my way. Really want to study. See ya!" I *pulled* the library door open and walked in. Lorna, Nancy, and Tess glided through the wall. No bruises or bounces for them.

Inside, the place was deserted. Seriously, who came in here for a free period at this time of the day anyway? Any sensible person would be at home if they didn't have to be in class until ten a.m. Which was exactly why hardly anyone had a free now. The faculty knew they might as well write *another hour in bed* on your schedule.

Lorna looked around. "This place is a ghost town."

I forgot I was in David's body—again—and laughed out loud. So loud it echoed around the room. Weird. I'd done that—made that sound. I'd been invisible for so long, it felt bizarre to be able to disturb the Living without apparating or Jabbing or—

"Shhh!" said a muffled voice somewhere in the stacks.

"Oh, great, we're going to get lectured again," Tess said. "Nancy, let's ditch this body and continue detecting without it. The boy's holding us back."

"You're David, aren't you? David Maher?" the voice asked.

Depends on your definition of "are."

A small sandy-haired girl poked her head around the end of the C aisle. She walked over to the library's main desk and looked up at me with a shy smile.

"Yes. Do I know you?" I asked. Better play dumb.

"I've seen you around," she said. She straightened some papers on her desk so that they were at right angles to a neat pile of books and on an exact level with her stamp. "It's very early to be in here. Can I help you with something in particular?" she asked encouragingly.

Man, this was not helping us at all. It was time to make a move.

"Nah, that's nice of you, but I'll get out of your hair." I turned David to walk him out. Remembering to *open* the library door this time.

"So what else did you do around here, Feldman?" Tess bounced through the wall. "You know, for *fun*. Or were you such an ardent member of the Little Blond Boy Appreciation Society that you couldn't fit anything else into your packed schedule? Though I guess all that gazing and hand-holding and hugging must have been pretty intense."

"Wow, every wannabe stand-up within fifty blocks must be delighted you didn't live long enough to graduate high school," I said, pulling David's body up tall. "You're too funny. I'm not sure they could have taken the competition."

"Guys! Guys!" Nancy said, rubbing her temples.

"Actually I had plenty of interests, if you must know. For a start I was in the photography club," I said defensively.

"And let me guess who your favorite subject to shoot was," Tess said.

Nancy shot her the Look. "That sounds very creative, Charlotte," she said.

"It *was* actually. The photography room's just around there. Wanna take a look?"

"Oh, I can think of nothing I'd rather do," Tess said, giving me the fakest smile you can imagine. Lorna poked her in the ribs.

I walked David's body down the hallway and peeked inside

the club room door. Silence. No budding Leibovitzes in here. I stepped inside. And instantly felt like I'd been kicked in the guts.

On the wall—blown up a meter square and in pride of place—was the last photograph I'd ever taken. A portrait of David I'd snapped as we were walking home through the park. Usually I spent ages setting pictures up, worrying about the light, or what our teacher Miss Peters said made "good composition." But this time, I'd just clicked my camera without even trying. We'd been walking past the boathouse, and the background was a blur of lake and grass and early evening sun reflecting off the lens. David wasn't even looking at the camera; he was laughing with his head to the side. When I came to develop it, I kinda thought I'd have caught half his head or maybe just an ear. But as soon as the picture came into focus, I realized it was probably the best photograph I'd ever take. Just looking at it, you could feel the autumn air and the breeze and the sense of it being Friday and us having two full days before we had to go back to school. Miss Peters made me enlarge it in the lab and put it on the wall as the shot of the month, which totally made me feel more proud than I wanted to admit.

"Charlotte, did you take *that*?" Lorna asked, standing beside me. "It's way cool. He doesn't look like an idiot in it at all."

"No, I guess not, he—"

Thud!

I whirled around to see a pile of pictures cascading out of Mina Anderson's hands and spreading like a fan as they fell onto the gray tiled floor. She bent down quickly and started to pick them up in a panic.

"David!" she said. "You scared me. What are you doing in here? Oh . . ." She stopped bobbing and scooping for a beat—long enough for her gaze to move from David's body to my photograph on the wall. "I guess you came to see that."

"Sorry, who is this girl again?" Nancy asked.

"One of Charlotte's friends from the photography club," Lorna whispered, like Mina could hear her. "She came to the funeral. She sat just behind lovely Ali."

"Wow, were all your friends this *cool*, Charlotte?" Tess asked, eyeing Mina's calf-skimming skirt.

Ignoring them, I strode over to where Mina was half crouching and started to help her pick up the pictures.

"Really, you don't have to do that," she said in a small voice. "I can clean up my own mess and . . ."

I stopped short. The pictures. They were all of me. Me in Club. Me waiting for David outside class. Me trying to get into my locker. David and I sitting on the lawn. I recognized them— they were the prints from a portrait shoot we'd done for a school project. Miss Peters had paired us up and told everyone to "try to catch your subject off guard—so it's natural." I remember thinking Mina had done a great job when I saw her prints. I'd had no idea she was snapping away. I just hadn't seen all of them before. I didn't know she'd taken so many.

"What the . . . ?" Nancy said.

"Looks like someone had a girl crush on you," Lorna whispered.

"No, no, it wasn't like that," I said in David's voice.

Mina looked at David strangely and quietly picked the remaining photographs up. She gently carried them to the table. "I guess you think I'm strange," she said quietly. "I was just making copies of these ones. Charlotte told me she really liked the shots, so I wanted to have more." She stopped suddenly, realizing how that could sound. "No, I mean I . . . I thought maybe Mr. and Mrs. Feldman would like to see them. To have their own set." She looked up and shyly made eye contact with David. "If you don't think that's out of line, that is. Or it's not too soon."

I'd always had Mina pegged as a kid I'd never hang out with outside club—she was so quiet she made Maggie Simpson look vocal—but maybe I'd been wrong? After all this was a super-cute thing for her to do.

"I'm sure they'd love it," I made David say. Lorna and Nancy nodded while Tess rolled her eyes. "But maybe take Ali with you. You know my, I mean, *Charlotte's* friend?" Mina nodded. "They've never met you before after all and you don't know where the Feldmans live."

"Good idea." She carefully packed the photographs flat in her red tote. "It's so easy to get lost on the Upper West Side." She looked down at the final picture of me she was holding in her hands. "She had such a lovely smile. I'll just never understand why this had to happen, will you?"

"Oh, please can we get out of here before she starts a collection for the Charlotte Memorial Lab?" Tess said.

"No," I said to Mina, turning my back on Tess. "Right now I don't know why this had to happen. But if I have anything to do with it, that won't be the case for very much longer."

Chapter 23

I'D LOVE TO SAY SAINT BARTHOLOMEW'S cafeteria wasn't a high school cliché, but that would be an out-and-out lie. Where you sat said just as much about you as what you wore and who you dated.

The best tables were right by the sliding doors that led out onto a small courtyard where we could eat lunch in the summer. So obviously Kristen and the Tornahoes bagged them. But, come May, that all changed. The cool kids moved outside and those next down the pecking order could move a table closer to the doors, so us mere mortals could watch Just-Call-Me J and Kaitlynnn flirting with whatever boy they were into that week.

The windows were like some TV screen onto the life you could have had. If only your parents earned more, your hair was less blah, or you didn't still need braces.

David used to say we should study the cafeteria in biology,

because it was a great example of the animal pecking order brought to life. I used to think that was clever. Now, I had a sneaking suspicion that—were I not possessing my ex's body at the very moment—he'd be sitting by the doors. And freaking loving it.

Air, sunlight, and cheerleaders' saliva being well-known cures for grief and all.

By the time you hit the area past the cash registers called SS (Social Siberia), there were no windows and the only audible noise was the hum of the backup refrigerator. Which was where Lorna was pointing to now.

"Oh! Oh! Oh! There's that weird kid," Lorna said, bouncing.

"Which weird kid?" I asked.

"You know"—she put her hands on her hips—"the weird kid who was watching cheerleader practice yesterday."

I shook my head.

"He was sitting on the benches. To the right of you. You probably didn't notice because you were talking to Ed—"

Nancy turned around. "Head? Charlotte was talking to *head*?"

"Oh, she's always talking to herself *in* her head, haven't you noticed?" Lorna said. "Sometimes, when Charlotte goes quiet and looks all moody, I ask her, 'Is there anything I can do to help?' And she'll say, 'No, Lorna, thanks for asking but I'm just talking to myself in my head.'"

Call the drama teacher over, we have a new winner for Ad-libber of the Year.

Tess looked at us as if we were certifiably insane. "And again, which weird kid, Lorna?"

"That one." She pointed at the back of the room again and mouthed a "sorry" at me.

Phew. She might not be loving the fact that Edison seemed to want to be my new BFF—or whatever he was—but at least Lorna wasn't about to issue a press release about it to Nancy.

I scrunched up my eyes and tried to focus on SS. Nope, no one there but a couple of the science club geeks getting off on their homework assignments. No, wait, there was a kid behind them: Brian.

"Yeah, he is strange-looking," Tess said as Brian took his unidentifiable wheat sandwich apart, filled it with potato chips, and poured sugar on top. "Why would he have been at cheerleader practice? Do you know him?"

Oh good, because Tess needed even more ammo from my relationship résumé to beat me up with.

"Yeeeessss," I admitted. Nancy looked at me expectantly, like Brian could be the break we'd all been waiting for. I was sooo going to have to level with them. "About ten years ago, we kinda might have dated for a minute." I closed David's eyes and waited for the shitstorm.

"You dated him?" Lorna asked, shocked. It was like someone had just told her that *American Idol* was a fix.

"Well, there's quite a lot of him to love," Tess said, giggling.

"Charlotte, why don't you go talk to him and check out why

he was watching the cheerleaders," Nancy suggested. "We should be looking for anything out of the ordinary after all."

Course. I could do that. Go talk to Brian. Who I hadn't even locked eyes with in the hall since we were, what, eight? Brian wouldn't think there was anything weird going on if David—who he never spoke to either—just walked on over to shoot the breeze.

"You don't seriously think Brian is in any way responsible for my death?" I asked.

Nancy gave me her best have-I-taught-you-nothing? look. "I don't know, Charlotte," she said. "He was your very first boyfriend. I can't believe you didn't tell us about him before. You said you didn't have any exes . . ."

"OMG, I dated him for, like, a week when I was still a fetus! Plus he's not an ex—he's . . . Brian."

A guy who was currently adding ketchup and mustard to his sugar sandwich.

"We still needed to know about him," Nancy said. "What if he never got over you and couldn't handle seeing you so happy with David every day?"

OMG. "Wait, he did say something strange yesterday," I said, remembering. "When I was by the bleachers. He didn't know I was there of course, but when Kristen was ragging on me, he made this super-weird comment about how he thought I was 'smoking hot' and he wished he could have told that to me."

Lorna's eyes grew wide. "I think he was totally still into you, Charlotte. What if he was so, like, consumed with jealousy and rage about you dating David that he pushed you under the F train? Like, if he couldn't have you, then no one could. What if he's secretly this *brilliant* criminal mind and he's been plotting your murder every day since you spurned him when you were six? What if it's made him hate all women, so now he's stalking Kristen too? What if she's next?"

We all looked over at Brian with a new respect.

He dropped his open sandwich on the floor, ketchup and butter side down, sighed, and put it back together again without even checking for floor fluff.

"Get a move on, slow butt," Tess said. "Your Key may await." She Jabbed David hard in the ass.

Hmmm, I wonder who taught her that trick?

I stumbled forward, tripped over a chair and just pulled up David's body before he nose-dived into Drama Drew's lunch. Alanna, who was sitting with him, raised her eyebrows at me in disgust. Who knew they were friends?

A couple of kids behind me giggled.

Whatever, I strode over to Brian's table and manfully (I hoped) put my hand on one of the many empty chairs.

"Dude, is this seat free?" I asked.

Dude? Dude? Where had I gotten "dude" from? David may be male but he was not a stoner surfer. He did not say "dude." Okay, so very occasionally he did, but it was one of those things about him that I tried to ignore. Like the fact he had a Kelly Clarkson album on his iPod.

I straightened up, coughed, and very deliberately looked at the chair and back at Brian again. I wasn't asking twice. Guys did not beg.

"Sure," Brian said. His voice was a lot lower than it had been in second grade. Which is down to something called puberty, Charlotte.

"Take a seat." Brian pointed. "Why not?"

I sat. Right, now what? Just roll on in with a *stalked any good girls recently?* Which was Tess-level rude. And he had bought me a pack of Hershey's Kisses as a present once. Thankfully instead of the real thing.

"So, dude," I said. Must stop that. I was one testosterone hit away from grabbing my crotch and asking if he thought Megan Fox was "smoking" too. "I saw you at the cheerleading practice today. You a fan of the blues and yellows?"

"Ha!" Brian laughed and sprayed the table with a few choice pieces of the sugar, potato chip, and (yep, that looked like . . .) turkey sandwich he'd been eating.

Lorna made a dry-heaving noise.

"Of course I'm a fan, man, if you know what I mean." He leaned over the table and nudged David in the ribs. "Just never thought there would be any point hanging out near women that fine"—he somehow made *fine* last for three syllables—"because they'd never be interested in someone like me. I'm hardly their type."

Fair point.

"Thought I'd be stuck with the likes of *that*." He pointed at Mina, who was heading, lunch tray in hand, in the direction of Ali's table. "But since last Monday, well, a whole load of us back here are wondering whether all that's changed," Brian said sleazily.

Um . . . what?

"Dude . . . You are a Legend," Brian said as he leaned back in his seat, crossing his arms behind his head. He was wearing a T-shirt with *Dr. Horrible's Sing-Along Blog* emblazoned across the chest (along with a light splattering of sandwich juice). I silently thanked myself that I had no idea what that was.

"Seriously, we—every guy who dines in SS—salute you." Brian belched.

"Hey, that's really nice of you, man, but mind telling me why?" I asked. Maybe I was being slow, but what had David done to get such props?

"Why? *Why?*" Brian laughed. "It's like the cheermeister doesn't even know what he's achieved," he said to himself in awe under his breath.

Delighted he could shed some light, Brian straightened up to explain. "So we all thought you were just another pretentious loser."

Good thing David couldn't hear this because that would ouch.

"But recently we are *loving* your work," Brian said, punching David's arm. "You have gone from zero to hero, remedial to Romeo."

Hey!

"Your girlfriend died, sorry about that, by the way. Charlotte was really cool—and definitely smoking—and you somehow persuaded the hottest girls in this school—in this *city*—to hook up with you. Respect does not even begin to cover it," Brian said.

Oh my.

"So you were watching the cheerleaders yesterday because...," I prompted.

"Because if someone like you can get three Tornadoes to date them, then there's hope for the rest of us," Brian said. "Seriously, ever since you've been walking around here looking all vulnerable, there's been a sea change. It's out with the meatheads who'll get into a college just because they can throw a ball and in with *homo sensitivus*. Guys like us! Those women cannot get enough of you. Which means it's only a matter of time before they can't get enough of us too."

And again, oh my.

"So you were hanging out at cheerleader training because you think the fact I've hooked up with a couple of hotties means you now have a chance with them too?"

"Freaking yes!"

"Seriously?"

"Seriously," Brian said in the most serious voice he could muster with a mouth full of sugar sandwich. "You've paved the way. You're like Bill Gates with Windows One-point-Oh. Yesterday, I was in the science lab and Jamie didn't pretend to barf when I asked if she needed help with her assignment. She actually *smiled* at me, dude. Do you have any idea what that means for geek-slash-hot girl relations? You should be knighted for services to guykind."

And if that happened, Brian should be crowned Earl of Disillusion.

"Hey, well, I'm glad I helped," I said, standing up.

"Sweet. Hey and, dude, we're all going to vote for you for Scream King too. It's the top story on my blog and Anthony over there tweeted the entire *Dungeon Master* group last night." Brian actually winked at me. "It's a slam dunk. You have to win. We've gone viral."

"No, really, don't do that," I said. "I'm not the Halloween dance type." And I really didn't want David to be.

"Dude, you're not getting this," Brian said, exasperated. "None of us are the Halloween dance types—this is why we have to get you crowned. To make a point. Show those lax boys who's boss." He looked over at a group of jocks braving the October courtyard in their shorts. What was that supposed to prove anyway? They were, like, tougher than the weather? "Plus, they've booked the ballroom of that hotel uptown—what's it called?—the Sedgwick. It's going to be awesome—it's where they filmed *Ghostbusters*, you know the scene where they catch the Slimer for the first time?"

Trust Brian to be the only person in my class to know that. I slowly walked David's body out of the cafeteria and down the hall to his locker.

I could feel the other dead girls' presences trailing behind me.

"We can cross Brian off the list too," I said. "The only person he's likely to stalk is Chris Pine at a *Star Trek* convention."

I opened David's locker and grabbed a pen. "Don't forget about Shylock and Spencer," I wrote on a piece of paper taped to the inside of the metal door. "And sorry about your head."

"What are you doing?" Nancy asked. "That really is not necessary."

"I know, I just feel . . ." I looked at my new friends—and Tess. ". . . like I need to get out of this boy now."

I stepped back and jumped clear out of David's body. He shuddered like a cartoon character who'd had a bucket of water thrown over him.

"Hey, David, it's only October, man. If you're so cold maybe you should start wearing more clothes," Leon Clark, the lacrosse captain, said as he walked past with one of his jerk-off friends. All wearing shorts. Of course. "Or you could just man the hell up." They belly laughed.

David looked around in confusion, like he'd just been woken up from a really deep sleep and even his mom couldn't make it better. I guess the last thing he could remember was getting ready that morning—before I possessed him.

The bell rang and David jumped. He looked at the clock on the wall. Three p.m.

"What the . . . ," David said, suddenly realizing that he'd lost six and a half hours and stumbling slightly.

"Are you enjoying this as much as I am?" Tess asked. "Because if I were you, I would be squeezing every last drop of F-you out of the situation."

David looked at his open locker—which he couldn't remember getting to, much less opening—and started piling books out of his bag back into it. He was officially having a mind-freak of a day. He looked up to see the note about Shylock and Spencer, screwed up his eyes trying to make sense of everything, and ran his hand through his dirty blond hair. As he did, he touched his forehead and flinched, sucking in his breath in pain.

Yep, that would be the library-door injury. Oops.

He looked at the note again, rereading the line about his head. David hugged himself with his arms, then slammed his locker.

Like that would shut a door on the weirdness and make it melt away.

David stood, staring at the closed, gray, graffitied door for a few seconds more, then bolted down the corridor and out onto the street.

"Do you think he'll be okay?" I asked. Damn! There was definitely a hint of giving-a-crap in my voice. After all the stuff he'd pulled, why wasn't I done with that?

"*Do you think he'll be okay?*" Tess mimicked back at me. She rolled her eyes. "Feldman, just when I thought you were getting a backbone . . ."

"David will be fine," Nancy cut in. "He's going to be disoriented, sure. We have just stolen a day of his life. It's way, way longer than a routine possession."

"That is nothing compared to all the time you wasted on him, Charlotte, so don't feel bad." Lorna gave my shoulders a little squeeze. Did I mention that I loved her?

"He'll just put it down to overtiredness or sunstroke," Nancy added authoritatively.

"There is no sun today, Nancy. It's raining out," Lorna pointed out.

"Oh well." Nancy shrugged and ported home.

As she did, a slight breeze blew up the hallway. A Halloween dance poster fell off the wall and dropped onto the floor in front of us with a swoosh.

"The dance is tomorrow night," Lorna said. "October thirty-first: it's almost your deathiversary."

Great. Bring out the streamers and balloons.

Chapter 24

I PORTED BACK TO THE ATTESA STEPS, KNOWING the others would have gone straight into HHQ. They'd probably assume I'd made the rookie mistake of misfiring myself and would catch up with them soon.

I wanted things that way. That was *my* plan.

I'd never been the Garbo gimme-space type (well, unless Mom was asking for a play-by-play of my day the second my schoolbag hit the floor). But right now, I just wanted a few minutes alone. Without Nancy instructing or Tess bitching or Lorna fussing with her hair.

I considered walking over into Washington Square, but from the Attesa steps, I could see there were a ton of dogs in the exercise run, excitedly yapping away. I had enough noise in my head. I didn't need any more. Instead I sat down on the gray stone and tucked my knees up to my chin.

The more I tried to zone out, the more worried I felt. Before my death, my pulse would have been racing as I thought through everything. Fat chance of that now. Instead all I had left was this low-level panic, where I couldn't pinpoint exactly which of the insanely hideous events of the last week was upsetting me the most.

It was like that feeling you have when you get to school and wonder if you've left your straightening irons on and they're going to burn down your parents' apartment, or if there's a test you haven't prepared for.

I let my head drop forward and massaged my temples with my fingers. Like that would help.

Through the window below, I could hear Nancy talking to Lorna. Well, more *at* than *to*. Even though I couldn't make out whole sentences, the tone of Nancy's voice told me everything I needed to know: She was debriefing her sidekick (she'd never talk to Tess like that), figuring out what conclusions they could draw from today, hypothesizing what the Agency should do next.

I could picture what each of them was doing without even peeking in. Lorna would be good-naturedly nodding along, but actually fantasizing about what she'd wear to a Halloween dance if she got the chance. Nancy would be writing *Brian* on the blackboard, then scholarly crossing his name out, then chewing on the end of a red piece of chalk.

And me? I was out here wondering what I was going to do with the rest of my death.

I'd seen enough bad cop shows. I knew that time was running out. The longer a murder went unsolved, the harder it became to crack. And I'd been dead five days and counting. By the time the trees in the park lost their leaves, I'd be nothing more than a cold case. Filed away by the Agency in one of Nancy's dusty cabinets, while newer dead girls with solvable murders checked into the hotel—and, like Tess, I'd have to stand by and wonder what made them so special that they could find their Key when mine was missing.

I sighed. Maybe I needed to focus on the positives instead. Was being here—in this world—really so bad? There were plenty of reasons to be glad I was dead. I'd never have to pay taxes, work a job I hated, grow old and wrinkly.

I forced a smile. It was better to be glass half full. Besides, maybe Lorna and Nancy were right to believe Tess when it came to the Big Red Door. Who knew what was on the Other Side anyhow? It might be all fire and brimstone.

A couple of kids ran by in pristine private-school uniforms holding their books in their hands. See, I'd never have to fail an exam again, either.

And if I did have to stay in one place forever, New York wasn't such a bad city to be shipwrecked in. What if I'd been murdered when I was visiting my grandmother upstate in her tiny one-bar town—they didn't even have a Whole Foods there. Not that I could eat Whole Foods anymore. But the point was that, in some places, there was zero to do. Nada. And I was not dead in one of them. There were a load of museums in New York I'd never even set foot inside, much less explored. And what about my favorite art galleries? And all their new exhibits? The books I hadn't read, and the bands whose (non-Brooklyn) concerts I could just sneak into—now I never needed to pay for tickets or get my parents' permission again.

I had so much to look forward to. So why did it still feel like my life was over?

Maybe because it was.

"Plotting how you're going to use your special powers to take down Manhattan, Ghostgirl?" Ed asked.

What was it with him and the sneaking-up thing?

Edison sat down on the step next to me. I looked around to check that Lorna and the others were still inside. I didn't need another interrogation about what was up with me and Ed today. It wasn't like I'd gotten a handle on what our friendship meant myself.

"Ghostgirl, superhero of the next world," Ed singsonged and waved his fingers in my face to get my attention. "Come on, talk to me. Maybe I can help. For a start, if you're thinking of storming the city via an army of sewer ghouls, I can tell you right now that that is a bad idea. I tried it back in '91 and—me?—I'm still here. Powerless."

Despite myself, I smiled.

"That's better," Ed said, returning my grin.

We sat in silence for the longest time. When I'd been alive, I'd felt kinda awkward with David if we didn't talk. Like I wasn't

275

entertaining enough or we'd run out of things to say. With Edison, it felt more like the talking was the less comfortable part. The silences were easy. While my head reeled, Ed stared forward, saying nothing. I hoped it was because he knew I needed time, but didn't want me to be alone.

"So what's really up?" he asked eventually.

Honestly? I didn't want to tell the other dead girls what I was thinking. It sounded stupid, complaining and whining about being stuck when they'd been here for so much longer. Sure, Nancy and Lorna acted like they could leave at any time, but could they really? And Tess? She just seemed to be bitter.

But Edison . . . He was so . . . weird and moody and funny and unpredictable. He didn't seem to have an agenda. Unless it was against colored clothes. He'd just tell me to shut up, if he thought I was being pathetic.

"It's my case," I said, concentrating hard on a spot in the street where the pavement had come loose. "It's been almost a week now and I'm—"

"Worried they'll never help you solve it?" Ed finished, nodding his head back in the direction of HHQ's window, where Nancy's voice could still be heard.

"Yes?" I said.

"Look, when I got here, I . . ." Ed stopped himself and mentally changed tack. "The other day, you asked me, does it ever get any easier. I've been thinking about my answer ever since, and I don't think I gave you the right one."

He looked at me intensely, his eyes flickering around my face, searching for something before he went on.

"When I arrived, I decided that life had taught me one very important lesson," he said eventually.

"Which is?"

"Which is that you can't control it." Ed dropped his eyes, took a pack of cigarettes out of his back pocket, and lit one up, shielding the flame with his hand. He really was one of those guys who made smoking look every bit as cool as your mother has always told you it isn't.

"When I was alive, there were all these *things*," he said, taking a long drag and flicking off some nonexistent ash, "these benchmarks or goals or whatever that were all set out for me—school, graduation, maybe college one day if I saved enough. All this *stuff* I had to do or it would be the end of the world."

He slowly blew out a smoke ring. "But the thing is that, when it did come—the end of my world—I had no way of stopping it. There was nothing I could do. No amount of studying harder, or getting in earlier, or flossing twice a day would have stopped it. My life ended and that was that."

Ed gave me a sad smile. "So, mighty Ghostgirl, my sage but simple advice to you is this: Don't sweat it. You couldn't do anything when the worst thing imaginable happened, so don't waste your afterlife worrying now—especially when you don't have a future to worry about anyway." Ed threw his half-smoked cigarette into the street. "If you're meant to go through the Door, you will."

We sat quietly for a minute, as I took what he'd said in.

Without another word, he scooted closer to me. So close our knees were touching. He leaned forward to brush a strand of my hair off my forehead. His hand was just a few centimeters from my face when something flashed in his eyes and he suddenly realized what he was doing—actually about to show me some affection when there was just the two of us here. Ed stopped, mid-sweep. His hand lay shell-shaped and motionless, agonizingly close to my face.

Suddenly I had the weirdest, clearest thought. I wondered if everything he'd done—the watching and the teasing and the scaring and the teaching and the actually opening up—might in some twisted boy way mean that Ed *liked* me.

And what if I might like him back.

I tried to look away, but it was like his eyes had mine in a boy tractor beam. His expression changed. He slowly moved his hand closer to my face, until he was tracing the contours of my cheek with his thumb—making it feel like it was under a heat lamp. Slowly he tilted his face and brought his lips down onto mine. The world whirled. And not in a way that made me feel ill either.

"Ahem!"

There was a loud cough from the Attesa doorway. Lorna bounced down the steps and stood in front of us, eyebrows raised so high they almost disappeared under her blond bangs.

We jumped apart like we'd been wrenched with a crowbar. Lorna stared at Ed strangely as he suddenly realized his hand was still raised in the air where it had been cupping my face. He snapped it back down by his side, turned his face away, and coolly took out another cigarette.

Act natural. She only caught you kissing Ed.

Kissing him. As in: On. The. Lips.

Lorna gave me a look that said she was in no way buying it. "We wondered where you'd gone," she said, pretending like she hadn't just walked in on what she'd just walked in on. What *had* she just walked in on? "Nancy was getting worried you'd misported—she was about to send Tess after you again. Aren't you glad I came looking instead? I said you were probably just taking a moment to yourself."

"Yeah, no need to worry or send out a search party. I was sitting out here, thinking and stuff," I said, refusing to meet her eyes and focusing really hard on that broken piece of asphalt again.

"And *stuff*," Lorna said.

Stuff.

Ed stood up and I felt a gaping space form beside me. I silently willed Lorna to leave and for him to sit back down. I needed to know if I was right about us or as delusional as Brian.

Which was stupid because the last thing I needed right now was another guy to jerk me around. If blue-eyed, straight Bs, mom's-favorite David could be such a fake, just imagine what damage confusing-as-hell Edison could do.

"I guess we should go inside then," I said to Lorna. "Get on with cracking my case. Or something?"

"Very good idea," she said, nodding hard. "Edison, will you be joining us? Or are you off to skulk in some shadows as per?"

"Oh, you know me," he said, "I pick skulking over working every time."

Ed saluted us both by touching an invisible cap, then walked off down the road, deliberately walking through two of the Living as he went. They both stopped, shuddered, and looked a little confused.

"Lorna, we were just—" I started.

Lorna put her hands on her skinny hips. "Charlotte, your *stuff* is none of my business. Though I'm a little surprised you're spending time on *stuff* after our chat yesterday. Just remember what I said about Edison. I don't trust his sudden interest in you. He's not normally like this with newbies and—"

"I know," I said, cutting her off and following her up the steps into the hotel. "You don't think he's being straight with me, but really we've been talking and . . ." I stopped. "You're right, I shouldn't be getting into this," I said, shaking my head.

So why, when I turned back and stared down the street to see Edison still watching me, did I want to run right after him?

Chapter 25

I DIDN'T GO BACK INTO HHQ LIKE LORNA ASKED me to. I couldn't face it. All that talk of clues and suspects and reading case files in the vain hope something would pop up after all this time.

Instead, I waited until Lorna padded down the stairs to the basement and snuck into the elevator. I went up to my room, crawled under the covers and closed my eyes. But of course sleep didn't come. I lay there, watching the shadows in the room lengthen until eventually the entire place was as dark as a room in New York City ever gets.

When I was a kid, Dad made up bedtime stories about the monsters that hid under "naughty girls' beds," ghosts and ghouls that only came out when it got dark. Even though I knew he was teasing, it still scared me enough to sleep with my star lamp on for most of second grade.

Now that I was one of the ghosts I'd been so scared of, the dark wasn't menacing anymore. It was a comfort. A break from the Living and the day and the whatever-the-hell had just happened between me and Edison outside.

I stayed there, lay like that, for hours and hours until slowly the sun came up, like someone turning on a dimmer switch to my room.

There was a gentle knock on my door.

"Charlotte?" Lorna said quietly.

I kept my eyes shut and pretended to be asleep.

"Charlotte," she said, louder this time. I didn't answer, so she bounced down on my bed, putting a hand on my back. "Ghosts can't sleep—remember?—so there's no point pretending you can't hear me."

Crap. I reluctantly rolled over.

"Please come downstairs," she begged. "It's the day of the Halloween dance. Nancy's got a new plan."

Like *that* was going to entice me.

"Is it as good as the one where I possess my ex-boyfriend, then a cheerleader tries to feel me up?" I asked. "Or this time, maybe I could have a ringside seat while my parents cry some more. Or watch while the head cheerleader shouts abuse at my best friend."

"Well . . ."

"That was all I needed to hear," I said, turning back to the window again. I knew I shouldn't be taking this out on Lorna, but now I'd awoken my inner brat, I couldn't put her back in her box.

"Please, Charlotte," Lorna said. "It's not good for you, all this moping up here on your own. I'm worried you're getting depressed."

I turned back over and pulled myself up on my elbow.

"Promise Nancy won't suggest any more possessions," I asked.

"Cross my heart and hope to die—again," Lorna said, a glint in her eye.

"Okay then."

We walked down the stairs to HHQ.

"Even so, we should trail David tonight," Nancy was saying to a bored-looking Tess. "We might not have found any concrete clues yesterday, but it did give us an insight into what was really going on in the high school. Maybe tonight, someone will relax and let out a secret."

So we were back in the land of *might* and *maybe*. Awesome.

The others very deliberately didn't look up when Lorna and I walked in. Which only had me even more convinced they'd been talking about me until they heard our steps on the stairs.

"One teeny problem," Tess said, drumming her fingers on the desk she was sitting on. "It's Halloween, so every kid going to this dumb-ass dance is going to be dressed up as busters or ghosts. How are we going to find David in costume?"

"Easy!" Nancy said. "He's meeting Kristen on the roof of the Sedgwick Hotel at eight p.m.—just before the Scream Queen and King are crowned."

David was *what*?

"And how exactly do you know that?" Lorna asked, her brow furrowed. "Charlotte possessed him all day long yesterday and Kristen didn't come over to talk to him once. We'd have noticed if they had made plans."

Nancy's smile faded. "I just know, okay?" she said.

Because that's an explanation. "Come on, Nancy," I said. "What gives? How do you know that?"

"I know that because I saw this note." Nancy walked over to the map wall and picked up a crumpled piece of paper from the table below it. Her eyes scanned it quickly as she reminded herself what it said, then she passed it to Lorna.

"'*Meet me at the top of the Sedgwick at eight p.m. Don't be late—I don't like to be kept waiting. Kristen*,'" Lorna read aloud. "Oh, and she signed it with three kisses and two pink hearts."

Of course.

"And how long have you known about this rendezvous, Nancy?" I asked. I could not believe she'd kept this from me.

"Not even a day," she said, giving me her best please-forgive-me eyes. "I found it yesterday morning when we were combing David's locker. It was taped to the inside of the door along with his schedule." Nancy shrugged. "I just thought that, seeing as we'd crossed Kristen off the potential murderers list, there was no point mentioning it. After the week you've had, I didn't think you needed another reminder that your boyfriend had moved on." She gave me a small, sad smile.

"Honestly, I'm fine," I said, and for the first time since I'd seen

Kristen and David together, I wasn't totally lying. "As fine as a dead girl can be."

I grabbed the note out of Lorna's hand and smoothed it out. See, I was *fine*. I could read it. It was only a stupid piece of paper that proved David and Kristen were going together tonight. Nothing I didn't know already. Nothing I hadn't heard them set up the other day, outside the locker room. It wasn't as bad as the-thing-I-saw-at-my-funeral. It wasn—

"Hang on," I said. "Kristen didn't write this."

Nancy and Lorna peered at the note over my shoulder.

"She didn't? What do you mean? How do you know?" Nancy asked.

I took the note and sat in one of HHQ's spinny chairs. "Last semester, Mr. Millington decided to 'mix things up' in chem class, so he split up everyone who usually worked together and made me and Kristen lab partners," I said. Six eyes watched me intently, hanging on my every word. "It was a total disaster. You know I'm useless at chem, right? Well, on top of that, Kristen played the diva and refused to mix any of the experiments in case the chemicals got on her hands and ruined her cuticles and—"

"I do see her point," Lorna said. "That's simply vigilant hand care."

"So I got her to do the report part instead, while I handled all the practicals." I ignored Lorna, Nancy-style. "But Kristen's handwriting is heinous—we failed one test just because Mr. M couldn't even read her notes. After that, I had to do all the writing *and* the mixing. I'd know Kristen's messy scrawl anywhere. And this is one trillion percent not it."

Lorna and Nancy looked at me in shocked silence. Even Tess didn't butt in. For once.

"But if that note's not from Kristen, who wrote it?" Nancy said eventually. "Why would somebody fake a note to David? If they wanted to meet up with him that bad, why not ask him outright?"

"Uh-oh." Lorna quietly sat down on HHQ's other spinny chair. "I think I've got it."

We all turned to stare at her expectantly.

"We're so stupid," she said, flipping her blond hair over her left shoulder. "I think we've been on the wrong track all along. Investigating the Tornadoes."

"What do you mean?" I desperately hoped we were finally on to something here. And Lorna wasn't about to send us down another dead end.

Lorna perched on the edge of the seat. Her eyes began to sparkle.

"You know Dolce and Gabbana did underwear as outerwear for Spring/Summer '10, right?" she said.

"No, and even if I did, soo?"

"Underwear as outerwear," Lorna continued. "It's when you wear your lingerie like it's regular clothes." She flipped her hair again.

"What does that have to do with my murder and who wrote this note—you're not making any sense," I said.

"I am!" Lorna promised. "It's a fashion amalogy."

"You mean *analogy*?" Nancy asked.

"That's what I said, a fashion *amalogy*." Lorna sighed in frustration. "D and G, they needed a new direction, some inspiration, so they turned an idea they'd been working on on its head. Instead of looking at the obvious stuff—like skirts and shirts—they focused on what you don't normally see instead, like bras and panties."

"And again, sooo?" I said.

"Sooo, you're not listening: What I mean is that maybe, just maybe, because we've been looking at this investigation in such a straightforward, obvious way, we've actually been missing out what's staring us in the face. Like, instead of looking at the skirts, we need to look at the bra tops."

"Pardon?"

"Instead of investigating the girls who *are* hanging around David, maybe we should be looking at the ones who *aren't*. Stop looking at the obvious suspects."

Tess, Nancy, and I gawked at her.

"You know Lorna may be on to something here," Nancy said eventually.

"Oh no, not you too." Tess rolled her eyes and walked over to the window wall.

"No, listen, all along we've thought that the motivation for Charlotte's murder could be that Charlotte had something her killer wanted—like David," Nancy said. "But then it became obvious that none of the Tornadoes would kill Charlotte to get to him."

"Exactly! See!" Could Lorna *be* any more pleased with herself?

"If Charlotte's murderer is that unhinged, then she's not going to lose her chance with David after everything she's been through to make him single."

"Carry on," I said. Nancy was starting to make sense. Not much. But enough.

"Like, if I'd killed you to get to your boyfriend, the last thing I'd do on the day of your funeral is let your family or the cops see me with my tongue down his throat," Nancy said. "I'd be clever about it; play the long game. I'd sit back for a while, and—just in case anyone was suspicious that you didn't slip under the F train because you're clumsy as—I'd wait, then *bam!* when the heat was off and I knew it was safe, that's when I'd make my move. That's when I'd go after David for myself."

"So what you're essentially saying is that my real killer is out there somewhere, biding her time?"

"YES!" Lorna and Nancy chorused.

"And you think that this fake Kristen note is from my murderer and she's sent it because she's decided tonight's the moment to let David know how she feels?"

"YES!"

"It makes total sense." Nancy took out her spiral notebook and scanned back over the pages like she couldn't believe we'd been so shortsighted. "It must have been so hard for her—all that planning, figuring out how to kill you, then as soon as you were gone, David got involved with the first girl who walked by."

"The first *three* girls," Tess said.

Did she ever miss a chance to be hideous?

"If she did kill you to get to him, your murderer must be mad at David—I would be," Nancy said putting her notebook away. "She must think it's now or never for them. She has to tell David how she feels before he gets serious with one of the Tornadoes—if that's possible—or she'll be back to square one. With the guy she wants, dating a girl who's not her. Again."

"And then we could have another murder on our hands," I said. "But who is *she*?" How could someone have liked David *that* much from afar? And, seriously, how had I not noticed he had a stalker on the loose?

"Nancy, much as I cannot believe I am about to say this, we need a Plan." Lorna jumped off the chair and put her hands on her hips.

"Yes. We need to work out who wrote this note," Nancy said, pacing back and forth. "We could go to the high school and find some test papers—they might have samples of the students' handwriting on them or we could—"

We didn't have time for that. My murderer was meeting David tonight. We had to figure out who she was before then. We needed to know what we were dealing with—and now.

Something was bothering me. There were two things in my head—two memories swirling—but I couldn't make them go together. What was the link? The note, the handwriting—I'd seen something somewhere before, I'd—

"Ohmigod," I groaned, feeling sick to my core. I looked at "Kristen's" note again. Crap, there they were—five of them, five totally obvious clues, staring me in the face like Lorna said.

"The letter," I said. "I think I know who wrote the fake-Kristen letter. We need to get back to the high school quickly, we've missed something *massive*."

Nancy paled.

"If the person I think wrote that letter did, then I'm not sure what she's going to do to David up on the roof. We better get going—before it's too late."

Chapter 26

I PORTED BACK TO THE HIGH SCHOOL AS quickly as my energy would carry me. David's locker was bolted shut. Damn. We had to get into it. We had to see what they said. If I was right, well, I didn't know what to think.

"Nancy, I need you to open this." I pointed at the locker as she materialized next to me with a small *pop!* Lorna and Tess appeared to my left a beat later. It was Saturday and the school was completely deserted. The seniors were probably at home putting the final touches to their costumes for the Halloween party right now. We didn't have much time before David went to meet "Kristen" on the Sedgwick roof.

"The combo is seven-seven-nine-one," I said. "I can move Living objects a few centimeters if I really try, but I don't have the know-how to do anything as complex as punch a code into a lock. You need to help, please. Quickly."

Nancy didn't ask me to explain what I'd just admitted—that I knew a trick she had never taught me. Instead she went to work on the lock. I watched, fascinated, as she concentrated, pushing her power down to her fingers, then carefully moving the dials on the lock into place. After just a few seconds, there was a small click and the lock sprung open. Nancy looked beat. Lorna took over, pulling the bolt off and dragging the metal door open.

"Promise you'll teach me how to do that if I end up sticking around?" I said.

"Deal." Nancy stood back, waiting further instruction from me.

"What are we looking for, Charlotte?" Tess asked. I looked over my shoulder, expecting her to be pulling a snarky face, but she looked genuinely concerned. Maybe it was the idea that she might be getting rid of me soon, but Tess hadn't been mean to me for at least thirty seconds. Weird.

I stuck my head into the locker. It was seven p.m.—dark at this time of year—and there were no lights on in the hallways.

"If I could see what I was doing, I'd be looking for those envelopes—the sky-blue ones we found the other day," I said. "There was a stack of them. Nancy held them up. Then we got distracted by Lorna finding the hair straighteners and . . ."

Nancy clicked her fingers and the lightbulb above our heads flashed on, flooding the space around us with light. I looked at her in disbelief.

"Oh, come on, Charlotte, you can't have been dead for as long as me and not have learned a few neat tricks," she said. "How do you think poltergeists do it?"

Cool. Maybe I should have studied my copy of the Rules after all.

Tess was rustling around in David's locker now, turning over pieces of garbage, paper, books . . . "Where are they?" she asked. "Nancy so had them. I saw her and . . . Aha! Here you go."

Tess pulled the handful of blue envelopes out of a pile of mess and held them up. "Are these what you mean?" she asked.

"Yes!" They were exactly what we were looking for. The key to my Key.

"I recognize those—they're the reminder letters sent to David from the library." Nancy's expression was confused. "Charlotte, you said they would be about his overdue books. What have they got to do with this?"

"Everything," I said. "Look at the writing on the front." Nancy and Lorna stared at the letters in Tess's hands. *For the attention of David Maher* was formally scribbled in that swirly girlie writing with circles above the i's.

"Now look at the letter from 'Kristen' again," I said.

Nancy took the two pieces of paper from Tess and kneeled on the floor. She smoothed them out to compare. I sat down on the tiles next to her.

"Oh," she said suddenly. There we go. Nancy had spotted

them too. "The circles—whoever wrote the Kristen note puts circles above their i's too."

"Exactly," I said. "And, unless I'm mistaken, the handwriting is totally the same, right?"

Nancy nodded. "Whoever wrote the fake Kristen letter wrote all these," I said, pointing at the pile. "And the only person in this school who sends out book reminders is Library Girl."

"What? That little sandy-haired sophomore from the other day?" Tess asked. "She looks so . . . *dull*. Could she really be a killer?"

There was a ripping sound. Lorna concentrated hard as she used her energy to open the first of the envelopes. She pulled out a single piece of light-blue paper, her eyes rounding under the yellow bulb as she started to read.

"What? What does it say?" Nancy asked impatiently.

"'*How I wish you could see the potential, the potential of you and me*,'" Lorna read.

"Wait there's more." Lorna concentrated on the letter.

"*I will possess your heart.*'"

"Weird, it sounds sort of like—"

"Lyrics from a song," I said, finishing Nancy's sentence. I recognized them right away. I'd played them a million times before—walking down Fifth to the subway, as I ran through the park on my way to school, at night when my brain was buzzing and I couldn't sleep.

"She's a fan of Death Cab for Cutie," I said. "Those are the words to their song 'I Will Possess Your Heart.'"

"'I Will Possess Your Heart'?" Lorna said. "If she only knew."

"Let's see the next one." Nancy ripped open the next letter in the library-stamped pile. "We need a little more evidence than just some dotted i's and smitten song lyrics."

She began to read.

"I wish I was special,
You're so very special."

"That's 'Creep' by Radiohead," Tess said. "I'd know it anywhere. They're one of Edison's favorite bands."

"And David's," I said, our eyes clashing. Had Library Girl been following him to know that?

"I've sooo never heard of them, but I can still figure out what those words mean," Lorna said. "Imagine if you'd tried to, like, bare your soul in verse and the guy you made a fool out of yourself for didn't even get it—or acknowledge you. I'd be upset."

"You know what? It's actually kind of a shame that David was too lazy to open her love letters, because he would have gotten a total kick out of playing guess-the-tune," I said. "So these notes, do you think they were written before I . . . died?"

"There are, like, fifteen in here," Nancy said, counting them up. "I think it's fair to assume she must have sent those over a time span longer than the last week. She could have been sending them for months. Getting angrier and angrier the longer David didn't talk to her about them."

What? Like angrier and angrier until she decided enough was enough and she had to push me under the nearest subway train? Awesome. So my boyfriend's laziness could be partly to blame for getting me killed.

"Oh, get a load of the call-the-cops-iness of this one," Lorna said. I read the next note along with her.

"There's no escaping me, my love.
Surrender."

Despite myself, I shuddered.

"Um, do you think she sent that . . ."

"Just after she pushed you onto the track?" Tess said. "The whole 'everything is perfect now' part—could be interpreted that way, couldn't it?"

I shuddered.

"Or it could just be Library Girl saying that she wants David to be happy." Trust Nancy to try to see the sunny side. "Oh, who am I trying to kid? And isn't that the same band whose music your mom was playing at your funeral, Charlotte?"

Tess gave me a smirk. I ripped open the next letter. You didn't have to be a music appreciation professor to figure when she sent this.

"Er, guys," I said. "I think she must have written this one a couple of days ago. You better listen up."

"Been here all along so why can't you see?
You belong with me."

"Oh! Oh! *Finally* one I know!" Lorna said. "It's 'You Belong with Me' by Taylor Swift. I LOVE that song."

"I've always thought there was something latently unsettling about Taylor Swift's music, and now I know what it is," Tess said.

Was it just me, or would Tess actually be kinda fun if she wasn't such a card-carrying nightmare of the Krueger kind?

"Okay, so we think Library Girl sent David these weirdo love-lyric letters," Lorna said, bringing us back down to earth for once. "And it sounds like she's pissed that David doesn't know she's alive. But that doesn't mean she's going to do anything to hurt David tonight."

Nancy walked over to me. "Is that the last letter she sent?" she asked slowly.

"No, there's one more." I waved the final baby blue envelope in the air. "Want me to do the honors?"

"It only seems right," Tess said, meeting my gaze.

I ripped and started to read. But as soon as I had, I sort of wished I'd left the final envelope untouched. I recognized the song from the first line. This was not good. Not good at all. Oh God, she'd chosen another of David's favorite bands, My Chemical Romance. She'd sent him the lyrics to "Dead."

"And if your heart stops beating, I'll be here wondering did you get what you deserve?" I read. I heard my voice shake.

"Uh-oh," Lorna said.

There was a moment of silence as we all took it in.

I looked up at the clock on the wall: Seven thirty p.m. We had to move—fast.

"Dead Girls, we've got thirty minutes to get over to the Sedgwick," I said. "Thirty minutes before David goes up on the roof to meet Library Girl and she tries to convince him one last time that they're meant to be together—"

"And if he says they're not, he 'gets what he deserves,'" Nancy finished.

"We'd better hurry," I said, "because—much as I might have wished for it a week ago—I don't want David checking in to the Attesa tonight."

Chapter 27

"THIS IS BEYOND HUMILIATING," LORNA SAID IN a muffled voice. "Finally, I get to put on a new outfit and you stick me in *this*?"

"Hey, I'm sorry, but they were the only things I could find at such short notice," Nancy said. "It's Halloween, you know. All the good costumes were rented out weeks ago."

"That the best you can do?" Leon Clark called out, cracking up. "My five-year-old brother made a better costume than that. I mean, dudes, did you swipe those off your own beds?"

The other lacrosse guys laughed along with him. The team was decked out in expensive-looking Ghostbuster uniforms, just like the ones the guys in the movie wear: light gray jumpsuits, big black army boots, and proton packs on their backs to blast away spooks. They looked good.

"I hope those things don't work for real or we're in trouble," Tess said, pointing at the proton packs. Whoa, was that a . . . joke?

"Who's under there anyway?" Leon asked, trying to lift up the white sheet covering Nancy.

"No one you know!" she said, bouncing backward to avoid Leon's hand.

The lax boys laughed even harder. "Hey, Leon! Whatcha doing? Get in here!" another Ghostbuster called from over by the Sedgwick Hotel's door. "You're missing the party."

"There's no party until the Leonmeister arrives!" he shouted, turning his back on Nancy and Lorna. He ran over to the other Ghostbuster and gave him a fist bump as the lax boys bundled into the hotel.

"Phew," Nancy said. She and Lorna were standing shyly in a two-girl huddle. Nance had done her best, making sure the white sheets they were wearing went the whole way down to the floor— so that none of the Living would notice these ghosts didn't have (visible) feet. Even so they looked totally lame.

On the way over from Saint Bartholomew's, Nancy came up with a plan. Of course. We were going to split up into two teams. Tess and I were to remain invisible—so, if we needed to, we could follow any of the Living unseen.

Meanwhile she and Lorna were going to go into the party disguised as students—in costumes that the Living could see.

"These outfits are our safety net," Nancy told Lorna. "You

have to remember that we're dealing with the Living here, not one of us. If David is in trouble, we might need to play by their rules to get him out without disturbing them and causing a scene."

"She's right," I said. "What if we need to, say, call the cops on Library Girl? You can only ask one of the students or teachers to do that if you're in disguise. Otherwise, if one of us suddenly materializes as an apparition on the dance floor it'll freak everyone out. They'll be more ghost sightings on the news than questionable anchor hairstyles. And that we don't want, right?"

Standing outside the Sedgwick Hotel now—the old building from *Ghostbusters* where our Halloween dance was taking place tonight—I had to say I was glad I'd got the non-dress-up role.

Two Slimer ghosts—of very differing quality—lolloped by. One kid had rented a massive lime ball of a suit, complete with a flopping pink tongue and ectoplasm that dripped from his arms as he moved. The other was wearing jade skinny jeans and a T-shirt with 'Prepared to be Slimed!' scrawled on the front in green fluoro marker pen.

"Even booger-boy over there looks better than us," Lorna moaned.

"Excuse me, ladies—or is it gents?" a guy said as he walked by Lorna and Nancy. He was all ripped suit trousers, messy shirt, and crooked Clark Kent glasses.

"What's he meant to be?" Lorna asked. "He doesn't look very ghostly to me."

"Oh! I know!" Nancy said. "He's the Keymaster! Haven't you seen the movie?"

We all looked at her blankly. Maybe I needed to send Nancy on a cross-dimensional date with Brian? They seemed to have a lot in common.

"In the movie, one of the Living characters gets possessed by a hellhound and becomes the key to another dimension," she explained. "Well, kinda."

The Keymaster strode straight through me. We both shuddered. David.

"That's him. He's here and dressed as the Keythingy," I said. "We have to go in, follow him. Quick."

We entered the hotel lobby—Lorna and Nancy being careful to use the dark wood revolving door rather than just walk straight through it—and waited in front of a large gold elevator.

"I really hope no one pushes me," Nancy whispered. "They could go straight through us, and all that would be left would be two sheets on the floor."

"Shhh!" I said. "We need to pay attention. See where David's going."

Alanna Acland, dressed as some ghost called Gozer the Gozerian ("That's the movie's bad guy," Nancy whispered. "It's an ancient entity from another dimension.") in a tight white jumpsuit, had spiked up her blond hair, put in red contacts and emptied half an Urban Decay counter on her face. She joined us.

We all clambered into the elevator, the real ghosts being careful to stand at the back so no one touched them. David pressed the button marked Ballroom, where the party was taking place.

As soon as the doors opened, he dissolved into the crowd.

"Charlotte, Tess, follow him!" Nancy said. "We can't lose him. We'll be over here by the refreshment table. Trying not to get noticed."

"There's no chance of that in these costumes," Lorna muttered.

I ran after David, narrowly missing a collision with Drama Drew, who made a very convincing Stay Puft Marshmallow Man. (I suppose he did have access to the entire drama club props store.)

"Hey, David," said a girl in a frayed lace dress and white wig. She looked like something from Elizabethan times. Though her face was painted deathly white and a fake knife—covered in blood—poked out of her back. Cool costume. "How are you? Are you doing okay?"

David turned and his face softened. "Ali, how are you?" he asked.

I did a double take at my old best friend. Oh yes, she *was* in there. She looked so different, older somehow, but still Ali.

"I'm holding up," she said quietly. "I spent the afternoon with Mr. and Mrs. Feldman, actually. They said you haven't been around to see them, which I couldn't believe. They asked how you were doing." She gave David a searching look, which even I could see under all the face paint. "I told them you seemed fine. That you had a lot of new friends helping you out."

David shuffled uncomfortably. "I've been keeping busy," he said, rubbing his cheek and smudging the dirt he'd applied there even more. "But it's been difficult."

"It hasn't looked *that* difficult," Ali said. "If anything it looks like you've been having the time of your life."

For about the fourth time this week, I wished I could hug her.

David flushed, then looked at his watch. It was 7:55.

"Actually Ali, I have to be someplace right now. But let's catch up another time, yeah? Talk about Charlotte, keep her memory alive."

He bolted before Ali could think of a worthy comeback.

"As if," she said to herself, turning on her heel.

"Charlotte, we've got to keep going or we'll lose him in this crowd," Tess said.

She was right. The party was filling up. A girl from my lit class was manning the table where you could vote for the Scream King and Queen. Skeletons and spirits were projected onto the walls, so they flew around above our heads. And there were steaming "traps"—the boxes used to contain caught ghosts—all over the dance floor. Just in front of us, Leon and Jay were pretending to catch a sophomore girl with their proton rays. I seriously hoped they didn't get a date out of that.

I spun back around to find that David had somehow gotten away from us and was heading for the elevator again. There were so many students in front of us. We couldn't get through. There was only one thing for it. I looked at Tess and we exchanged a smile.

"Go!" she shouted.

We ran through the crowd, bashing through my class as we went. Behind us, we left a kinda Mexican wave in our wake of confused kids shivering for a second, then wondering why they'd felt the AC had suddenly turned on. We braked at the elevators, just as David pressed the call button.

"Hey, sexy!" Jamie and Kaitlynnn strutted over, blocking David's way. "You're not leaving already, are you?"

Kaitlynnn was wearing the shortest red dress I'd ever seen, with a tiny little cape on top. Jamie had paired fishnets with a pink princess dress. If princesses didn't believe in wearing skirts, that is.

"Hey," David said, looking them up and down. And back down again. Well, that was where your eyes were drawn to. "You do know the theme is *Ghostbusters*, right? What are you guys dressed as?"

Kaitlynnn smiled smugly. "We thought we'd be different, so I'm Little Dead Riding Hood and J is Ghouliet!"

"Get it?" Jamie asked. "Ghouliet! I'm here looking for my Romeo."

Tess and I groaned. "Could she at least have put a dagger in her breast or carried a bottle of poison for authenticity?" Tess asked.

"You expect that much?" I asked her.

"Well, you both look, um, great," David said. "And I totally want to catch up with you later, but right now I've got to go and find Kristen. Sorry."

"I thought you were picking her up from her town house?" Kaitlynnn asked.

"Come find us later, please," Jamie said with a wink. So much for my rash "confession" putting her off. "I demand a dance."

"Would I let you girls down?" David asked, smiling his most winning smile and pushing the elevator button again.

Creep.

"Nancy!" I shouted in the direction of the refreshment table, where Lorna was suspiciously eyeing Brian as he attacked a bowl of "eye scream." "David's going up onto the roof. If we're not back in fifteen minutes come on up and save us or something."

"Wait!" Nancy called, running over and dragging me away from Tess's earshot. "Charlotte, there's something I've been meaning to talk to you about."

"Nance, this isn't the time. David's about to get in the elevator and—"

"I know, but please, please be careful, Charlotte. Don't use any powers that we don't know are safe."

"Any powers? What do you mean?"

Nancy eyeballed me. "Don't play dumb with me, Charlotte Feldman," she said. "I'm smarter than Kristen and her cronies. I know you've been hanging out with Edison."

"We were just . . ."

"Stop, I've seen him talking to you. Like the other day, when he was by the bleachers." Crap, had everyone noticed that? "And—from your guilty expression—I'm imagining there have been quite a few more meet-ups than that. Look, I know how frustrated you are that finding your Key is taking some time." Nancy looked me straight in the eyes, which would have been more dramatic if she wasn't peering through two hastily cut holes in that old sheet. "I can guess what he was teaching you." Nancy sighed. "There's a reason I haven't told you about certain things, Charlotte. They might not technically be illegal, but they're not covered in the Rules for a reason—not every ghost can handle them. Please remember that there could be repercussions."

David hit the button again.

"Nance, you have to trust me on this," I said, keeping my eyes on David. "I won't do anything stupid. But if it comes to a matter of life or death—well, I can't promise I won't do anything. I'm sorry."

The elevator door was opening. David was getting in.

"Fine," she said in a tight little voice. "I trust you, but please be safe. We're here to call on the Living for help if you need us."

"I know. And thanks," I said, running over to Tess.

The doors were shutting. We had to move.

"Here we go," she said. "Let's bring home your Key."

We jumped through the doors.

The last thing I saw as they closed was a small ghost walking slowly across the room, shaking her head every step of the way.

Chapter 28

BONG, BONG, BONG, BONG, BONG, BONG, bong, bong...

The bells in Saint Bartholomew's Church echoed around the city as David stepped out of the elevator. Eight p.m.

"Showtime," Tess said.

"Kristen?" David called out into the darkness. "You up here, you crazy girl? What's with all the notes and the mystery? I could have just picked you up in a cab like everyone else."

The roof was silent but for the noises of the city below. We were nine stories up, but that was barely kneeling in New York terms.

"Kinda claustrophobic up here, isn't it?" Tess said, looking around. For once I totally agreed with her. It was suffocating.

Our eyes began to adjust to the light, which was only coming from the glare of the buildings around us. There were a couple of old broken tables up here and some rain-rusted chairs. Overgrown plants dominated one corner of the space. The roof didn't look like it was hotel-guest ready. It felt more like a disused scrap yard than somewhere you wanted to hang out.

"It looks like no one's been up here for months," I whispered to Tess.

"Which, at the risk of sounding like Nancy Bossy Pants, isn't exactly making me relax," she said.

David must really have wanted to see Kristen. Because if I'd been him, I would have turned right around.

I scanned the roof. Dead girls and ex-boyfriends aside, I couldn't see anyone else up here. But then, I couldn't see a whole lot.

"Maybe Library Girl's just playing a trick on David, to get him back for not noticing her or opening her letters?" I said.

"Charlotte, if she's the one who pushed you, I think that's about as likely as Ed not using sarcasm as a defense mechanism." Tess walked to the edge of the roof and looked down at the street below.

I wasn't sure I'd heard Tess use his nickname before. The way she did was different from how she talked about Lorna or Nancy. She sounded less . . . neutral.

"Edison *is* kinda difficult to figure out." I opened my mouth before I could stop the words escaping and instantly regretted them. I hardly dared make eye contact with Tess.

A strange look passed over her face. Tess turned and sat on

the roof's edge, swinging her feet over the side. I wondered what would happen if she slipped and fell. Nothing could hurt her now, but would she scream? Or calmly fall to the concrete below, then pick herself back up again, like something from an old *Road Runner* cartoon. I wondered if the sidewalk would stop her. Or if she'd fall straight through it and down into the subway and sewers underneath.

"Do you want to figure him out?" Tess kept her face turned away from me.

I felt myself blush in the darkness. I hoped she wouldn't whip around and see.

"No, it's-it's not that," I said, stuttering. "It's just that it's strange, him living with us in the hotel, but not being part of the Agency. I wonder what he does with his time. That's all." I tried to make my voice sound confident and final. Like that was it. Mild curiosity. Conversation over.

"He was here when I got to the Attesa, you know?" Tess said, looking out into the night. There were no lights on in the office just below us. It made the building look sad and empty. "We're the two longest-serving residents."

I kept quiet and let Tess carry on talking. Was this why Nancy had put her on my team? To make us talk and maybe she'd see that I wasn't so bad after all.

"If things go your way tonight, you could be gone—you'll never know what this is like," she said. "Some people never go over to the Other Side because they don't want to, but some of us aren't lucky enough to find our own Keys." She looked back at me with an exhausted expression in her eyes.

"Then let's make sure Charlotte isn't one of them, shall we?" Edison ported onto the roof next to me with a *pop!* and half smiled. "What, you really thought I was gonna miss the big showdown?"

There was a screeching sound as the fire-escape door creaked open. Tess jumped up. Light, watchful footsteps echoed on the metal steps.

"Kristen? Is that you?" David called into the darkness.

Step by step, more and more of the person who'd just opened the door came into view. Her sandy hair caught the moonlight as she climbed up onto the roof.

"You're not Kristen," David said unnecessarily.

"You're going to wish I was," she said as the fire door slammed below her.

Chapter 29

"SORRY, WHO ARE YOU?" DAVID ASKED AS LIBRARY Girl walked across the roof toward him. She wore a simple black knee-length dress and tan wedges. She'd carefully tied back her hair in a ponytail, but already wisps of sandy curls were breaking free. She'd even put on some mascara. Library Girl must have been preparing for this moment all day. For the first time—seeing her in the moonlight instead of buttoned up and scowling in the library stacks—I noticed that she was actually really pretty.

Pretty unhinged?

Her face fell. "Who am I? Who am *I*? This is *exactly* what I'm talking about," she muttered to herself. "After everything I've done." She stopped, realized she was rambling and focused on David again with an intense smile. "Come on, do you really still have no idea who I am, David?"

"Um, no," David said, looking at her as if she were potentially a psychiatrist's-couch escapee. "I'm up here waiting for someone special, actually," he said. "There's this girl and we're sort of dating. Well, she, like, *really* wants us to be. She'll be along any second, so you might want to leave before then—I think she's got something big planned, so we'll need some alone time."

How rude.

"The girl you're 'sort of dating'?" Library Girl said. Her smile faded. "How can you be 'sort of dating' someone? What's wrong with you? Your girlfriend only died last week and already you've 'sort of' replaced her? You seemed so into Charlotte every time I saw you together in the library."

David clicked his fingers in the air. "That's where I've seen you," he said. "You're that sophomore who works in the library! I remember you now."

"You do?" she said, her voice switching back to happy mode.

"Yeah, you're always in there, like a busy little bookworm."

She shook her head indignantly. More curls escaped. "A *what*?" she asked, upset.

"I mean, you must work real hard in there," David backtracked. "I've never even seen you in the hallway or the cafeteria."

"Maybe that's because you weren't looking hard enough," she said. "Maybe I've been in all those places all along." She put her hands behind her back and swung her hips.

"Look, it's nice to meet you properly and all, but my date, Kristen, you know, the head cheerleader, she's going to be here any second." David looked at his watch.

"Really?" Library Girl asked. "Are you sure about that?"

David nodded like a dumb puppy. Library Girl walked over to the roof edge where Tess, Edison, and I were standing. She was a couple of inches shorter than me, with a birdlike build. Could my murderer really look like this?

"And how do you know? What did Kristen do? Leave a note in your locker asking you to meet her up here?"

"Yeah, she did actually," David said, starting to look confused.

"Before the Scream King and Queen were announced?"

"Yes, but how do you know—"

"And was it on pink notepaper, like this?" She pulled an identical piece out of her pocket.

She had David's full attention now.

"With little kisses and hugs under her name?" Library Girl asked.

"Yes, but . . ." Somewhere inside David's head the cogs crunched into place.

"The note—it wasn't from Kristen, was it?" Watch out, David was up to speed now. "It was from you." He pushed his dirty blond bangs off his face. I noticed a purple bruise where the library door had hit. "But why? I've never really spoken to you before. Why did you pretend to be Kristen to get me up here?"

Library Girl sighed and sat daintily on the edge of the roof beside Tess. Ed shot me a WTF? look. I felt like I was part of some weird open-air play—the kind that takes place around the audience. How would I know when I heard my cue?

"But David, you and me, we go way back," she said. "Don't you remember me at all?" She swung her feet back and forth, banging her heels on the brick. It was weird to see her out of our usual uniform of plaid skirt and blazer. "We were at summer camp together in seventh grade, and we slow danced to Maroon Five. We had that connection."

Now David was really looking at her like she was not playing with a full deck.

"It was only one dance, but you asked me my name. I thought, there and then, that you were the cutest boy I'd ever seen." She smiled at the memory.

"Whoa," Edison whispered.

"Um, I remember camp and the dance, but I don't remember Maroon Five and I don't remember you," David said. "I'm really sorry, but it was, like, five years ago. And I sometimes have trouble remembering what I had for dinner last night." He smiled apologetically.

Library Girl ignored him and continued her story. "Then I moved schools—to one downtown—and you stayed on the Upper East Side. To be honest, I thought I'd never see you again. I mean, how many kids live in Manhattan? I can go weeks without going to my old neighborhood. I lost contact with a lot of my friends from that time. So imagine how excited I was when—all these years later—you transferred to Saint Bartholomew! I could tell it was you right away. I'd know those sea-blue eyes of yours anywhere."

Okay, so now she was creeping me out too.

"And that's when I knew," she said, looking up at him now. "That's when I knew we were meant to be: It was *fate*."

"Um, there's obviously been a mix-up," David said, trying to back toward the stairs and way away from the psycho sophomore. "Maybe I should go downstairs. Kristen's gonna be pissed if I miss the Scream King crowning. And if you've ever seen her mad, you know we don't want *that* on our hands."

"Oh, I took care of her already." Library Girl jumped off the wall and ran to block David's path. "I left Kristen a little locker note too: one telling her you'd pick her up from her place at eight fifteen." She looked at her watch and smiled. "Which would be around about now. I guess she's waiting there, all alone. Boo hoo. The thing is, it's taken me so long to get this time on my own with you, David," she said quietly. "I didn't want Kristen popping up and ruining it."

"And I *have* tried to talk to you before," she said. David was not getting away from her and down those stairs. "Like that time Camels on the Freeway played amateur night at Arlene's—I came up to you after that and said how great I thought they were."

"You did?" David asked, momentarily distracted simply because someone had heard of his stupid band.

"Or when you had that lit essay on Fitzgerald due. You spent hours in the library researching it, and I saved all those extra books for you to make sure you got a good grade."

If what she was saying wasn't so goddamn stalker, it might have been kinda cute.

"And when we walked past each other in Rockefeller Plaza all those times on your way to class, I always waved hello."

"Really?" David was looking creeped out again. As Library Girl was speaking, she'd edged a few steps closer to him. He backed away even more—not realizing he was heading away from the stairs and toward the other end of the roof.

"Is it just me, or is she *Girl, Interrupted* wacko?" Tess asked. "Like, worse than all the cheerleaders put together?"

I couldn't say anything. The words were stuck somewhere between my brain and my tongue.

"And we have so much in common," she said. "Emily Dickinson's my favorite poet too. I know you love her because you've kept her book out even though you're racking up fines on it every day. I adore the Clash and the Stones and Nirvana. Every time I see you in a new band shirt, it's like you've looked on my iPod and worn it especially for me. So I thought, I have to get David on his own so I can finally talk to him—we're made for each other. I figured you hadn't read my letters because they were in library envelopes. So that's why I planted the Kristen note in your locker. To get your attention. To get you up here."

"Oookay," David said, taking another step away from her— and another one closer to the edge. Why wasn't he looking where he was going? "I'm really glad you did, because it's been super-nice catching up, but I think we should get back to the party now. Though you're not dressed for it, are you?" He motioned down to her black dress. "Maybe we could talk another time? Like when I stop by the library maybe?"

Library Girl turned her back to him. Her shoulders slumped. "Maybe we could talk? Maybe you could stop by? Is that all I get? A *maybe*? I really hoped it wouldn't come to this," she said under her breath.

Uh-oh.

Library Girl whirled around. Her eyes weren't soft anymore, they were blazing.

"I think someone just flipped the switch." Edison had a worried look on his face I'd never seen before.

"You see, David, I really hoped this would work out between us. But now I'm not so sure. And I've come too far to let you just go back down those stairs and make out with some reality-TV star wannabe, after all the work I've put in." She took two more steps toward him. David was way too close to the edge of the roof for comfort.

Tiny as she was, Library Girl stared him down. "I'm sorry . . . ," she said, and pushed David in the stomach so hard that he fell backward onto the concrete floor, less than a hand's span from the nine-story drop. She was strong for such a little thing.

"But if you don't want to be with me, I don't want you to be with anybody else." She raised her arm, ready to lunge again. Oh God, she had a knife. David was so shocked, he couldn't get up.

"Charlotte, if you don't want Blondie sharing your room in the Attesa, we need to do something—and fast," Tess said, shaking me out of my trance.

This was it. This was my cue. I looked from the psycho

sophomore to David and back again. He might have hurt me more than anyone else in my entire death, but I didn't want him to be murdered too. I had to do something.

And that's when the burning started. In my toes, up my legs, my belly, my arms, my shoulders, until my head felt as if it were on fire. A familiar pink glow began to illuminate the rooftop. But it wasn't a light. It was me.

David yelped. "Charlotte? B-But you're, you're . . . ," he stuttered. "This has to be a joke. A sick Halloween joke." He looked desperately around the roof. "Are you in on this?" he asked Library Girl. "Who's doing this? Make it stop, *please*."

"It's no joke, David," I said, raising my arms and walking toward him, to show that I was a real ghost and not just a light show like the ones zooming around the ballroom below. Was it wrong to be kinda happy that he looked so terrified?

"I'm here to avenge my death," I said slowly and deliberately. "I can't rest until I know who killed me. I have to make my murderer pay."

"Murderer?" David said. His face was even whiter than mine. "But I thought you fell under the F train. Charlotte, I thought you tripped."

Library Girl dropped the knife and stumbled away from David, like a drunk person. She could hardly walk. She couldn't take her eyes off me or stop shaking. Suddenly I got what the expression "you look like you've seen a ghost" meant. Not so brave now are you?

I motioned for Tess and Ed to Jab David away from the edge of certain death. They stood on either side of him and gave my confused ex a couple of less-than-gentle pushes to the safety of the center of the roof.

I turned to Library Girl, who was sitting in a crumpled heap on the floor, shaking. Really, was she going to give in this easily?

"You!" I said, pointing at her and floating over. "I am here for YOU."

Too much?

"Please." Her whole body quivered like a frightened animal's. "Please don't hurt me. I'll do anything. Anything you want. Just don't push me over the edge. Don't kill me. There's so much more I want to do with my life. It can't end now."

I crouched down, so I was on eye level with her. I wanted her to look at my face. Right now, I was so mad, I could hardly speak.

"You know what? There are hundreds of things I've never done," I said. "And I can never do them now."

Her eyes slowly rose up my face until they finally found the courage to meet mine.

"I never visited another country, or stayed out past eleven," I said. "I didn't get to watch the sun rise, or drink a cocktail that's been properly mixed for me by a barman, instead of Ali swiping stuff from my parents' liquor cabinet. I won't get to see my friends graduate. I'll never dance at my prom. I can't ask my mom for advice when things get tough, and I'll never give my dad another hug. I'll never download the Arctics' next album or wear something other than my horrible school uniform again." I felt my voice catch. "I was only sixteen—*sixteen*—I had everything to live for. But I didn't get to live my life. So you tell me: Why should I let you live yours?"

Library Girl's eyes welled and she began to sob. Whatever. Her waterworks were not going to get to me.

"Don't talk to me about missing out," I said. "Not when someone took my life before it had even begun." I was beyond angry now. "All I want from you is the truth. I need to know what happened to me."

Her eyes were defeated and red. "I didn't have anything against you as a person, Charlotte," she started. "But I knew he would never notice me with you here."

"Ladies and gentlemen, we may have just cracked young Feldman's case," said Tess. Edison motioned for her to shhh.

"Go on," I said. Oh God, I thought.

"There was a day, weeks before you died . . . David came into the library," she said. "He gave me the biggest smile." She actually grinned herself at the memory, through the shakes. "I thought, finally, *finally*, after all these years, David knows who I am. I'd tried so hard to get his attention, but it was like I was invisible."

"I know the feeling," Tess said.

"I knew that if I could just get him to talk to me, he'd realize we were meant to be together," she said. "And now he'd noticed me—it was my time. So while he was studying, I went over to say hello." Her face clouded over. She looked over at David, who sat crumpled in the center of the roof. "But by then you had snuck in. David was sitting with you, and you guys were"—she looked disgusted—"*making out.* I told you to stop, threatened you with calling a teacher and getting a detention, but neither of you seemed to care. You carried on kissing. And when you walked out of the library, you were holding hands. That was when I knew—if I was going to get to him—I had to get you out of the way."

I'd been waiting seven days to hear someone say those words— every night when the world was asleep, I lay there agonizing about who my murderer could be—but now that Library Girl was saying them, they didn't feel like the prize I expected. Instead it was like I was having to deal with my death all over again.

"Go on," I said slowly.

Library Girl sat upright. "I started following you, every day for a couple of weeks . . ."

How hadn't I seen her? Why hadn't I turned around or caught her out of the corner of my eye. I guess that, even if I had, I wouldn't have noticed her. What she said was true: Compared with the Tornadoes or the drama club or even Brian and his sugar-sandwich-induced bulk, she was one of the invisible people.

"It wasn't difficult." She twisted a stray curl around her finger. "You always took the same route home. At first I didn't know what I was going to do to you. I thought about putting pills in your coffee—you always had a cup of that in your hand—

but then I figured that they'd do an autopsy and the cops would pick up the drugs and know it was murder. And I couldn't have that. How could I get close to David if I was in jail?"

My glow faded a little. My energy was shrinking. I hadn't won even if her words gave me my Key. It was horrible to hear this.

"I knew I had to make it look like an accident so that no one would be suspicious," she said. "But what kind of accident could it be? Then I saw you and David after class one day. You were walking across the road and you tripped..."

"I remember it. I grabbed your arm." David's voice was taut. I'd almost forgotten he was here.

"You were both giggling—laughing at your clumsiness—while he teased you about how that happened all the time and how you would hurt yourself one of these days if he wasn't there to catch you when you fell. And that was all I needed to know. I had my method, my alibi. I thought about pushing you under a cab, but that might not have killed you." She shuddered. "What if you'd just been injured and David spent the rest of his life caring for you, like Cary Grant in *An Affair to Remember*? I'd never get between you then."

I hated how much she'd thought this through.

"No, a cab wouldn't do. I needed something faster. Something heavier. Something fatal. Like a subway train." Library Girl smiled at her own ingenuity. "So I waited until you were traveling home on your own that day. It helped that you were wearing those stupid high-heeled boots that you couldn't walk in." She looked at my feet, noticing for the first time that I was wearing them still now.

She lifted her eyes back up to mine; they were cold now, expressionless. I knew then for sure, before she even admitted it, that she'd done it, she was the one.

"Then I got right behind you, on that crowded platform, and when the train came in, I pushed. And that's when you—"

I screamed. A horrible, loud, last-noise-on-earth scream. It was a noise I'd only made once before. Then. For a second I was back there, back on the platform. As the wind sucked back my hair. The F train chugged. My foot felt wet. Headlights in the dark. A sharp push. Someone screamed. Heat. Then nothing. Until I came to and saw Nancy's face.

Until I realized my life was over.

I looked over at Edison. I forgot the platform, the confusion, and Nancy. Instead I remembered what he'd taught me at the river. I remembered the lights dancing on the water, the gulls bobbing up and down, the silence of the night, and everything he said. His most important lesson of all.

The burning inside me began to change. All my pain and hurt and anger—at Library Girl and Kristen and Jamie and Kaitlynnn and the Blondes and David and even Tess—traveled down inside of me, until I wondered if there was anything left.

Then it started to rise.

I got hotter and hotter and hotter until I thought I was burning. The light around me turned from pink to a toxic neon green. Ectoplasm began to drip from my arms. I felt my spirit grow and rise off the roof.

This wasn't apparition, this was different. I was stronger than I'd ever been.

And I was going to take this bitch down.

Chapter 30

"YOU ARE MY MURDERER." MY VOICE WAS louder than before. It echoed around the skyscrapers, like thunder in a summer storm. "What gave you the right to steal my future?"

I was at least nine feet tall. I raised my arms high and green streams of light shot out of my palms, the lime glow reflecting in the windows of the buildings around us. David let out a whimper and covered his eyes. I loomed over Library Girl, my ectoplasm dripping on her freshly laundered dress.

"The cops might not know what you did," I said, "but I do, and I am going to make you pay."

Library Girl said nothing. She just sat in the same upright position, gently quivering.

"Um, Charlotte," Tess said, bending down and waving an apparited hand in front of Library Girl's face. "You can stop with the second-rate Stephen King script regurgitation. You got her confession. Plus I think you may have finished her off already."

"What?" I boomed.

"She seems to be in a catatonic state of shock." Tess Jabbed Library Girl's arm, but she didn't react. "I think you've scared her cuckoo."

Oh.

I floated down to her level. Library Girl's eyes were glassy, her pupils unmoving. The only sign she was still alive was the gentle rising and falling of her chest and the occasional blink. I'd made her pay all right. The entrance fee to the nearest psychiatric unit.

"Is she going to snap out of this?" I asked. "Should I feel bad?"

"Bad?" Edison asked. "She KILLED you, Charlotte. She just admitted it. And you're worried about her future mental health?"

There was a sob from the other side of the roof. David. I had to talk to him. I had things I needed to say. I looked over at Edison, who was watching me intently, his expression as impossible to read as ever. This wasn't a situation *Seventeen* magazine prepared you for: what to do when you're haunting your ex, but the guy you've just kissed has ported there too.

I'd deal with Edison later. This might be the only chance I had to talk with David. I floated from Library Girl to where David was sitting. He jumped back.

"Charlotte, I-I-I can't believe it," he stuttered.

Was he on the verge of tears? I hoped so. He looked so small and helpless. My anger cooled and my shape shifted from zombie to apparition again, the glow around me switching from emerald to rose. I looked more like the old Charlotte now. The one he used to love.

"I can't believe the little sophomore from the library *murdered* you because she liked *me*." He shook his head in disbelief, his bangs falling back over his eyes. "This is all my fault—I should have realized the effect I have on women *years* ago."

There was a time when I thought he was the hottest, cutest, coolest guy ever. And I would have let him get away with a comment like that. But not anymore.

"Yes, it is your fault," I said. "David, everything is. You owe me. Big-time. And not just for saving your life back there. But for getting hot and heavy with half the school before I'd been dead for a week."

"You know about that?" he said with a small sniff.

I nodded, unable to hide the fact that I was still, really, majorly bothered about it.

"The truth is I missed you. And Kristen was just there. She was comforting me. Nothing happened, Charlotte, honest."

"Oh, please," I said, sinking down to face him. "David, I might be dead, but I am not stupid. I've been watching you. I know everything—and every*one*—you have done over the last seven days. I know about Kristen in the chapel and Jamie in your room and Kaitlynnn in the hallway and . . ."

David's eyes were wide. "You saw all *that*?"

"Oh yeah and sooo much more." My hands found their way to my hips. "I'm a ghost, David, it's, like, my job to spy on the

Living." I took a second and tried to calm down.

"Honestly, this is me you're talking to now, so no more BS," I said firmly. "Why did you do it? We were choosing colleges based on how close they were to each other. You were supposed to be my soul mate."

David bowed his head.

"The way you've acted . . . ," I said, shaking mine, "I need to know: Did you ever give a shit about me in the first place?"

I looked at him, dreading yet desperately waiting for his answer. And totally aware that Edison was watching us closely all the time.

"Yes, of course I did. Please don't ever think that I didn't care for you. I love you."

David tried to touch my arm, but his hand went right through it. He sucked in his breath.

"I loved being with you," he said, "but our whole thing was that we got each other so much, we didn't care about what anyone else thought of us. You were like no other girl I'd ever met. You weren't into malls or matching your nail polish to your hair band or whatever. When we were together we talked about *stuff*. Like bands and authors and artists. Important stuff."

God, was it wrong to be hating old Living me right now? Because David kinda made her sound like a total jerk. No wonder Ali didn't want to be around us 24/7.

"Then you died and I was devastated." He sighed. "And I guess I didn't know who I was anymore without you. I couldn't be David without Charlotte. Not the David you loved anyway. So I started to care what other people thought."

He lifted his head to look at me. "Then, just when I was feeling super-low, all these girls who had never noticed me before wanted to be *with* me. It was like nothing I'd ever felt before. I guess I got a little carried away . . ."

It was strange looking into his eyes and having him look back. I'd spent so much of my death imagining him staring at me the way he was now. But it didn't feel like it used to. Too much had changed. I'd changed. And the only thing I was certain of was that I could never go back.

I saw Edison shake his head in disgust.

"Imagine if the tables were turned," David said, changing tack. "What if some psycho freshman had fallen for you and pushed *me* under the F train because he couldn't stand to see us together. Then imagine if, while you were hurting more than you'd ever hurt before, the hottest guys in the school—like Leon and Martin and Jay—started asking you out. Can you honestly say you wouldn't have acted exactly the same way as I did?"

I looked into David's big blue pleading eyes. And I thought about what he'd just said.

For, oh, about half a second.

"Yes, I can," I said with total certainty.

David flinched.

"You can go back to that party now, David. And you can get your Scream King crown, dance with Kristen, and wait for

331

Kaitlynnn and Jamie to paw you the second her back's turned. You can finish high school being Mr. Popularity. When you run out of girls in Manhattan, you can go to college and find a whole heap of new muppets there. But I want you to remember one thing: As long as I am in this dimension, I will never forget the way you have treated me. And I—" I said, about to launch into another verbal attack.

Oww! I doubled over in agony, then snapped back up again. What was *that*? Something was wrong. Something peculiar was happening to this world.

David was looking at me strangely. Like, even more strangely than he had when I'd been zombiefied. The pain started again, burning through me, then just as quickly ebbing away. The roof was wiggling. And the buildings around us, they weren't standing at attention anymore. They were leaning toward me. Closing in.

I sat down on the concrete floor trying to steady myself. I felt someone port next to me. Was it Ed? Tess? I couldn't tell. Everything was blurry.

"Charlotte?" David asked, looking around. "Where did you go? You can't just disappear. I need to talk to you. I have so much to say to you. I . . ."

His voice sounded like it was coming from inside a cupboard. Muffled, like when your mom yells at you to get out of the pool when you're underwater.

I felt hot. And—if I didn't know it was impossible—sweaty. I looked down at my arms. The pink glow had gone, but somehow my hairs were actually standing on end. I might not have done a whole load of extra Rules book study, but I knew *that* should not be happening.

"Ed?" I called out into the blackness, but he didn't answer.

I lay on my back and stared up at the night sky. The Empire State Building swaggered above me as if it were going to tumble in, bringing the Chrysler with it. The whole world was collapsing and there was nothing I could do. It couldn't be ending. It had already ended. So why was I . . .

Then everything went black and still.

All I could hear was silence. And all I could feel was wind in my hair.

Chapter 31

I OPENED MY EYES, SLOWLY, ONE AT A TIME—AND found myself safe and sound in the lobby of the Attesa. With a shiny new key in my right hand. Weird.

Oh. It wasn't just any key, was it? It was *my* Key. Somewhere inside I instinctively knew it. The Key that could take me to where I—like all the other dead girls who'd been lucky enough to leave this planet without having to have to deal with unhinged librarians and bitchy cheerleaders on the way—should rightly be.

"OMG! OMG!" Lorna screamed as she ran over and hugged me so hard she nearly sent me flying through two hotel walls and outside. "I've been so worried about you! We've all been so worried! But you're back! AND. WITH. A. KEY."

Until now, I didn't know ghosts had the vocal ability to talk in that octave.

"OMG! Nancy, Charlotte's got her Key! This is absolutely the height of amazingness! So, so, so this must mean—"

"This must mean that, not only did I haunt a heartfelt confession out of Library Girl," I said, as Lorna bounced up and down in front of me, "Tess and I also saved David from her too. But not before scaring the *life* out of that cheating Class-A douche bag though." Lorna's eyes had grown worryingly wide. "Well, not literally," I added. I didn't want her to misport with excitement. "I'm not *that* bitter. So how did I get back here? The last thing I remember I was up on the roof, then it all went black. And now I'm here. I didn't port myself."

I turned my golden Key over in my hand. So this was the baby that would open the Big Red Door. It had swirls along the handle that matched the ones in the Attesa's lobby and three prongs at the fob end—a long one sandwiched between two shorties. Pretty.

"Your Key pulled you back here after Library Girl confessed and you solved your murder," Nancy said, standing beside me and eyeing it. "They seem to have a few powers apart from those of the usual door-opening variety. You know, it doesn't matter how many times I see one of these things—and I've seen quite a few since we started studying the old case files—"

Lorna sighed loudly.

"It's still so exciting when another pops up," Nancy said. "Can I hold it?"

I handed my Key to her and she stroked the swirls greedily,

then abruptly stopped. "It's lovely, but it doesn't feel right," Nancy said firmly. "When I get mine, it will."

She handed it back to me as if it were a teeny, fragile newborn baby.

"So how did you guys know to split?" I asked.

"Tess came down from the roof and said it was time we left," Lorna said. "The police came. David must have called them, and we saw them taking Library Girl away. I don't know what you said to her, but I don't think she'll be normal again for, like, ever. The Living can deal with her now. I'd totally had enough of watching your heinous classmates try to eat each other's faces, so we ported back here. We didn't even hang around for the crowning of the king and queen."

"I'm surprised you're in such good spirits," Nancy said, looking at me carefully. "Tess was muttering something about Edison getting upset and ditching her on the roof. Did something happen up there?" Nancy gave me a look that said she knew exactly what had happened—and she was not happy about it.

"So when are you going to use it?" Lorna cut in, trying to distract Nancy. If I ever needed a personal pit bull, I was hiring Lorna. "Your Key, I mean."

"I suppose I should use it soon, but . . ." I tried to think straight. After everything that had happened—Library Girl's confession, confronting David—my mind felt like it was operating in a fog. "It's just that, after all the dead ends we've hit over the last few days, I wasn't expecting to find it today. I was starting to wonder if

I'd *ever* find it. And now I have it, I . . . It's not like I need to pack before I leave but . . . When you think about it, I've only been dead for a week. I'm still trying to get my head around that."

I trailed off and gently laid my Key on the low table by the Door, tracing its outline with my pointer finger. It looked so normal, but just being near it made my teeth buzz. I could feel its power. It was almost as if it wanted me to go through the Door as soon as inhumanly possible, so its work was done.

I just wasn't sure I was ready for that yet. I couldn't go back to my Living life, that much I knew. If the last week had taught me anything, it was that there was nothing for me there anymore. But the idea of starting a new one, one that I knew even less about? That terrified me too.

Tess clomped up the HHQ stairs. There was something in her expression that made me feel uneasy and weak.

"Oh, stop messing around with all your existential tormented-teen crap and get an afterlife, Feldman," she said, her eyes flashing. "Just put the metal thing in the little hole in the Door, turn it a bit, and things can get back to normal around here. I'm sure even someone with your limited intelligence can manage that."

So our truce was off then?

"Guys." I ignored her—so, she was bent out of shape about me hanging out with Ed; still, the whole *Heathers* act was t.i.r.e.d.—and focused on Nancy and Lorna instead. "Do you mind if we get some air?"

Nancy scowled. "Charlotte, you are dead. Ghosts don't

need air. Or water. Or food. Or cookie dough ice cream with marshmallows and extra rainbow sprinkles. So going outside to 'get some air,' especially at a crucial moment like this, is a totally pointless exercise and—"

"Nance?" I said. "Can you shut it? For once in your perfectly ordered life? I just want a few minutes to think before I do anything rash. Like moving from one dimension to the other. Or eternally damning myself by accident on the way."

"Right."

Lorna, Nancy, and I walked down the Attesa steps and onto the street.

"Some air," while physiologically useless, was so what I needed. Outside, everything instantly felt better. Night had turned to early morning while my Key had been dragging me back. The city was awake again, people were making their way to work and the sun was playing peekaboo from the top of the park's arch.

When I was alive, autumn was always my favorite time of year: when the city had cooled down enough to eat ice cream without it turning into a shake before it hit your mouth. It suddenly occurred to me that—apart from when I was apparition or getting pulled by my Key—I hadn't felt heat or cold since I'd died. Instead I was always just right, the kind of snuggly warm you get five minutes after you pile into bed.

"Limbo to Charlotte, come in, Charlotte," Nancy said. "Seriously, don't stress. It's perfectly normal to feel this way when you get your Key. We had a guy once who lay with his head under his pillow for *six* weeks before he opened the Big Red Door. He'd get within three steps of it, freak out, and run back to his room. Four other new ghosts went through before he had the guts to do it. You can stay here as long as you like. There's no checkout policy at the Attesa."

I raised an eyebrow at her. "Sorry, bad joke," she said. "What I mean is that you don't have to do anything until you're sure you're ready. Take your time. When it's right to use your Key, it'll feel right. That's what everyone says, anyhow."

I heard a scream behind us and turned to see three college freshmen drunkenly stumbling down the street. They were trying to drag their friend along and, I figured, back to their dorm to sleep it off. So I wasn't the only one who'd had a seriously late night then? I had to use every ounce of my energy to resist the urge to run on over, possess drunk boy, and make him perform a Riverdance, just to freak out his friends.

I smiled to myself. Being a spook was waaaaay more fun than it ought to be.

"Just look at me and Lorna," Nancy said. "I know how I died. And I'm pretty sure that whoever blew up our townhouse at ten p.m. did it thinking my parents were inside. Not many people knew they'd gone to the ballet that night. My dad, well, he's a lawyer and he'd recently made sure some dangerous guys had gone to jail. I'm sure if I dug around it wouldn't take long to figure out which one ordered the hit."

Whoa. "I'm sorry, Nancy," I managed. There was so much I

wanted to tell her but the right words just wouldn't come.

She gave me a small smile. "Don't be. I could get my Key if I really wanted. It's just that I, personally, feel I can do more good by hanging around here for a while. Helping a few more people, you know? The ones who, without the Agency's help, might not get to the Other Side."

"More Dead Girl Detecting, right, Nance?" Lorna said, giving her a playful shoulder nudge.

"No one has to make excuses. I get why you're still here," I said. "You both have your reasons for wanting to stay. And I would not dream of questioning them." I sighed. "Right now I need to figure out what I'm going to do next."

Lorna gave my arm a squeeze. I swapped a smile with her. "I guess, in a way, for three girls who've been murdered in gnarly circumstances, we're pretty lucky," I said. "We all think we can go through the Door someday. Whenever we decide that will be. We haven't given up hope. Not like Miss Bitter in there"—I motioned back inside at Tess—"who seems convinced she's staying here forever, and that gives her a license to be a jerk."

Drunk boy puked his guts up right across the street from where we were standing. Eww. It kinda killed any hope of a moment of quiet reflection.

"Charlotte, can I say something?" Lorna asked.

I nodded. "Of course."

"Um, well, Nancy and I were talking, and we were both saying how—even though you've only been here a few days—we've really loved having you around. It's been way nicer than normal." Lorna gave me a shy smile.

"You're such a natural detective," Nancy said. "The way you thought to go back to those letters in David's locker and sensed that he was in immediate danger. It was brilliant. I would have played it by the book: come back here, done some research into Library Girl, built up a profile of what she was likely to do. If we'd done that, taken the slow-road"—Nancy shuddered—"things might have ended very differently for David."

"Though his murder would have been a cinch to solve," Lorna said, bobbing her head.

Nancy gave Lorna a shocked look. Then—suddenly—the pair of them started giggling. And before I knew it—cheating-boy-slut ex or not—so was I.

"You're fun to have around, Charlotte," Lorna said when she'd composed herself. "Please say you'll stay. For a few days longer at least?"

Fun? The teen queen thought I was *fun*? I'd never been called fun before. I used to think "fun" was lame. "Fun" was for girls who thought Girl Scouts was neat and not a ritual humiliation forced on children by parents who wanted them out of the house.

"You've got eternity on the other side of the Door—what's a few more weeks here?" Lorna said.

"Plus you're a brilliant asset to the Agency," said Nancy, as always, all business. "Much as I hate to admit it, maybe we need someone who's a bit more impetuous than I am around here and isn't afraid to bend the Rules. *Sometimes*."

"Oh. My. God. Did you just say the Rules aren't always to be obeyed?" asked Lorna. "Nancy Anne Radley, I am so going to remind you of this the next time you're all 'Nooo, you can't go into Barneys Co-op and start possessing girls just so you can know what it feels like to try on Lanvin.'"

"No! I didn't mean that, I simply meant . . ."

As Lorna and Nancy carried on arguing, I quietly clicked my fingers, employing Edison's Lifesaver trick to block out the sound of their—increasingly shrill, it had to be said—voices. See, not everything about Ed was bad after all. Pretentious, yes. Black, totally. Hot, uh-huh. But not *bad*. He would have to have been an utter saint not to have found a way to get some peace and quiet stuck in limbo with these two. The way he turned up on the roof to check that I was okay—that was kinda cool. Plus, if it wasn't for Ed's extra lessons, off curriculum as they'd been, Nancy was right—David would be somewhere very different now.

Like here, with me. I found myself hating the thought of that when, just days ago, being with David again was all I wanted. Or all I ever thought I did.

Being dead, I thought as I watched Lorna and Nancy silently squabbling, it wasn't the end of the world after all. In that moment, it kinda felt like a beginning.

Chapter 32

I LEFT LORNA AND NANCY OUTSIDE AND SLOWLY walked back up the Attesa steps. As I came into the lobby with its checkerboard floor and red velvet drapes, I thought back to my first day here. Opening my eyes to see a bespectacled Nancy trying to be all serious, but unable to hide her concern, me not knowing where I was or how I'd gotten there. I'd felt so lost, so scared. Like I'd never find my place again.

Even now—now I had my Key—I shuddered at the memory.

"Wow. I'm not sure that I can do this. I've thought about this moment for so long and now it's here, I'm actually having an attack of morality. I can't get the stupid Rules out of my head . . ."

I did a rabbit-in-the-headlights stop. That was Tess's voice, but she wasn't talking in a tone I'd ever heard her use before. This wasn't default Tess: snarky and dripping with I-don't-care-if-you-vote-me-Least-Likely-to-Give-a-Shit. This was different.

Really different. Tess sounded almost . . . unsure of herself. Scared about whatever she couldn't do.

I looked around the lobby. Where was she? I could hear her, but I couldn't see her. She must be tucked around the corner, standing by the only place out of my line of sight: the Big Red Door.

Right where I'd left my Key.

"Tess, come on," said another lower voice. "You don't need to do this. We can still find your killer."

Edison. I was sure of it. But why was he . . . My stomach fell and my legs became weak. What were he and Tess discussing?

"Hayes, you know that—more than anyone—I cannot stand to watch another ghost go through the Door. And watching Little Miss Emo having this big afterlife crisis about whether to put her Key in the damn lock or not. It's pathetic."

Tess sighed loudly.

"But stealing her Key?" Edison said. "Sending yourself through the Door instead of her? Even I know that's a whole big bag of wrong."

Oh God.

"Whether you believe Nancy's stupid Rules or not, we don't know if it even would work," Tess reasoned. "What if I tried to use Charlotte's Key and it didn't even fit in the Door when I held it? Or if I went through, then burned in some hellfire or whatever? Like I repeatedly tell those dimwits out there, we don't know what's on the Other Side. But it's something *really* powerful, and whatever it is could have set up a booby trap for dead girls who steal Keys and don't play along."

I wanted to move. Desperately. I wanted to shout. I wanted to tell Tess that—no matter how she felt about me—she couldn't be considering this. But I was glue-sticked to the spot. She couldn't betray me like this. Please, no.

"It's your decision, Tess." Edison's voice was measured, level. It was the same tone he'd used when he was teaching me the Jab and all those other tricks. "All I wanna point out is this: If you use her Key to go through the Door, she'll be stuck here *forever.* Can you really do that to another person?"

"Hey! What's with you?" Tess asked in an angry whisper. "I might be getting nervous, but I am going to do this. You know that. We had a deal."

WTF?

"We never had a 'deal,'" Ed said quietly. "I'm not some Wall Street asshole. I don't make deals with anyone."

"You promised that you'd help me to get out of here," Tess said. "It's been six years and I still don't have a clue who killed me. Six years, Ed. SIX. The trail's gone cold. The police gave up trying to find my murderer long ago." Her voice caught. "You knew the plan—you were supposed to befriend her, make her trust you—then when she got her Key, you'd help me to get it. Of course the irony is that all your work was a waste of time—I didn't bank on her being stupid enough to just leave it lying on a table where anyone could pick it up. Whatever, the point is that you promised to help me. So don't get all 'can you really do that to her?' on me now. You have no right. You owe me that much."

"Tess, please . . ." Edison sounded broken. "We've been through this. Sure, I might have played along with things at first, but I didn't think you were seriously going to steal the girl's Key. You can't do this to Charlotte."

Played along? So Tess was the reason why Edison had been showing me the ropes? My stomach lurched.

"No? Then what about what you did to me, Ed? You and your brother?"

I heard Ed pace across the floor. "We've replayed that night a million times, Tess. It was no one's fault. I didn't know you were going to be there."

"Oh, come *on*. I always waited for Matt outside the restaurant after his shift ended," Tess said. "I was his girlfriend. It was what I did."

Wait, Tess had been dating Edison's *brother*?

"Well, you shouldn't have been there that night," Edison snapped. "He should have called you, told you to stay away. He knew how dangerous that place was. That's why I went on that final job in his place. If he cared about you he'd never have let you anywhere near it."

"Thanks, Edison." Tess's voice was scratchy. "Out of all the things you've said to me since, that's got to be one of the worst."

Ohmigod, was I hearing this right? Tess was there the night Edison died? So Lorna was right after all. They had known each other when they were alive. Just not in a way any of us could ever have guessed.

"I'm sorry," Edison said. "I'm sorry you were there that day and I'm sorry you looked through the window after the gunshot went off . . ."

"I heard a bang. I was worried about Matt. I didn't know they'd hit you. I—"

"I'm sorry one of the gang thought you saw who killed me. And I'm sorry he shot you too."

Oh. My. God.

"And I'm sorry—most of all—that Matt didn't protect you in the first place by calling and telling you not to meet him that night," Ed said quietly.

"I was in a coma for five days and he never visited." Tess's voice was little more than a whisper. "Five days. You remember? Those first five days you were here before me?"

"It would have been too dangerous for him, Tess, you know that . . ." Edison coughed quietly. "We've discussed this. Let's not go over and over it all again. Please. Your death was a tragic case of wrong place, wrong time. I'm not the reason you're still here, that you haven't gone through the Door. So don't try to use that as an excuse for what you're about to do to her."

"But it *is* your fault," Tess said, her voice stronger now. "If you'd just helped me trail the guys who Matt had worked for in my first days in the Attesa, we could have figured out who shot me—and you. I could have gotten my Key. We both could. But instead all you wanted to do was watch over your stupid, selfish brother and your mom."

"I had obligations," Edison said. "You could have taken up that Lyndsay girl's offer of help."

"Her? As if! What use was she with all her 'read the Rules' and 'don't disobey'? She was the original bossy boots. Worse than Nancy could ever be. No, Ed, me being stuck here *is* your fault." I could imagine her slowly shaking her head, her brunette waves bouncing with every word. "I deserve a break. I deserve to leave. And I need you to get out of my way, so I can pick up Charlotte's Key and go through the Door."

"I can't do that." Edison's voice was firm.

"Can't? Or won't? I don't see why it matters to you what happens to some stupid new girl? She's only been around a week— it'll be years before she feels the way I do. What do you care anyway? You're not usually this way with newb— Oh." Her tone switched. "Oh, I see now."

I heard Tess's feet spin on the floor. She must be turning to face him full on. "You have feelings for her, don't you?"

"No," Edison said.

"Don't lie. That's why you showed up on the roof, isn't it?" Tess ranted. "That whole white knight act wasn't to back me up; it was because you didn't want me stealing her Key! You were never going to help me, were you? All the cozying up to her, the extra lessons—they weren't so you could gain her trust—you actually *like* Charlotte."

There was a silence. I wasn't sure I was ready to hear what would fill it.

"No, well, it started as that but . . . she's *different*," Edison said.

Was I? Tess sighed with frustration.

"You can't take this from her." Edison changed tack. "Look, what if we take a Key from the next one? Wait for someone evil? Someone who doesn't deserve out of here?"

"I thought I had your word," Tess said in a low voice. "Guess I was wrong."

I heard a scuffle, the movement of feet, then scraping. Metal on wood. Which had to mean Tess was—oh *no*—picking up the Key. *My* Key. My only way out of this world. I might not want to use it yet, but that didn't mean I never would. I couldn't let Tess have it. I had to stop her.

I willed my legs to work and sprinted across the tiled lobby, skidding into the alcove where the Door was—just in time to see Tess putting my key into the hole. Edison stood frozen behind her. "Charlotte, this isn't what it seems, we—"

I ignored him. "Tess, please, please don't do this," I said. My voice sounded like someone else's.

Tess spun around. A pained look passed over her face. Her pupils were so large, her eyes looked black in the shadows.

"Charlotte. I guess I should have been ready for you to appear just at the wrong moment—as always." She was trying to keep her voice steady, but it wobbled a little as she spoke. "It would have been much easier, for both of us, if you'd stayed away. You didn't need to see this."

"Tess, please." I swallowed hard. "I know we haven't been the best of friends, but this? You can't go back from this. I heard you two talking . . ."

Edison's eyes met mine, then darted to the floor.

"You know this is wrong," I said. "You don't have to do this."

"No, you really don't," said a solid voice behind me. My backup girl. Nancy.

"Just put Charlotte's Key back on the table," Nancy said, in a determined tone I'd never heard her try on Tess before. "You can search for your killer again—and this time the three of us will be here to help. With all the things we've learned recently, I know we can find him or her." Nancy's eyes were kind, but her expression resolute. "There must be clues you've overlooked, leads we can look into, lessons we can learn from other cases."

Furls of smoke began to slide under the bottom of the Door. The locked glowed.

"Plus, the last time you tried to solve your murder, I wasn't around," Lorna said, flanking me on the other side. She lowered her voice to a whisper. "And, you know, I'm secretly the smartest one here." She smiled, trying to lighten the moment, to show Tess that if she took my Key out of the lock now, we'd forgive her. It would be okay.

We stared at Tess. Not one of us daring to move. She was motionless: a stone statue holding a Key she didn't dare turn, as three pairs of eyes bore into her, silently begging her to do the right thing.

The smoke danced across the white and black tiles, skipping over Edison's feet.

"I can't stay here forever," she said to Nancy. "Watching dead girl after dead boy check into this hotel, get their Key, and leave. Watching the lucky ones go naturally when their time is right. Watching the Living I knew grow old, then move on. Watching all those people do what I'll never do. Achieve what I never can. Get the hell out of here."

The edges of the Door took on an amber glow, like the end of one of Edison's cigarettes. I felt the floor beneath me gently vibrate.

"You won't be here forever. I promise you." I took a small step toward her. The Door hummed.

Suddenly I knew what I had to do. "If you return my Key, I won't use it until we've found yours." I knew what I was offering her, the terrible pact I could be making, but in that moment, I wanted to help. With my Key in her hand, I finally knew what it was like to be Tess. The hourly horror she must feel, knowing she could never complete what she came here to do.

Tess turned and looked at me. "Really, Feldman?" she asked, out of habit breathing hard. "You'd do that for me? You'd damn yourself to an eternity in limbo, just to help—when I've been nothing but horrible to you since you got here?"

"I would," I said, staring her down, willing her with everything I had to drop my Key.

Her face became a mask. She tightened her grip on the metal fob and began to turn.

"Tess, please, I'll help too," Edison said. "I'll do everything I can this time."

Tess squeezed my Key in the lock. The Door started to gently tremble. A puff of green smoke shot out from under it. Tess gasped, as if suddenly aware of what she was doing.

She whimpered and jumped back like she'd been burned— with the Key in her hand and out of the lock.

The Door groaned as the smoke sucked back under it, like a vacuum cleaner in reverse. Instantly it returned to its usual painted hue. Tess collapsed onto the Attesa floor in a ball of sobs.

Maybe I should have walked out right there and then, given her the kind of speech I gave David or at the very least hit her. But suddenly hearing Tess's cries, I knew I couldn't. Instead I ran over and held her tight until she was all wept out.

"I had to be mean to you." Tess was beginning to speak normally again now. "I knew if I started to like you even a little bit, I couldn't go through with it. Guess I'm even lamer than I imagined." She sniffed and gave me the ghost of a smile.

Lorna bobbed down and stroked Tess's hair. "We'll figure this out," she promised, as Nancy joined the hug.

"Hey, Ghostgirl," Edison said, breaking the mood.

I looked up and found his green eyes. "What?"

"A word." He beckoned me to where he was now standing at the curtain's edge. Nancy gave me a small nod and took Tess's head from my lap to hers. I stood up and ducked behind the red velvet.

"Exactly how much of that conversation did you hear?" Edison asked as I reached him.

I pulled the curtain back an inch and looked at Tess sitting broken in Nancy's arms. She seemed so fragile now. "Enough to know that you haven't been totally honest with me." I let the curtain fall back again and turned to face Ed. "But that you had your reasons and you tried to make it right."

His eyes softened and he stared me down for a beat longer than was necessary. I tried to move, to go back to the others, but my feet felt as if they were tacked to the tiles.

"And the very last part," he said, leaning a little nearer, "were you close enough to hear that?"

My arms went weak and hundreds of bubbles formed in my chest. Was that a ghost thing or a girl thing? Maybe it was a side effect of my Key. I managed an uh-huh.

Edison's palm found my elbow. I tried not to shudder. He broke my gaze and looked down. "Look, Charlotte, you've got a lot to deal with right now. You and the blond band boy . . . You have history. I get it. I saw how he was looking at you up on the roof. If you still want to—"

"No! Ed, I know the David thing looked bad." I tried to move toward him too, but the air between us felt dense like sponge. "But after everything that's happened, I really wouldn—"

Waaahhhh! Waaahhhh! Waaahhhh! The sound of a siren blasted through the lobby.

I shot back with surprise, almost tumbling over. Edison steadied me, pulling me back onto my leaden feet. The bubbles fizzed where my heart used to beat.

"Charlotte!" Nancy called out. We spun around and ran back to the other side of the curtain.

Nancy jumped to attention. "I hate to change the subject," she said, looking down at Tess, "especially at a moment with quite as much gravitas as this, but it seems"—she pointed to a light flashing madly above the Attesa's front desk—"that any second now we're going to get a new arrival."

Nancy grabbed my hand and quickly pulled me over to the old-fashioned mail chute at the front desk. I was too confused and beat and *what just happened?* to argue. Tess and Lorna followed behind.

A letter sealed with red wax appeared. Nancy tore it open.

"A seventeen-year-old girl's just been murdered . . . ," Nancy said, skimming quickly, "coming out of the Hudson Library Bar, up by Central Park. According to this, someone deliberately pushed her in front of a cab. Oh! A bit like you, Charlotte . . ."

For such a star pupil you'd have thought Nancy—at some point before now—would have taken a lesson in tact.

"And she'll be here in twenty minutes." She tucked a curl behind her ear and stared down at her watch. "So we should, you know . . ."

I looked at Nancy and Lorna and smiled. "Get on with what we're here for?" I asked.

Since I'd died, the one thing I'd learned was that nothing was what it seemed—not my boyfriend, not my life, and certainly not my death. But if you had friends to help you through, well, maybe none of that mattered. Maybe it would be okay.

"Come on," I said, grabbing Lorna's shoulder and silently giggling at her face as I dared to ruffle the arm of her perfect blue Marc J dress. "It looks as though I'm the newest member of the Dead Girls Detective Agency. Whether I like it or not."

Tess, Lorna, and Nancy hurried down the stairs to HHQ.

"Hey," Edison said, grabbing my hand as I walked past and pulling me close, "I happen to like it very much."

JOIN
THE COMMUNITY AT

Epic Reads
Your World. Your Books.

DISCUSS
what's on
your reading
wish list

FIND
the latest
books

CREATE
your own book
news and
activities to share
with friends

ACCESS
exclusive
contests and
videos

**Don't miss out on any upcoming
EPIC READS!**

**Visit the site and browse the
categories to find out more.**

www.epicreads.com